SONG OF THE BIRD PIPE

Steven W. Wise

Fear both the heat and cold of your heart.

J. R. R. Tolkien

authorHOUSE®

AuthorHouse™
1663 Liberty Drive
Bloomington, IN 47403
www.authorhouse.com
Phone: 1 (800) 839-8640

Cover Art Photo © Terry Martin

Published by AuthorHouse 11/16/2017

ISBN: 978-1-5462-0911-9 (sc)
ISBN: 978-1-5462-0910-2 (e)

Print information available on the last page.

This book is printed on acid-free paper.

Contents

CHAPTER 1

Don't stop 'til Jesus grabs you by the hand

The gallows, March, 1886, Fort Smith, Arkansas

Hattie Wax stood near the front of the half-circle of gawkers who had come to watch the hanging of the young cowboy. On her right shoulder was a large parrot adorned with plumage much like the flowing dress worn by its master—greens and yellows and touches of blue, embellished by slanting rays of the rising sun, cut low, framing deep cleavage. Wild red ringlets draped the collar. On the woman's head sat a great purple hat, cocked toward the bird, with a low brim and long ostrich feathers hanging like tiny tree branches laden with rain. Her features were ordinary—wide-set green eyes, longish nose, thin lips, yet men had stolen glances at her since she was twelve. Thin black tattoos began at the corners of her mouth and bisected her chin, but did not meet, each ending with an ornamentation that resembled a musical note. Ten steps behind her, standing alone, was the Indian called Rufus, whose dark, steely eyes swept slowly back and forth over the crowd, his head barely moving. Beside him stood a tall, wild-bearded man known only as Lucian, his huge hound sitting on its haunches at his boots. The Indian reached down with his right hand and allowed the dog to nuzzle his fingers for a moment.

The hangman, Apsel Graf, stood on the gallows, awaiting the three men trudging toward the staircase. He was not a tall man, yet appeared so in his perfectly tailored black clothing, his back, ramrod stiff. A pair of Colt Model 1862 Police revolvers hung cross-draw style over his hips. Despite the morning chill of late March, he wore no hat—as was his wont—oiled hair combed straight back. He wore a full dark beard, neatly trimmed, his eyes deeply hooded under woolly brows, framed by angled lines that appeared as inscriptions in flesh. He was forty-two years in age, and for the past twelve he had been the Chief Executioner for the Western District of Arkansas. It was commonplace for pedestrians on the boardwalks of Ft. Smith to cross the street before reaching him.

The stairs of the gallows creaked with the weight of the squatty, black-clad preacher—big Bible in hand—closely followed by the condemned cowboy, merely a boy in both age and demeanor, and behind him, Sheriff Josiah Colley. Colley shuffled the cowboy and the preacher into position, and then stepped back. Hangman Graf placed his left hand on the boy's shoulder as he whispered in his ear for several seconds, and then patted gently. The cowboy had the pasty face of a sad, bewildered child who had been scolded too harshly for a minor misstep. It was when the preacher began to pray that Hattie turned her head slightly to the right and whispered.

She smiled grimly as the parrot shifted its feet and spoke loudly and distinctly with the voice of a woman. "Poor boy poor boy poor boy."

The preacher stopped in mid-word. "God of mer…" Sheriff Colley and Hangman Graf stared down, and Colley shook his head, feared what might follow. The boy's eyes did not move. The preacher said, "Have you no shame, woman? Please allow this to proceed…for the sake of the condemned…for everybody."

"*This!* Preacher man? Just what is *this*?" Those near her moved away, and some of the women murmured in agitation. "Let me tell you what *this* is. It's a cryin' damn shame is what it is. This poor boy gets a snootful and still manages to get the best of one of the most worthless son-of-a-bitches in this territory—the kind that the great judge has come to rid us of—and what does the judge do?" She turned, pointed to the open second floor window of the stone courthouse building, behind which Judge Burleigh Plume looked down, his arms akimbo. "He sends the boy to hang. And I'll be goddamned if there's justice in that, much less a lick of sense!"

Sheriff Colley took a step forward, spoke in even tones. "Sooner or later, the judge is going hold you in contempt for disturbance."

"Well, Sheriff Colley, that'd make me and him perfect even with each other, wouldn't it? But he don't have the balls."

"No balls no balls no balls no balls."

She nodded her head. "Even Hector knows."

Sheriff Colley moved toward the top step. Hattie said, "Stop, I'm near done. Just gonna help the boy, since apparently the preacher ain't havin' much luck with his prayin'."

"Be quick about it then, and leave."

"Son, look at me." He moved his eyes first, then his head. "You close your eyes tight and think on bein' astride some sweet filly of a girl and you don't stop till Jesus grabs you by the hand."

The preacher said, "Your blasphemy will send you…"

"Oh, shut up."

"Shut up shut up shut up."

She turned on her boot heel and the bird's wings fluttered as she stomped away.

Sheriff Colley turned to the preacher, who nodded and said, "Well…I…uh…well, I've already prayed." Colley sucked in a long breath and said to the young cowboy, "Dillingham, do you have any last words?"

Dillingham, eyes clamped shut, did not speak. Hangman Graf moved quickly and drew the black hood over his head.

Hattie Wax heard the explosion of noise as the trap door opened. "Ride on, cowboy…ride on." Hector stirred but did not speak.

Hangman Graf watched the Indian called Rufus and his companion Lucian, followed by his hound, as they approached. When they were within twenty yards, Rufus turned and walked quickly away, but Lucian raised his right hand and touched the brim of his hat. He wore an old duster reaching to the toes of his boots. A tattered bowler hat was crammed down to the top of his ears, white hair stringy and loose in the cold breeze. Reaching nearly ear to ear was a mustache a woolly inch thick, and above it, offshoots winging up from his nostrils. A plum-sized wad of tobacco was nestled between his teeth and left cheek.

Hangman Graf met the man and the dog, reached down and rubbed the fleshy folds behind the hound's ears. Lucian said, "He was a youngun, looked like, 'fore you hooded him."

"Just a boy."

"Ummm. Did he leave tolerable."

"I talked to him, tried to ease him."

"Well, I 'spect Hattie Wax helped too with her useful thought."

Graf raised his eyebrows, slowly shook his head. "That is a strange woman…even for a whore." He shook his head. "And that Indian always with her…he is worrisome."

"Strange?" He chuckled. "They all are…from whores to church ladies…and I've knowed several of both kinds and some in between back when I had my juices. And far as the Indian is concerned, Rufus ain't a bad one to have keepin' an eye on you, 'specially when you're mouthy as Hattie Wax. I've knowed him a good while now."

Graf looked away toward the tree line beyond the edge of town, and Lucian sensed that he wished to be alone. "I think me and Mose had enough of town for one day." He turned, took a few steps before turning back to Graf. "You're a good man…with a hard job."

"Your judgment is lenient, others would disagree." Graf turned and walked toward the trees.

Lucian watched him for a full minute, and then said,

"I'll tell you, Mose…even for a hangman, he's too damn sad in the eyes."

Apsel Graf walked into the shade of the trees and chose a tall elm to lean his shoulder against. He closed his eyes, waited for the dreamy moments to come, waited for her to take form on the inside of his eyelids, as it always did following a hanging. Then she came—the tender artistry of eyes, nose, mouth, the rise of her cheekbones, the yellow flow of hair—and though gravid with the girl child, she moved precisely as she had in life—liquid, feminine—two decades past. She advanced in fragments of time and space, and Graf knew that she would halt at a distance that would only allow him to read her visage, though he longed for her to come nearer. She stopped, the space between them a chasm of unknowable breadth, yet, thankfully, maddeningly, he was allowed a moment to lock his vision on the exquisiteness of her face as she beckoned him with forgiving eyes. Quickly, she withdrew into the shadows, and Graf's arms remained outstretched long after she had vanished.

CHAPTER 2

The new girl coming

The sprawling two-story house sat two miles from the edge of town, and fifty yards from the Arkansas River. Tall cedars and red pines mixed with black walnut and oaks stood like giant sentinels around the buildings, and between the hardwoods, chokeberry and buck brush thrived, forming a barrier that opened only to a single-entry lane. The house had a wrap-around porch with a wide swing suspended from the ceiling. Behind the house stood a lofted barn, a corral, and a log cabin, and beside the cabin was a big garden. Just how Hattie Wax had come to own such a property had been a matter of gossip and conjecture around the territory for a dozen years, and from time to time, and for her amusement, Hattie had leaked tidbits that ranged from outrageous lies to truth. She sat alone in the swing, shawl wrapped over her shoulders in the chill of late night, listening to the sound of hooves that signaled the approach of Sheriff Josiah Colley.

Sheriff Colley dismounted at the hitching post near the porch, walked up the four treads and sat down beside Hattie. "Good evening." He tilted his hat back, revealing a wide, creased brow, and under it, blue eyes that Hattie had always considered oddly soft for a man whose trade was dealing with violent men. He wore a thick, droopy mustache peppered with grey that hid his top lip, and with ends that hung wild to the bottom of his jaw line.

"And the same to you, Sheriff." She reached down beside the swing and picked up a bottle and two shot glasses, passed a glass to Colley. "Let's cut the night chill and warm up the insides."

"I like that idea."

The neck of the bottle chimed against the rim of the glasses, and then the glasses chimed against each other. They tipped their heads back and took the whiskey in a single gulp. He said, "And one more for good health and long lives?"

"We've already had both more than we deserve. Don't want to appear greedy."

"Appear? To who?"

She raised her free hand to the sky, waved it around for a moment. "The Great Sorter, Josiah…there has to be a great sorter of all this activity down here."

"Based on my experience, he ain't much on orderliness, sorter or not."

She scoffed, "'He', is it? You so damn sure of that?"

"Well, if he is a she, it makes even less sense." He lifted his empty glass. "To hell with all this deep thought."

She filled his glass, then hers, and they quaffed the whiskey. He said, "My, but this is fine to the tongue."

"Everything is fine here," she said. "You know that. Let the commoners drink rot gut and rut down on The Row."

"I suspect that they are doing that right now, and keeping two of my deputies busy in the doing."

"And then maybe they get in front of old Judge Plume… God in a black robe…in a month or two?"

Colley shifted his weight, grumbled, "You need to stop that activity. That was the second time in less than three months."

"Maybe I will, maybe I won't. Depends on what the dead one walkin' looks like, and what he did."

"And that bird…shit almighty, Hattie. You're going to rile Judge Plume sometime bad enough that he'll send me to lock you up."

"And just what would you do, Sheriff Colley?"

"I don't want to think about that."

"Oh hell, if the old bastard ever tried that I'd figure a way to get inside of his britches, and then I'd have him forever, because we both know damn well that his haughty wife would skin him if she found out."

Colley laughed from his belly. "The truth is that you just might at that."

She reached over and placed a hand on the inside of his thigh. "Enough of this talk. Let's proceed upstairs and get you busy makin' me richer."

"Talked me into it."

They stood, and she picked up the bottle and took his glass. She said, "One more thing, a favor…and I'll make it up to you in memorable ways."

"You have my full attention."

"There's a new girl coming to see me about working here, name of Iva Lockwood. I'm told she's a real beauty, which ain't a particularly good thing in our line of work.

And...she was cloudy in her letter about why she's leaving St. Louis. I'd appreciate you and your men keepin' an eye out for her when she gets here. She'll be on the 2:10 from Little Rock next Tuesday. Long yellow hair, green dress. She won't be hard to pick out."

"Not a problem." He paused, cocked his head, "You got Rufus on this too?"

She nodded, "I couldn't do without that Indian."

CHAPTER 3

The scent of lilac in her hair

The train chugged to a halt and hissed great billows of steam. The Indian Rufus stood at the corner of the depot, his hands in the pockets of an old duster that touched his boot tops. His right hand rested atop a Colt Dragoon revolver in forty-four caliber. Inside the duster, and sheathed on his right hip, was a bone-handled knife with an eight-inch blade.

Rufus shifted his eyes but not his head as he saw Sheriff Colley walk to his vantage point at the opposite corner of the depot. When Colley stopped, he met Rufus' gaze, but only for a moment. Neither man acknowledged the other. The passengers began to appear from the train cars, and soon only a few remained. The woman appeared with the shimmer of the afternoon sunlight on her emerald green dress. She wore a dark gold bonnet, and below it spilled long locks the color of wheat straw. She carried a bag in each hand, and when she reached the boardwalk she sat them down, looked about.

Rufus walked toward her, and when she saw him, clasped her hands together at her waist, smiled easily until he stopped in front of her. "Mr…Rufus, I believe?"

"Just Rufus."

"You were not hard to spot."

"Same for you."

"Very well…just Iva for me."

Across the street from the depot, Apsel Graf shouldered his way through the doorway to the general store, and as he turned to walk away, a flash of emerald green caught his peripheral vision. He turned his head and allowed the entire vision to form. It appeared to him as a moving portrait of feminine beauty—flowing rather than walking—and he stood mesmerized as the yellow-haired woman followed Rufus to the buggy. Just before the buggy disappeared around the corner, Rufus looked back over his shoulder at Graf, but the staring man did not notice, his mind filled with only the moving vision, again and again.

Rufus and Iva had ridden for over a mile in total silence, yet for reasons that Iva could not fathom, the silence was not uncomfortable. She pilfered another look at the Indian. His nose was aquiline, his skin the color of burnished bronze in the afternoon sunlight. A finger-wide scar traced a jagged line from his right eyebrow to his jaw line. Raven hair was worn in a thick braid that hung halfway down his broad back. His voice rose from his chest rather than his mouth—a low rumble, like distant thunder.

She said, "Is it far?"

"No."

The horse clomped away another hundred yards. "Have you…uh…worked for Miss Hattie long?"

"Yes."

Iva nodded, raised her hands from her lap for a moment and then lowered them. "I'm a big city girl most all of my life—Kansas City, St. Louis, and Baltimore before that. I imagine it'll be different down here."

The carriage covered another hundred yards before Rufus said, "Places are different, people are not."

Iva looked past the horse's ears as it cleared the last bend in the lane and saw a woman standing on the front porch of a sprawling house. A great, multi-colored bird sat on the woman's shoulder. When the carriage stopped, Rufus hopped off, went to Iva's side and helped her down.

Hattie walked down the stairs and took Iva's hands, said, "Welcome to my house, Iva."

"Thank you, I'm so glad to be here."

"Hector, where are your manners?"

"Hello hello hello."

Iva laughed. "Hello to you, Hector. What a beautiful bird you are."

"I know I know I know."

Hattie huffed a laugh. "Don't make him worse."

Rufus walked toward the stairs with Iva's bags. Hattie said, "I think Rufus has a treat for Hector." The man paused beside Hattie and the bird hopped to his shoulder. Hattie said, "Last room on the right."

"Treat for Hector treat for Hector treat for Hector."

Hattie pointed to a swing and said, "Join me."

Hattie and Iva settled in the swing and Hattie toed the floor gently as the chains creaked a faint rhythm. They turned their heads toward the sound of the front door opening, and then watched the little woman, wiry and agile, approach with a glass in each hand. Her mulatto skin was the color of cinnamon, her features delicate and feminine, though edged with age. Hattie said, "Iva Lockwood, meet Dilla—a lady in all ways, who I can't imagine doing without."

Iva smiled, nodded, and said, "I'm pleased to meet you, Dilla."

"Same to you, Miss Iva. You needs somethin' while you're here, you jus holler."

"*While you're here.*" The words registered in Iva's brain with a twinge of disappointment. "Thank you, I…uh…hope that is a long…while."

Dilla turned, took three steps, then turned back around. "Roast chicken for supper, and dumplins outta this world."

Hattie sipped from her glass, allowed the silence to gather. "She didn't mean anything by that. If I didn't want you here for a long time I wouldn't have invited you."

Iva blushed. "Oh, I didn't…mean…"

"I know what you meant, and it's alright." She patted Iva's arm. "Dilla knows that a long time ain't forever, but it's not like you think."

Iva fingered the rim of her glass. Hattie continued, "My girls are special, not Row girls."

Iva said, "Row girls?"

"They call it The Row, in town. Several houses—all rough—cowboys, drunks and the like. I imagine you know plenty about all that."

"More than I care to remember."

"Well it ain't like that here. I won't tolerate it. Nobody goes upstairs without a nice chat with me first. And nobody goes upstairs that hasn't parted with a serious chunk of his wallet…and that gets me to the 'long while' part." She paused, took a long sip of the tea. "My gone girls write me, Iva. One writes from San Francisco and tells me what the ocean looks like at sunset. Another one, from a big cattle spread in Montana, where her husband rides beside her and treats her like the Queen of Sheba."

Iva looked down at her glass, then back up at Hattie. "I never dreamed like that."

"You can dream now. Your looks…good gaaawd! Maybe you're with me three years—four at the most—and you're staked to a new life where you pick the man, not the other way around."

Iva shook her head, raised her eyebrows. "My looks…"

"Don't tell me…more of a curse than a blessing, huh?"

"Something like that."

"Don't worry about the other girls. First place, it ain't like they're something the cat drug in. And more than that—and you know this—there's a hundred ways a woman can get a man to latch onto her whether she's a beauty or not. Don't worry…there won't be any jealously. You'll soon be like sisters, and when Sally leaves next, you'll likely cry, and her too."

Hangman Graf walked up the back stairs of the boarding house that stood at the corner of Third and Mulberry Streets. His room was on the corner of the second floor. The room was spare and orderly—the made bed in the corner, a high-backed chair with wide cushioned arms in front of the fireplace, an old roll-top desk with a low chair. In the center of the room sat a small table with a chair on each side. He placed the crate on the table and then sat down in the high-backed chair. From his vest pocket he withdrew a silver locket and flipped it open. The likeness of a woman stared through time at him until two decades faded away. Haunting beauty, soft eyes, yellow hair. He carefully swept the tip of his forefinger over it, then closed his eyes and sat motionless until the scent of lilac in her hair came to him.

CHAPTER 4

A vis'tation from Mister Rufus

A flicker of foreboding passed through Hattie's brain when the tall man in the white Stetson hat walked up the staircase with Iva. It was his hand in the small of her back; the fingers were busy—like the legs of a great spider—rather than resting comfortably in the manner of a typical wealthy patron, but she let it pass. Their preliminary conversation had gone very well. He was a merchant passing through, and had learned of her establishment by a strong recommendation from an associate in Kansas City. His tailored suit was immaculate, his beard and hair neatly trimmed, flecked with gray. He introduced himself with a little bow as Wilton Concannon, and Hattie was certain that the name was not fictitious. It was the way of such men.

It was when the man hurried down the stairs that Hattie knew that she had made a mistake. She found Iva in her bed, clutching her crumpled gown to her bosom, her eyes cold and distant, betraying no emotion despite the quivering of her lips. Hattie nestled beside her, said, "What'd he do, Iva?"

The gown slid down. Deep red bruises, soon to purple, and around the nipples, bite marks, two of which leaked tiny rivulets of blood. A sound like the hissing of a snake escaped Hattie, and then she said, "Should I fetch Doc?" Iva shook her head. "Dilla will be up here directly to tend you. You all right till then?" Iva nodded, pulled the gown back up.

Hattie banged open the kitchen door, and when the black woman looked up from her dough pan her broad features turned instantly from inquisitive to a fret. Hattie said, "Dilla, get up to Iva's room. Heat some water and take things for a poultice."

"Yes 'um." She reached for a hand cloth and began to scurry about the kitchen.

Hattie found Rufus behind his cabin, perched on a seat that he had fashioned from a tree stump. He was whittling a hickory stick, a foot long and an inch thick. Roasting on a spit over white coals was a rabbit carcass. Hattie walked up behind him, but he made no move to rise, nor did he look up.

"Some rabbit?" he asked.

"I'm not in a dining mood."

"Ummm..."

"I have a chore for you and it needs done tonight."

"The chore?"

"At the hotel you'll find a man registered as Concannon. He abused my new girl." Rufus shook the hickory leavings from his hand. "What part of her?"

"Her bosom."

Rufus looked up at her. "Will she heal?"

"Yes…but it will take a long time. I want it made even." He nodded as he resumed his whittling. "What you makin'?"

"A bird pipe."

"For what?"

"The little songbirds that are coming back."

"What will it sound like?"

"You will know when you hear it."

"Ah…your soft side, huh?"

"I have one."

"Maybe…but not tonight." She turned and walked away.

Iva cried softly now as Dilla gently placed the poultice over the worst of her wounds. "Miz Iva, you shoulda yelled out when that man started actin' like dis."

"I know, but it happened so quick, and he put his hand over my mouth…I just…just…"

"You hush now, child. Dilla's gonna fix you so good and gonna get you a toddy for sleepin'. You gonna be fine soon now, don't you worry no more."

Iva buried her face against the woman's shoulder, shuddered, said, "What if he comes back?"

"Oh he ain't never passin' this way again, child. I know that. I know how these things work."

"He's rich, he gets what he wants."

A mirthless chuckle rose from deep inside the woman. "You ain't been here long enough to know. I have. What he gonna get be a vis'tation from Mister Rufus, that's what he gonna get." The chuckle rumbled again. "He ain't never gonna be back dis a way. Never."

Two hours past midnight, Rufus, moccasins on his feet, stood in the lobby shadows, listening to the rhythmic snores of the night clerk, his head and arms resting on a small table behind the front desk countertop. Tied to Rufus's side was a buckskin pouch. He moved silently until he stood over the open registry book on the front desk, looked down and found the name written in flourishing longhand, "W. Concannon," and beside it the number "14." The big key ring hung from a nail behind the desk, and he picked it up carefully. Inside the room, he took a match from his pouch and struck it with a thumbnail, lit the oil lamp. He moved to the bed, poked Concannon in the ribs, and when the man rose up, slammed a fist into his chin. From the pouch, Rufus took two strips of cloth, one longer and thicker than the other, and two short lengths of rope.

Concannon stirred, began to struggle against the ropes that bound his wrists and ankles and the gag tied over his mouth. Rufus slapped the side of his face, said, "Lay still, there is nothing you can do now." The man's eyes bulged whitely as Rufus ripped open the night shirt, pinched Concannon's left nipple and said, "Very touchy, ain't it?"

Concannon's body bucked and then stiffened as Rufus lowered his head, slowly sucked the nipple past his teeth and bit it off. The odor of urine drifted up with the muffled cries. Rufus waited for him to stop writhing, and then took the long cloth strip and bound it around the man's body, positioning the thickest part over the bleeding wound. "I have greased the cloth so it will not stick when you change it. It will heal, but it will take a long time—just like the woman's."

Concannon grunted now, angrily, as Rufus knew he would. He leaned forward, touched the tip of his nose to the man's forehead. "This is the way it will be now. I will untie your ropes and then disappear from your life, and tomorrow you will get on the train, ride away, never again to come close to Miss Hattie's place. If you do not do this, or if you go to the law, I will come again into your life and chew your cock and balls off and leave you to bleed out." He paused, waited for a moment. "Do you understand?"

Concannon's head bobbed up and down, and Rufus untied his bindings. He looked up at the bed post, on which hung a silver-studded holster and gun belt, and in the holster he saw a bone-handled Schofield revolver. He took it down from the bed post and looped it over his shoulder as he slipped from the room.

The trembling man remained in the bed for a quarter of an hour before he got up to pour himself a drink from the whiskey bottle that sat on the night stand.

The morning light seeped into Hattie's room. She ran a hand over her face, filled her lungs with air, pushed down the blankets, and arose. In his cage in the corner of the room, Hector stirred, fluffed his wings. "Miss Hattie get up Miss Hattie get up." Hattie stood and walked to the table on which sat a porcelain bowl of water and a clean hand towel. Beside the towel she spied a small piece of oil cloth, folded over, and a shiver ran up her spine like a scampering mouse. She unfolded the cloth and looked down at the nipple and the dried blood turning to black.

"Well, Hector…a man should be able to pleasure himself without actin' like a goddamn animal."

"Goddamn animal goddamn animal goddamn animal."

CHAPTER 5

'Cause I don't know whose fucken son I am

An hour past sunset, the thunderous, irate voice of Emma Dunstan rolled up the stairs to Hangman Apsel Graf's ears, and he pushed away from the table, opened the door. Another voice, much younger but equally strident, clashed with hers as Graf clambered down the stairs. The door to the kitchen stood open, and blocking it was the wide backside of the woman. Graf looked over her shoulder and saw the boy, crouched forward, his right hand clamped around a greasy chunk of ham hock. A short-billed cloth cap reached nearly to his eyes; his mouth was set in defiance. His cheeks were hollow, and his head was too large for his shoulders, his waistcoat tattered and filthy. His homespun trousers exposed skinny, white shins, and his socks flopped over the tops of brogans caked in dried mud. He appeared to Graf as an angry clown shrunken into a boy's body.

Emma said, "I've been missing things in this kitchen for three days, and now I know why! Damn street waifs!"

Graf eased his way past Emma and walked to the door leading to the dining room, closed it and turned around. He looked at Emma. "Was it just food?"

"Who knows what the little shit took. He could've snuck all over this place…rooms and all."

Graf looked at the boy. "Well?"

The boy said nothing, shifted his hateful gaze from Graf to Emma, then back again. Graf said, "I'll deal with him."

"I'd appreciate that. Hard enough to make ends meet around here without…this!"

Graf turned to the boy, said, "Put that down and come with me. I have some food in my room."

Emma said, "Well, he can damn well take that hunk of ham too, now that he's grimed it all up with those paws that's been God knows where. You ought to beat him, not feed him, you ask me." Then she stomped from the room.

Graf opened the door, put a hand on the boy's shoulder and guided him to a chair at the table. He went to the cupboard and took down a jar of molasses and a half loaf of bread, from which he cut two thick slices. He sat the food on the table along with a spoon, and then sat down across from the boy. "Help yourself."

The boy dipped the spoon into the molasses and heaped it over a slice of bread, and with four mouthfuls, devoured it. He repeated the process with the other slice of bread, wiped his mouth on his coat sleeve and looked at Graf, who said, "Now, back to my question. Was it only food that you stole?"

The dark eyes shifted and he licked his lips, wiped

them again on his sleeve. He reached into his coat pocket, pulled out a silver broach and a necklace with a small cross pendant, and tossed them on the table.

"And that's all?"

He nodded.

"What is your name, son?"

The voice was prepubescent, but hinted at a deepness to come. The words spilled out with the hurried cadence of a city dweller. "That's what I go by."

"What do you mean?"

"Son…that's what I go by."

"That's not a real name."

"It's mine…I took it for myself."

"Why?"

He narrowed his eyes. "Cause I don't know whose fucken son I am."

Graf tilted his head back, passed a hand over his brow, puffed out a long breath. "You don't sound like you're from around here."

"I come from New York on an orphan train."

"I've heard of them. Didn't some family adopt you?"

"Tried. I didn't trust the way the old man fingered my arms when they lined us up on the platform at the train station in Little Rock. Soon as we got a mile outta town and the road went through woods I was gone like a flash. I could hear the old bastard hollerin' at me, but he'd as soon caught a rat as me." He paused, couldn't suppress a little laugh. "Then I just went back to the station and hopped a night train to here."

"How old are you?"

"Ain't sure."

"What you are is old enough to get into some real trouble for breaking into places and stealing things besides ham hock."

"I don't break into places. I can pick locks clean as a whistle with no more'n a little piece of wire."

Graf shook his head. "That woman down there has been my landlady for a long time, and when I give these things back, that'll be the end of it…as long as…"

"I ain't gonna bother this place no more."

Graf tapped his finger on the table. "The pick wire. You're not going to bother *any place* anymore."

Son dug it from his coat pocket and laid it on the table. "That might be hard to do."

"It won't be hard for you if you're locked up."

The boy squirmed in the chair and looked away for a moment, then at the door. Graf said, "Go ahead and run like the rat again, but sooner or later, you're going to be back in the same pickle, and maybe the next person is inclined to take a board to your head."

The narrow shoulders slumped as he pulled off his cap, and uneven stalks of brown hair sprang up. "What you want me to do?"

"The head law around here is Sheriff Josiah Colley. I work with him now and then, and I can tell him of your situation in the streets, and that you want to mend your ways and find a place to earn your keep at."

"If there's another nasty old bastard feelin' me up, I'll be gone again."

"I'll make that plain to the sheriff."

"Why would he want to help somebody like me?"

"We've worked together for a long time."

"Good friends, huh?"

Graf raised his hands from the table and then quickly lowered them. "More like…business acquaintances."

"You a law?"

"I am…after a fashion."

"Chasin' bad people?"

Graf shook his head. "They're caught when I deal with them."

The words echoed in Son's head. *When I deal with them.* "What's that mean?"

Graf folded his hands and looked the boy squarely in the eyes. "I'm the Chief Executioner for the Western District of Arkansas."

Involuntarily, Son's upper body recoiled from the table as his face flushed. "Jeeesuuuss Christ! The hangman." He puffed air past his lips, wiped his nose on his sleeve and shook his head. "Just my luck. I got the whole damn town to pick from, and I pick the place where the hangman lives."

Graf said, "It can be good luck. It's up to you. I just hung a boy not a great deal older than you. He mixed whiskey and a gun and did something stupid. You keep on like this, maybe one day it's you up there with me." He paused, waited for Son to look up, but he kept his head down. "But it doesn't have to be." Graf flicked a hand toward the door. "Leave if you want…or let me see if I can help you."

Son looked up, picked up his hat, rolled it in his fingers, and then tugged it back on his head. He reached into his coat pocket, pulled out a small wad of tobacco and bit off the corner. He rolled it around until he settled it with his tongue behind his lower jaw teeth. "I am kinda tired of this."

Graf said, "Well, that's a start. I'll make you a pallet in

front of the fireplace. You can stay here until we find you a place."

"Ever do this before…for somebody like me?"

"Never had the chance."

"You got a spittoon anywhere?"

"No, but I'll find you something."

"Thanks."

Son shifted his body on the thick pallet, pulled the blanket up to his chin. Weak light from a street lamp leaked through the window curtains. He said, "You awake?"

"Yes."

"What should I call you?"

"Graf is my name. That'll do."

"Alright."

"What should I call you?"

"What I told you—Son."

"What is your true name?"

"Floyd McCarty…far as I know."

"But you don't claim it?"

"Never fucken will."

"I understand." He paused. "You need to work on your mouth. Starting tomorrow."

"That'll be a bitch to change."

"That's plain enough, but start tomorrow. It's a requirement."

"Whose…yours or the sheriff's?"

"Here's another thing to work on—don't ask so many questions. You're not in a questioning position."

"Just one more?"

"What?"

"What would you do if I was to be gone in the morning?"

"If you were gone in the morning, I would hope never to see you again, because I fear that if I did, it might be at the same gallows where I saw the last condemned young cowboy take his last breath."

"I ain't got anymore questions."

"Good."

CHAPTER 6

I'll slap you 'til you're snottin' all the way to your feet

Hattie heard the approaching horses and walked to the front parlor window. The lanky man she recognized as Lane Tilley, one of Colley's deputies. Riding a paint pony beside him was a boy— hunched forward, bobbing like a cork on choppy water, both of his hands filled with mane. She stepped onto the porch and waited for the horses to stop.

Tilley smiled widely, tipped his hat, said, "Afternoon, Miss Hattie." His eyes wandered past her for a moment as his gaze swept over the upstairs windows.

"Deputy." She looked at the boy, who had straightened his posture. His face was flushed and he struggled to breathe evenly. "Who you got here?"

"I got one that ain't ready to work in your corral yet, that's for sure." He chuckled. "Says it's his first ride, and I've seen evidence to support that."

Tilley dismounted and pulled a folded note from his vest pocket. "The Sheriff asked if you'd look at this."

Hattie took the note, unfolded it and after reading for a few seconds, said, "I expect you'd be more comfortable on the ground, youngun. Let's all go sit on the porch for a spell."

With both hands, the boy adjusted his grip to one side of the pony's mane and then slid down with a thud from his brogans. Hattie motioned to the swing and they sat down, with Son in the middle. She read the note, folded it back, and tucked it into a dress pocket. "Well, youngun'…got yourself quite a start in town, huh?"

Son rolled his eyes toward Hattie, but said nothing. She said, "Hummm…so I'm supposed to call you 'Son'…son?"

He nodded, fidgeted with the bottom of his waistcoat.

"You can call me Miss Hattie." She paused, waited for his reply. "Surely that little pony didn't bounce so much air from you that you can't talk."

"Alright…Miss Hattie."

"Deputy, tell the sheriff that I'll see how this new hand works out for a couple weeks or so, then we'll talk again." She looked down at Son. "I might want to give him back."

Tilley stood, tipped his hat, said, "Really good seein' you, Miss Hattie."

"Come back and see us again sometime."

He grinned. "I'm savin' up."

"You do that, Deputy. Be worth it."

She watched with Son as the man mounted with a flourish, turned his horse, and trotted away.

"Well…Son…what I have here is a little ranch. My help is a lady named Dilla, who can do most anything around this big house that needs doin'. And my only hand is named Rufus, who can do most anything that needs doin'—anywhere. We keep a nice corral, sell a horse or two now and then, keep a few beef cattle, and he's good about making things, fixing things…" She toed the floor with her boots, waited for the swing chains to begin their little song. "And then…I have some ladies that stay with me here…"

"I know 'bout the rest."

She snapped her head toward him. "Just what is it that you think you know, little man?"

Son drew in a breath, knew that had run his mouth too soon. "I mean…well, it's just that…hell, Miss Hattie, I grew up runnin' the streets in New York. I didn't mean no harm."

"Ah…a boy beyond his years, it seems. How old are you?"

He shook his head. "I truly don't fuc—I mean, I don't know, Miss Hattie. I think twelve."

"Let me tell you what's different about this… establishment…from what you think you know. I don't want for my girls to stay here any longer than they have to. This ain't like the places you've seen in the city. It's respectable, and we make a lot of money, and when one of the girls gets a good bank account, she empties it and heads off with every chance to make a new life. And that's the end of that speech."

The chains sang louder. "There won't be many rules, but there is one that you don't ever mess up on, and it's this—I ever hear you call my house a whore house, I'll slap you til you're snottin' all the way to your feet."

"I understand."

"Other than that, you treat everybody with respect, do

whatever me or Dilla or Rufus asks of you, and don't go upstairs unless one of us is with you."

"I understand."

"Now—you stink like a gut wagon. After you meet Dilla and Rufus, he'll show you the wash pump beside his cabin. We're fresh out of small clothes, but Dilla and Rufus will figure something out until she can wash and mend..."—she waved her hand from his neck to his shoes—"that. There's a room built on the back of Rufus' cabin, and that'll be yours for this tryout. And, bet your hungry."

He nodded. "I am."

"How does a big ham sandwich and a glass of sweet milk sound?"

Son licked his lips, and then said, "Really good."

"Alright then."

She pushed up from the swing, waited for Son to stand with her. He said, "Why you doin' this for me?"

"You need to work on your questionin' and just concentrate on answerin' what your elders ask." He lowered his head. "But I'll answer that one. Nobody ever helped me much. Maybe that's why I like helpin' other people who need a hand."

"Thanks."

"Save it. You haven't tried to work with Rufus yet. There's a reason that little room stays mostly empty." Son widened his eyes and his brow furrowed. She waved a hand, said, "Ah...he'll be alright. Just don't back talk him. Now... you ever meet a parrot?"

"Never seen one."

"That's about to change." They got up from the swing. "And I know there's one more thing you're dyin' to ask about but are afraid to." She smiled as she traced the tattoo on her chin with the tip of her forefinger and thumb. "Go ahead and look close."

Son studied the tattoo, marveled at the perfect lines and symmetry. "Never seen such a thing on a woman."

"Not even in big old New York City?"

He shook his head.

"Well…I'll declare…I like that, I do indeed."

CHAPTER 7

A stricken man

Rufus laid a flour sack on the wagon bed, and as he bent forward to pick up a crate he saw Hangman Graf approaching along the edge of the street. He did not acknowledge the man until he had placed the crate in the wagon. Expressionless, he looked at Graf.

Graf said, "I have something to be delivered to Hattie Wax." He held out a sealed envelope.

"About what?"

"It's a private matter."

"You never had a private matter out there before."

"That's none of your business."

"Everything out there is my business."

"Just deliver the note."

Rufus shook his head. "You can't see her for a while anyway."

Graf felt the blood rise to his cheeks. "Who do you mean by 'her'?"

Rufus ignored the question with a smirk. "She got roughed up. Wait a couple weeks. You want her, chinch up your balls and ride out there like any other hard cock." He turned back to his loading.

"Who hurt her?"

"A stranger."

"From these parts?"

"No." Rufus let the silence grow for several seconds. "Paid him a visit in his hotel room. It's all settled."

Graf nodded, tucked the envelope back into his pocket, and then turned and walked away.

Rufus opened the back door to Hattie's house and walked into the kitchen. Dilla looked up from the stove. "You need somethin', Mr. Rufus?"

"Go get Miss Hattie for me. I'll be out back."

In the back yard Rufus struck a match with his thumbnail and lit a thin cigar. He drew the smoke into his lungs, and then exhaled through his nostrils. Hattie walked to his side, took the cigar from his hand and drew on it, puffed her cheeks as she shot a stream of smoke into the dusk. Rufus said, "The hangman wants to see your new girl."

"The hell?" She looked at Rufus. "Knock me over with a feather."

Rufus shrugged his shoulders. "Just a man."

"Word does get around quick I reckon."

"It wasn't the word."

"What then?"

"He saw her when I got her at the depot."

"Ah….lust at first sight." She took another puff, then handed it back to Rufus. "Doesn't seem like him to ask you about all that."

"He didn't. Tried to give me a note for you, but I knew what he wanted."

"So you didn't take it?"

He shook his head. "Wasn't in the mood to be a note-passer for the hangman."

"Damn. That would've been interesting reading." She pulled her shawl around her shoulders, laughed. "Well, he's outta luck for a while anyhow."

"Told him that."

"Wonder if he'll show up later?"

"He will."

"What makes you so sure?"

"He wanted to know who roughed her up."

"Goddamn…a stricken man. Sees her one time and turns into a white knight. Amazin'."

As Rufus began to walk away, Hattie said, "Wait, let me have the cigar. I need to smoke and think on that for a time."

"Why don't you think on why it is that you took in a stray pup and gave him to me."

"Maybe because you don't seem to get along with grown help."

"Horse shit. You just feel sorry for him."

"And what's wrong with that?"

"Maybe nothing…maybe everything."

"How you two gettin' along?"

"He's still afraid to talk to me."

"That's about the start I figured on."

"I may leave it like that."

CHAPTER 8

The hangman cometh

Two weeks later, at three o'clock in the afternoon, Graf rode a tall dun gelding down the lane to Hattie's house. He was dressed in a black woolen suit with a grey vest over a starched white shirt, and his boots were well polished. There were no other horses hitched to the post, and he dismounted and wrapped the reins around the post. He walked up the stairs and stopped in front of the door, drew in a deep breath, exhaled evenly, and rapped the door knocker.

Hattie opened the door. "Well, do tell. The hangman cometh."

Graf nodded deferentially.

Hattie stepped onto the porch, closed the door behind her. She motioned toward the swing. "Sit with me a short spell."

They settled into the swing and Graf folded his hands at his waist. Hattie said, "I know who you're here to see and I won't mess with you about it. She is a beauty."

"I…uh…would just like to meet her."

Hattie huffed and turned her head toward him. "You'd be the first that just wanted to…talk with her."

"Be that as it may."

The piano notes—soft and melodic—drifted to the porch. "She even plays the piano, sings like a bird, and she's sharp as a new nail, hangman."

"She plays beautifully."

"Whether you want to just talk to her, or you think of something else more interesting, the price is the same—forty dollars gold coin, or sixty dollars worth of those national bank notes." She flipped her hands. "I ain't no great truster of the government."

Graf withdrew a small purse from his vest pocket and pinched out two twenty-dollar gold coins, and then dropped them into Hattie's open hand. She said, "I know it's none of my business, so you may not answer, but I'm a curious sort. Why her, why now? She's not the only beauty that's passed through town—hell, even The Row has an accident now and then."

Graf stood, needlessly straightened his coat. "It is an old story."

Hattie's eyes probed his, and something passed between them, though neither could identify it. "She reminds you of another woman."

Nearly imperceptibly, he pursed his lips, tilted his head an inch, but said nothing. Hattie said, "One way or the other, every goddamn thing on earth is an old story, hangman." She laughed. "I don't do introductions, so you can proceed inside…and talk." She pushed up from the swing and began to walk away, but Graf said, "How is the boy working out?"

She stopped and turned around. "Still here. So…alright I reckon, considerin' that he spends most of his time with Rufus."

"Indeed."

She turned back around and entered the house, left the door open.

Graf walked through the doorway into the parlor. Two women, dressed in colorful gowns, sat on a couch beside the piano. Graf nodded toward them, but his eyes did not leave the back of Iva's head. The women exchanged a quick glance, smiled at each other, and then stood and walked away. The piano music continued for several seconds, ending with a long, soft note. Iva swiveled gracefully on the bench and looked up into Graf's eyes. Lightly brushed onto her lips was carmine dye, and a touch of rouge highlighted her cheeks. She wore a soft purple gown, with a wide, white collar and on her feet were slippers that matched the gown. Her hair was gathered into a tight bun, held together with three silver stick pins. She held out her right hand and said, "Good afternoon, sir. I'm Iva."

Graf, momentarily speechless, raised his hand and took hers. "I'm so…very pleased to meet you." Her fingers were soft and warm and she withdrew them slowly—a fading caress. She gathered her feet to get up, but Graf shook his head. "I would like for you to play more."

She swiveled back into position. "By all means. Your preferences?"

"Along the lines of what you were playing."

She laughed easily. "Oh my, I must confess that I was piddling on my own. "She paused, her hands resting in front of the keys. "Strauss…*The Blue Danube* perhaps?"

"Perfect."

Graf sat down on the couch and she began. She played the entire piece flawlessly, and Graf knew that if he had been in a seat at a concert hall, there would have been little difference in what he heard.

The last note sounded and then faded away. She turned to face him and cocked her head as if to ask his opinion. Graf said, "Marvelous…I…uh…just marvelous."

She said, "Let me finish for you—marvelous for…one of my profession." Graf opened his mouth to reply, but could find no words. Iva said, "Forgive me, I couldn't resist the tease. I'm impish that way. And besides, it is a good question even if you didn't actually ask it." She leaned forward. "Am I forgiven?"

"You are."

"Good. I might answer it sometime. Now, what shall I call you?"

"Apsel."

"My, but that is an interesting name."

He risked a little smile. "So my parents thought."

She stood and extended her right arm. "Shall we carry this conversation up to my room?"

Graf stood and she placed her hand on his forearm, and then they walked to the staircase, began to climb.

The kitchen door cracked open a few inches and Hattie peered out. Behind her, Dilla looked over her shoulder and said, "She know that's the hangman?"

"I didn't tell her, and I doubt he did either."

"That man gives me the shivers."

"He gives me some too, Dilla, but his gold in my pocket feels as good as any damn man's. What's more, he's right near handsome up close, and I didn't figure that." She cocked her head. "Maybe that makes him spookier yet."

"Least ways, I don't reckon you're frettin' about him gettin' rough."

Hattie slowly shook her head. "Not a chance in this world of that."

Ten minutes after Graf rode away, Hattie tapped on Iva's door. Iva opened the door. "Come in. Sit with me."

"Always like to see how a first visit goes." With a glance, Hattie saw that the dye on Iva's lips was perfectly even, as was her rouge, and that her hair remained pinned in a tight bun.

Iva turned up her palms, widened her eyes, smiled with bemusement. "He never touched me. I feel guilty about making money off of him."

"Not me. Time is time, no matter what a man does with it." A little laugh escaped her. "I didn't believe him."

"He told you that he just wanted to talk?"

"Yep, said he just wanted to meet you."

"Why me—sight unseen?"

"He saw you when Rufus got you."

"He ever been out here before?"

"Not once."

Iva flopped back on the bed, crossed her ankles and locked her fingers. "He seems like a very interesting man, but now that I think on it, he didn't tell me all that much about himself. He just wanted to know about me. I liked him."

"He tell you what he does for a living?"

"He said that he works with the District Court."

"He's the hangman—and a busy one at that. Goddamned old Judge Plume sees to that."

"In a thousand guesses, I'd have never come up with that."

"Our business is full of surprises."

CHAPTER 9

He made not a sound

For over three weeks, Son had followed Rufus around as the man went about his tasks, with no more than a score of words being spoken, and most of those by Rufus. The boy took his meals in the kitchen with Dilla, but Rufus was seldom at the table, preferring to gnaw on jerky at noon and then roast meat on his spit in the evenings. Son had gained weight and had new color in his cheeks. He marveled at the spring in his step, the regular way of things, and had striven with all his being to please the dark man whose wide back he always seemed to be staring at. He mostly fetched and toted, but when Rufus bent over a task, the boy tried mightily to understand the how and why of his actions.

They slogged in the barnyard now, Rufus behind a feisty half-grown bull calf, prodding him with a fist as they approached a gate. Rufus flicked a hand forward, said over his shoulder. "Gate."

Son hustled to the gate and opened it, but when he released it, the gate began to swing back. He reached for it at the same time that the calf jammed its head through the opening, pinning his right forefinger between the post corner and the animal's jaw. Son grunted in pain as he jerked his finger free. Rufus pounded the calf's rump again as he quickly herded it through the gate, and then closed it. When he turned back, Son was staring at his mangled finger, and Rufus saw his face blanch white, his knees buckling. He grabbed him around the shoulders and headed toward the back door of the house.

Rufus opened the door and guided Son to the table. He hooked a chair leg with his boot, pulled it out and sat Son down. Dilla rushed to the table. "What happened?"

Rufus said, "A finger."

Dilla scooted a chair close to Son and sat down. "Let me see here." She gently lifted his right hand from his lap, leaned in for a close look. "Mr. Rufus, I need that towel over there by the pump."

Rufus handed her the towel and she folded it, placed half under the hand and half over it. "You need to go get Miss Hattie."

Hattie stormed into the kitchen, closely followed by Rufus. She hurried to the table, lifted the towel and put it back down. She went to the pump and drew a cup of water. "Little man, I need to pour water on this so I can see better." He nodded. She dribbled water over the wound as she leaned close. From the second knuckle forward, the top half was mostly stripped of flesh, the nail completely gone. Showing whitely were the jagged ends of broken bone. "Goddammit, Rufus!"

Son said, "Wasn't his fault." Rufus turned to walk away. Hattie said, "Wait, we're gonna need your help—if you don't mind."

Hattie looked at Dilla, who shook her head in a silent answer. "Son, more than half this finger is ruined, won't ever be anything but a bother. It's a long ride to town and there's no guarantee Doc will be around. And even if he is—wouldn't be much different than what we can do here." She looked at his face, waited. He said, "Go ahead."

Dilla got up from the table, walked to the rack of utensils hanging on the wall, and took down a heavy pair of scissors. From a cupboard drawer she took a piece of linen and quickly cut several strips and then she dropped them and the scissors into her apron pocket. With one hand, she snatched up a small can of coffee grounds, returned to the table, and sat down.

Hattie said, "Let's lay your hand up on the table…that's it…real gentle. Keep the towel over it."

Son said, "It's too quiet in here. I don't want to hear my heart."

Hattie said, "Well…I…uh…"

"Could Miss Iva come down and play for me—loud and happy?"

Hattie popped up and within a minute, several sets of footfalls sounded on the stairs. Before Hattie sat down again, the notes rang from the piano and with them the soprano voices of four women sang out the first lines of *Camptown Races*.

"Thanks."

"You can thank them all later. You'll be the wounded hero around here for a while."

He closed his eyes, waited. Rufus moved to his side and clamped a hand on each shoulder. Hattie took hold of his left hand as Dilla shifted in her chair. Son opened his eyes, raised his head, and looked up into Rufus's face. The pop of the bone and the whicker of the scissors came as one—discordant from the piano notes and the voices, but instantly lost in them. From the inside corners of Son's eyes, single tears formed and trickled down his cheeks, but his eyes did not leave Rufus's face, and he made not a sound.

With deft fingers, Dilla dabbed a thick coating of the coffee grounds on the stump and then bound it with the cloth strips, tying the ends together. She raised the hand up. "Need to keep it up, little man. Gonna throb like your heart's in it, but that'll pass in time. And I got poultices like magic, they are. Don't you worry. Worse part's over."

Son lowered his head, rested it against Hattie's shoulder, and for a moment he was certain that he would empty his stomach. But he drew deep breaths until the sensation subsided.

Dilla said, "You don't mess with this dressin', little man, just me or Miss Hattie."

Hattie said, "Dilla, let's get him up to my room. He'll sleep in my bed tonight."

They climbed the stairs with Hattie and Dilla locking arms behind the small of his back. Hattie opened the door and they guided him to the bed, laid him down on top of the quilts. Dilla slipped off his boots. Hector stirred, said, "Hattie and Dilla Hattie and Dilla."

Hattie said, "Mind your manners, Hector. This poor boy needs quiet."

"Quiet quiet quiet poor boy poor boy poor boy."

"He'll be alright now, Dilla. You come check on him every once in a while."

"Yes, ma'am." She placed a blanket at the foot of the bed and then left the room.

Hattie picked up a whiskey bottle from her nightstand, uncorked it and poured two fingers worth into a glass, and then filled it from a water pitcher. She sat down on the edge of the bed. "You ever get into any whiskey back in the big city?"

"Took a bottle off a passed out drunk behind a saloon once."

"What'd you think?"

"Didn't like it. But I did like the chew I got out of his pocket."

"Ah…you're too young to have a nasty brown mouth. You ought to stop that." She held out the glass. "This will be better than the alley stuff. Think of it as medicine."

Son took a tentative sip, scrunched his cheeks and mouth. "Whew."

"If it wasn't strong, it wouldn't do you any good. You finish this, and before night, I'll give you another dose. This first night, you'll need it."

He nodded, took another sip, bigger than the first. "I pissed myself at the table."

"I would have too, anybody would have."

"Even Mr. Rufus?"

She shook her head. "No, not Mr. Rufus."

That night the moonlight, white and clean, shown through the window pane, bathing the sleeping boy beside her. Hattie reached across his body, adjusted the pillows framing his wounded hand. The first notes— flute-like— floated upward, as if carried by the moonlight. They were short, yet melodious, like those of a songbird at dawn. She got up, walked to the window, but when she looked down, the notes stopped and she could not see him. She sat down in the chair beside her dresser, and waited.

The door opened silently and Rufus stepped into the room, closed the door behind him. Hattie motioned toward another chair, and he sat down. She pointed to the object in his lap. "What's that?"

"A sling from soft deer hide."

"I'll be damned."

"He has iron."

"That he does…and for a boy."

"If it is not there as a boy, it is not ever there."

Hattie released a long sigh. "Shame he's right-handed."

"He has three fingers, a decent stub, and a thumb. That is enough."

"Should he learn to shoot left-handed?"

"Not if his strong eye is his right."

"Middle finger on the trigger then?"

Rufus nodded. "He will never know the difference."

"You get him up on a horse yet?"

"No."

"Soon though?"

"Soon."

Close by and near the river, a pack of coyotes began to yip and howl, and within seconds another pack answered from a half mile away. The man and the woman listened as the intermittent chorus echoed back and forth for a full minute, and then it ended as suddenly as it had begun, the final howls fading into the night.

Hattie said, "Why do they stop so soon?"

"Say what they want and stop. People should be like that."

"Some are."

"Not you."

"No, but you are, Rufus. You're like the wild coyotes, and that leaves a lot of room for me to say all I damn well please." She got up and walked to his chair. "And you don't really mind that do you, my wild Indian?"

She smiled and slipped the gown from her shoulders, leaned over him, her breasts lightly brushing his cheeks. He raised his head, reached up with the tip of his forefinger and traced the lines of the tattoo on her chin.

"I got it perfect."

"You are a crafter. That's why I let you mark me."

His cat-like purr, deep and throaty, filled the room, and then he said, "But not the only reason."

He cupped his hands underneath her breasts, gently molded them together, raised them to his mouth, and flicked the hard nipples with the tip of his tongue. She leaned back, pulled up the gown, and then padded to the closet, stepped into a pair of low-cut boots. She snatched up a shawl from the foot of the bed, leaned over the sleeping boy for several seconds and listened to his deep, rhythmic breathing.

They left the room, and after they had walked through the kitchen and out the back door, Dilla stepped out of her tiny quarters and walked toward the staircase.

As they neared Rufus' cabin, Hattie pulled on his arm. "No, I want to go down by the river, just grab a tree and bend over, see if you're stud enough to make me howl at the moon."

"Pick a sturdy tree."

"Bold talk."

"We will see."

CHAPTER 10

Wallow…or move on

The women sat at the dining room table as Dilla served breakfast. A tall pot of coffee sat in the middle of the table, and around it were glass bowls of apple and peach preserves and a platter stacked with biscuits and another with bacon.

Sally, long black hair wild and tangled, tilted her head back and sniffed the aroma. "Be a wonderful thing if I could just sit here long enough to be satisfied with that smell without eating anything."

Belle, petite, fully dressed and coiffed, said, "Good luck on that, gal. You sniff while you pass the biscuits and bacon down here. And the apple preserves while you're at it."

Sally reached for the platter and the bowl. "I hate you, you know that, right?"

Except for Iva, they all laughed, and Hattie said, "No law against taking some nice fast walks down to the river now and then, Sally."

"I've been considering that."

Hattie said, "For over three years you have. Forget it.

You're too close to graduating. You can work on it out in California…maybe walk on the sand beside the ocean."

"I might just do that—settle on a rich widower who lost a fine big-assed woman."

They laughed again, but Iva only smiled, looked down and fingered the rim of her cup. Hattie looked at her, said, "You alright?'

"I uh…sure, fine."

"Hey, the boy's going to be fine, don't worry. He's tough…gritty city…like you."

Iva nodded. "I want to see him. Has Dilla already taken him some breakfast?"

"No. Go ahead and take him something. He needs to eat whether he wants to or not. He's gonna need a little whiskey for a day or two more, and I damn sure don't intend to make a drunk out of a pup."

Iva got up and cut open a biscuit, folded two bacon strips into it, and then spooned peach preserves on top of the bacon. She put the biscuit in her napkin and left the table.

Iva knocked lightly on the door, but heard nothing. She cracked the door open and peeked in. Son was propped against three pillows, and he turned his head toward her and rubbed his eyes with his left hand. He blinked her into focus. "Hey."

She said, "Hey to you, Son." She scooted a chair to his bedside and sat down. "Feel like a bite? Dilla's biscuits and bacon and peach preserves?"

"Maybe. Ain't sure where my stomach is yet."

"I understand. I'll put it on the night stand. How's the hand?"

"Hurts like a sonofa…I mean, pretty bad."

"Hang on. It will pass in time." She fingered the sling. "Miss Hattie come up with that?"

His face brightened. "Mr. Rufus made it for me."

"It's beautiful…and the leather work, oh my…"

"Miss Hattie says he'll make it into a pouch for me when I don't need this no more."

She smiled. "Tell you what. You need to get up and stir around some. How about let's go to the piano and I'll teach you some notes…left-handed."

"Alright."

She took his left hand and pulled him up to a sitting position, and then reached for his boots and put them on his feet. She wrapped an arm around his shoulders and steadied him as he got up. He looked down and closed his eyes for a moment, then looked straight ahead, leaning his weight against Iva. "I'm woozy."

"Figured you'd be. We'll just stand here until you're better."

"I've gotta pis…pee, really bad."

"Hold onto the bed post."

Iva reached down for the chamber pot and laid the lid beside it, placed it on the bed. "Here. I'll turn around and hang onto the back of your britches."

She waited as he fumbled with his trouser buttons. "I'm bad with this one hand."

"I'll help." She turned and reached around him, quickly unbuttoned him, and then put her hands back on the top of his trousers.

The stream of urine sang against the porcelain for several seconds and then churned as the level in the pot rose. "Whew."

Iva waited until he had covered himself. "More help?"

"Yeah."

She buttoned him back up. "Ready now?"

"Let's try."

The intermittent sounds carried to the dining room as an odd, yet pleasing, jumble of plunks and perfectly formed notes, and every few seconds Iva's voice carried on the notes before they faded into new ones. Sally picked up her biscuit and tilted her head back as she dropped the last bite into her mouth. One by one, she licked her fingertips, and then took a long sip from her coffee. "That one should have been a momma."

Belle said, "Maybe she was."

Sally said, "Bet not. What do you say, Miss Hattie?"

Hattie stood by the edge of the opening into the parlor so that she could watch the woman and the boy on the piano bench. "I say it don't matter if she was or wasn't." She listened to a few more notes. "All that matters is what I see now. It's like life in general, ladies—all that matters is now forward. The past is mostly something to be let go of."

Sally said, "Easy to say, hard to do."

"Maybe for some, Sally gal, but it don't change the fact." Hattie turned around, swept her eyes over all of them. "Wallow...or move on. Don't appear so hard to me."

Sally waited for Hattie's eyes to stop on her, knew that they would, but there was no hardness in them. Sally said, "I was about that boy's age when we lived in Richmond at the end of the war. Then the Union took it—or what was left of it. Pa done killed up on some road in Maryland, momma grieving her guts out, wondering what would become of me and my two little brothers. We packed all we had in a wagon pulled by a broke-down mare and headed west for an uncle in Missouri. As sorry an old son-of-a-bitch that ever drew breath." She looked away from Hattie, took another sip of coffee. "I hope he died rough."

Hattie said, "We all got our stories, and I ain't heard many happy ones around here." She shrugged her shoulders. "Just makes my point."

Sally looked back up. She smiled, and then laughed. "I think I'll have another biscuit and then barge in there and add my shitty voice to the party."

Hattie laughed with her. "Hell, let's all go, raise the goddamn roof."

CHAPTER 11

The edges of the great wonderment

With the first of May came the rain and the beginning of the heat. It was pleasant, except for the fact that it portended the sultry, suffocating heat of the summer to follow. Iva's corner room had two windows, and they were half raised, allowing the early evening breeze that had pushed away the rain to draw through. She sat with Graf in front of the window facing the river, their chairs touching, his hand resting on top of hers.

Iva said, "The river is up with the rains and it has raised its voice. I love the sound."

"Yes, it is a peaceful murmur."

She raised her fingers, interlaced them with his. "So like you, Apsel, my mystery guest—a peaceful murmur."

"Is that so bad?"

"It is not, but still a mystery."

"My feelings for you grow."

"And mine for you."

Graf felt the rush inside his chest, waited for it to subside. "I would imagine that I don't have much competition as…a conversationalist."

She squeezed his fingers. "I enjoy that greatly, but—that is not entirely what I meant."

The rush came back inside of Graf and he turned his head toward her. "Despite who I am and what I do?"

"You are an officer of the court, and to the men once condemned, the most important. I consider it to be an honorable profession."

"You are in the vast minority."

"That is fitting—it is where I have been all of my life."

Graf lifted her hand, studied the long fingers, the manicured nails. "Fingers created for the keyboard."

"Ah yes, the child prodigy, rising star in Baltimore… destined for greatness. I performed at many of the same venues as the great tenor, Granville Pollard—actually had the privilege of knowing him and his wife, Letha, quite well. Had I not left, we would have performed together at some point."

"And yet…along the way?"

"Along the way were parents so forceful, so domineering that…that I became lost to myself. And then a husband— an arranged thing between two prominent families—who became so jealous that I was afraid to so much as smile at another man. He is not much larger than me. A little weasel of a man, yet a popinjay through and through."

"A what?"

"Someone who struts around like they are an eagle, when they are more like a blue jay."

"I need to remember that word. I meet more than a few of that breed."

They listened to the river song, and in the oaks behind the house the breeze freshened and the leaves sang in the air with the river. "It doesn't seem like that situation is one that you could just walk away from."

"Oh, it wasn't, and even though it's been over five years, I still feel as if I'm running."

"How did you manage to get away?"

"I planned it for weeks. The particular night didn't matter—he slept in a drunken stupor every night. I gathered every small item of value and what little money was there and put it in a knapsack. And I put in a derringer and a Colt pistol, ball and powder, and two knives from the kitchen. The only thing of value the bastard ever did for me was to teach me the use of firearms." She glanced at him, smiled wickedly. "Ironic, isn't it? I would have happily shot him had he ever chased me down." The smile faded. "And then I just put on a set of his clothes and walked into the night."

"I am surprised that he, or one of the families, didn't send Pinkertons to find you."

"They may well have. But I chopped off most of my hair and hid it in a trash heap. I soiled my face and clothing— became the woman that none would recognize, and got on the early morning train pointed west." She raised her arms theatrically. "A new woman with a new name was born—Iva Lockwood."

Graf looked out the window and Iva watched his mind churn with the question that, more than any other, she knew he sought an answer to. There was no use in avoiding it; she would spare him the asking.

"And now, Apsel, you want the answer to the great question."

"It is none of my business. I have no right to ask it."

"There is no single answer, which is to say that there is no…justification, and I know that is what you would like to hear. A young woman driven to near madness, evil forces aligned against her, in hiding, running out of money…all that. That was a part of it, but not all." She stood and stepped to the window ledge. "What if I just wanted to be like the Arkansas River down there—wild and free, Apsel? Dependent on no one, answerable to no one, the past forever behind me."

He stood, moved behind her, circled her waist with his arms. "I understand the need to be free of the past more than you can imagine."

She wrapped her arms with his. "You loved once?"

"A very long time ago."

"But it does not seem so long ago, does it?"

"Some days it does, some not."

"And when you are with me?"

He shook his head. "It is very strange. It is both."

She turned to face him, placed her hands on his cheeks. "That is not strange, Apsel…it is not strange at all. What is strange is that I have lived twenty-six years and I have never kissed a man because I wanted to."

Graf whispered, "Do you now?"

"Yes."

They touched lips in the manner of teenagers first exploring the edges of the great wonderment—the forbidden element of life both tender and savage—once locked away and now freed. Their lips parted, tongues brushed, and the passion rose, and in their mouths was the salt taste of mingled tears. Iva buried her face against his neck and said,

"Carry me to the bed, Apsel, and make love to me like we were virgins with no pasts."

He swept her into his arms, cradled her for a moment, and then carried her to the bed.

They lay in tangled sheets, Iva's head nestled against Graf's shoulder. The sound of hammering carried through the open window and Iva knew that it came from Rufus's cabin, and she knew that he and the boy were working side by side. She got up and wrapped a gown around her shoulders. She said, "Come look."

Graf pulled on his trousers and joined her. In the light of a lamp hung from the cabin porch ceiling, they saw Rufus and Son huddled over what appeared to be an animal trap, the boy handing tools to Rufus whenever he held out a hand. Iva said, "I've come to adore that boy. He's like a grown man all scrunched up in a little body."

"He's a survivor. It turns out that I am very happy he chose my boarding house to steal from. Destiny should give him a good life." He paused, the discomfort growing inside his brain. "I have mixed feelings about Sheriff Colley sending him here. Hattie Wax—in her own way—is not a bad thing, but…Rufus…"

"He seems to have taken him under his wing."

"I know."

"Rufus is very quiet and very—efficient—at everything, it seems."

"Above all else, he is a Sioux."

"And that is why you have doubts?"

"It is believed by many in these parts that he rode in the Little Bighorn massacre."

"That was many years ago."

"Not that many." She felt his chest rise against her back as he drew a long breath and slowly released it. "After the war, I rode with the Army for a time, and almost stayed in. I could have been out there that day."

"But you were not. You should let it go."

"I know. Even Sheriff Colley has, and he lost a brother in the massacre. That should be enough for me."

"Enough of this talk. I don't want to spoil this night."

"I'm sorry." He leaned down and kissed her neck. "That is the last thing I would want."

"You are forgiven."

"I suppose that I should go now." It was more of a question than a statement.

"Stay longer. I don't care what she thinks."

"It is her house, her rules."

The sound inside of Iva's head was like rushing water, and then words came, as if spoken by another woman. "Only so long as I stay."

The thump of Graf's heart was a drum beat in his chest. He said, "My God, can this be real? What has happened here?"

"A dam has burst inside of me—that is what it feels like has happened."

He touched his forehead to the back of her head, drew in the fragrance of her hair. "You need to think on this for a few days…but…the thought of you being with another man…"

"I have no intention of being with another man—here or anywhere else." She walked to the dresser top and picked up one of the two gold coins. "This one is yours, the other Miss Hattie's, and the same with all those you have left."

He took the coin and said, "No, it is not mine, it is ours."

CHAPTER 12

Shadow and light, Miss Hattie

Hattie and Iva sat across from each other at a small table in Hattie's room. Hattie had listened to Iva talk for several minutes without interjecting a single word of her own. When Iva finally stopped talking, Hattie stared at her for several seconds before grabbing the neck of a whiskey bottle and pouring herself two finger's worth in a glass. She stood, walked to Hector's cage, cocked her head at the parrot, and then quaffed the whiskey. "Hector, this is a crazy thing I just heard. Crazy, crazy."

"Crazy Crazy Crazy."

Iva said, "I know it sounds…crazy…but I…"

"You should take up drinking, Iva."

"I don't do well with it."

"It would without a damn doubt clear up your thinkin' a good deal." Hattie returned to the table and poured more whiskey, and then rolled the glass in her fingers. "You think you've found yourself a gentleman in the hangman, but let me tell you something. A gentleman is just another goddamn man tricky enough to fool some women for a time."

"It doesn't feel like a trick to me."

"Of course it doesn't, that's the way tricks operate." She took a sip of whiskey. "Look here now. So you had yourself one magical screw. It happens every once in a while…even me. I saw more cocks than a fly caught in an outhouse for a year before it ever happened to me, but I had sense enough to let it go real quick." She took another sip, and then picked up a box of Lucifer matches, stuck one, and lit a thin, black cigar. She shot a precise jet of smoke a yard long. "How old are you, twenty-five, twenty-six?"

"Twenty-six."

"You need to add twenty to that before you can see men clearly. Of course you can't do that, but I'm already there, so I can see for you, if you let me. He's way closer to my age than yours. Hell, he'll fall apart long before you and you'll have to put up with his dying ass if you don't have the guts to put a pillow over his head—which you probably won't. Shovel spoonfuls of mush in his mouth, wipe his ass. Ah!"

Iva said, "It's because he's the executioner, that's what really bothers you, isn't it?"

Hattie emptied her glass, gave it a little shove with a finger, and drew on the cigar. "It's a consideration."

"Well it's not with me. Judge Plume is the one that puts them up there."

"It's spooky that any man would take up such a trade. There must be something wrong inside his head. For Christ's sake, I don't think the man has a single friend in town… shit…maybe old Lucian, the trapper, and his hound dog, but I've seen people cross the street rather than pass by him."

"That is beyond reason to me."

"You want to know what really bothers me, here it is: Any man that can spin a head as beautiful and smart as yours so damn fast…just by a few *talking* visits and one—I reckon—screwin', has got to be unnatural in some way, and it most likely ain't a good way."

Iva got up and walked to the window, looked into the swirling oak leaves, the sunlight filtering through like ever-changing latticework. "I'm not as naïve about men as you think I am. The first man that I thought I loved was my father—as it should be for any daughter—and he turned out to be a tyrant, which led to an arranged marriage to another tyrant, which led to my escape. Then I became mostly a kept woman. Oh, I tried a few regular houses, but I caused too many fights—between the girls and the men both." She huffed a mirthless laugh. "The men who kept me were mostly married, so I lived away from society, available during the day, when they could slip away from some bank or high place of business. And then, at night, I was afraid to venture out. I've always attracted too much attention."

Hattie said, "The damnable curse of beauty—something I've never had to deal with."

"Yet men are drawn to you."

"I have assets, but more than that, I know men better than they know themselves."

"Maybe most men, but not all."

Hattie ignored the remark. "Why did any of the rich keepers ever let you go?"

"I think it was my detachment. I found places to go in my mind while they grunted and pawed. It must have been like mounting a mannequin with a hole in it." A minute passed in silence. "Come look at something with me, Miss Hattie."

Hattie walked to her side, looked out the window. Iva said, "Look at the patterns of light and shadow through the leaves—there is as much one as the other. But all I have ever studied is the shadow—the shade of the oak—and I'm tired of it. The first time Apsel ever touched me it was with one finger to the back of my hand. And he *asked* me if he could. Can you imagine that? He had bought the right to open my gown and push me down on the bed and have his way, and he *asked* to touch my hand. I almost made fun of him, and then I realized that he meant it."

Hattie drew on the cigar, blew the smoke through the open window. "By God, but he's a slick one, I'll give him that." She shook her head, laid her hand on Iva's shoulder. "We ain't gettin' anywhere today, that's plain. But if I have to chain you to that oak out there, you're gonna stay here for a while until you have a chance to think all this over— castin' your lot with…him."

"Shadow and light, Miss Hattie. I'm sick of the shadow. I'm not entertaining another man."

"I know, but you can stay anyway." She glanced upward at nothing. "I've evidently gone soft over the years…in some ways."

The door to Rufus' cabin shut with a whump, and the women looked down to see Rufus and Son, side by side, walking toward the river. On the boy's left shoulder rested the big Winchester .44-40 rifle, the barrel pointed to the sky. He no longer wore the sling, but the stub of his right forefinger was still bandaged.

Iva said, "Guess we'll be hearing more shots from the river soon."

"We will. He says the boy is a quick study."

"Apsel says he is a survivor, and that he deserves a good life." She smiled. "I do so like that boy."

"Well, on that I can agree with the hangman. Then again, we all are and we all do, but it don't always work out." She flicked the ashes from the cigar. "You can verify that with him when you ask him what it feels like when he jerks the trap door lever."

"I don't see any need to ask him that."

"You will…sooner or later."

Iva turned away from the window and walked from the room.

CHAPTER 13

More horse than man

John Post Oak and the riders behind him rode at a trot along the riverbank until they were within a hundred yards of Hattie's house, and then they slowed to a walk. It was just before midnight and the quarter moon shimmered silver on the river, but Post Oak paid no attention to the beauty offered him. He was a man who had never sought the beauty in anything of the earth, or above it. All of the men rode with the practiced ease of years on horseback. The two white men were in worn saddles; Post Oak and the other three Indians were bare back, and even the Indians marveled at the union of Post Oak and his paint mount—two creatures perfectly attuned to the other, each formidable in its own right, yet together as one, a sight far beyond their ability to describe in words. The saddled men wore pistol belts and their Winchester rifles were in scabbards; the Indians carried their rifles tethered with short ropes tied to the rifle levers and their waists, and crisscrossed over their shoulders and chests were full cartridge belts. On Post Oak's head was a United States Army hat with an eagle feather in a snakeskin band.

Post Oak said, "Wait here."

The Indian nearest him said, "It is a waste of time. You will not get him away from his white whore. We do not need him. Why do you care?"

Post Oak turned his horse with the touch of a knee, looked at the man, held his eyes until he looked down. "Maybe I am trying to save him, but it is no matter to you." He paused, listened for a moment to the flow of the river. "You keep making speeches like that to me and we *will* need another man."

Rufus opened his eyes and listened to the sound of the coyote-like howl that came from the river. Within seconds there came another howl, shorter and closer, and then another closer yet, and then silence. He got out of his bunk, slipped into his trousers and boots, and then walked out of the cabin. He spied the man and the horse fifty feet behind the cabin—a portrait in shadow, edged in moonlight—and the singularity identified the horseman even before Rufus walked up to the horse and ran his palm gently from the great eyes downward to the sniffing nostrils.

Rufus said, "Where do you find such horses?"

"I have good eyes and I roam where I please and take what I want." With a liquid motion, he lifted his right leg and slipped off the horse, his moccasins barely making a sound on the hard-packed earth. He held out his right arm and they locked forearms and hands for a moment and then separated.

Rufus said, "It has been a long time."

"Yes, and it was a good train as I remember—many rich whites and two blue soldiers to scalp, and a finger bone from a stupid woman too proud of her ring." He sighed. "And then the dog-fucking Pinkertons came and made the trains a lot of trouble, but they are not on every train."

"And you still have the scalps and the bone."

"As sure as the coyotes shit in the forest."

Rufus said, "Why do you come?"

"To save you from all this." He swept his hand toward the cabin, the barn, and the house. "Doing chores like a red nigger for the great white whore, minding a child trailing after you. It is no life for a warrior like you who rode with Crazy Horse and all of us who killed yellow hair Custer and his soldiers at the Greasy Grass River, and who robbed trains and banks."

"And now you are on wanted posters, and you—or your body—is worth five-thousand dollars. And worse than the Pinkertons, the famous deputy named Hatch is after you."

"It would be money earned in hell…even for him. I plan to run a long stick up his ass and cook him slow someday."

"I told you when I left that I was tired of it all. What makes you think anything has changed now?"

"A hunch I reckon. After years pass, a man like you will return to his roots."

Rufus looked toward the big house and then back at Post Oak. Rufus said, "The woman…she is more like us than the whites."

"Hummm…so she has a hold on you."

"It is a hold that suits me."

"It is hard to hear you talk like this."

"You don't have to listen anymore."

Post Oak's eyes reflected the moonlight, appearing to Rufus as wolf eyes over the sharp, high cheekbones, and for long seconds he stared into them, wondered if he would feel the beginning of fear, but he did not. Post Oak said, "You are the only man that I could ever imagine fearing, and I am the only man that you could ever imagine fearing. We belong together."

"We did for a time."

"Say no more for now. I will be in these parts for a while. I have a good hideout, and there are stupid whites wandering through the wilderness, and those trains that carry Wells money. We will talk again." He mounted the horse, turned it away, and then back. "A woman is only a wet gash that satisfies until your cock goes limp."

"Some."

"All." He eased the horse away in a walk, but after a few yards he turned it back toward Rufus. "I have never told you about the blue soldier at the Greasy Grass River that I let live."

"None lived."

"I know, but this one should have. I rode up on him when he was on the ground, guns empty, wild-eyed, and I waited for him to cry out and plead with me, but he did not. He looked me in the eye and said, 'Fuck you to hell, you red bastard.' He was not like the others, running and crying for mercy, and I felt like the Great Spirit—with power to decide life or death—and I tipped my hat to him and rode away. I should have told our warriors to let him live and ride away… so that he could tell the story of our victory. We should have left one to tell the story from the whites' side."

"For what reason? The story was told in dead bodies for them to see. Besides, they claim all our victories are massacres and that theirs are noble victories."

"Ah, my friend, you have no story-telling in you—no desire to write history."

"That is true, but why tell me this now?"

"Because there is more history to be made...ours...yours and mine. There will never be another Greasy Grass River, but we will have our victories, and one day, after a good one, you and I together can decide who we might let live to tell our story."

He turned his horse a final time and disappeared into the night.

When Rufus reached his cabin, he heard the door to Son's room creak open, and they boy stepped out. "Finger got to throbbin', woke me up. I think I was layin' on it."

"Well, you ain't now. Go back to bed."

Son turned, hesitated, then turned back and said, "Mr. Rufus, who was that man?"

"Did you listen?"

"I swear not, just peeked around the corner."

"Just a man I used to know."

Son nodded, thought better of asking any other questions. "He sure looks right on a horse...like you."

"He is more horse than man."

Son studied Rufus in profile as he pondered what he had just said. He wanted to ask more, but instead he walked back into his room and closed the door.

CHAPTER 14

Content to just watch the watchers... for now...

Graf came on a Sunday, an hour past noon, in a buggy with a covered top. He tied the mare to the post, walked to the front door, and knocked. Sally opened the door, gave him a tiny nod, and stepped aside. "I'll go get Miss Hattie."

"No need for that. Just let Iva know that I'm here." She walked toward the kitchen, and he sat down in a chair beside the piano. Within a minute, Hattie opened the kitchen door and walked to the sofa and set down. She motioned to the whiskey bottle and two glasses on the end table beside her. "Too early for you to have a snort with me?"

"I don't use it."

"I don't either, hangman, I just drink it." She uncorked the bottle and poured herself a half glass, took a sip. "There now—smooth and hot. You don't know what you're missing."

"I do know. I didn't say that I never drank."

She lifted her head, looked up at the chandelier for a moment, then back at Graf. "Enough with the nice parlor conversation, huh? You and me ain't ever going to have such a thing. As a customer, you're as good as any other. But what you are now—and I'm cloudy as hell on that to tell you the strict truth—upsets me."

"I'm sorry for that, but I don't see why."

"You are not sorry and you wouldn't see. The prize is too great."

"So, you consider it as a contest—a tug of war—between you and me?"

"Reckon it is that in a way. But I don't want to keep her to make me money. Hell, I don't need money. I want her to stay for a while and make enough money to get away from this wild-ass territory and find a man to treat her as special as she is."

"And you don't consider me able."

"She can do a damn sight better than you, hangman."

"As far as the money is concerned, I am far from a pauper. I have lived very frugally for many years. The bank is happy to have me as a depositor—not as happy as they are to have you—I understand that. But that is not what really bothers you."

Hattie held the glass under her nose and drew in the aroma of the whiskey as she swirled it around. "I don't consider it a natural occupation."

"Nor do I consider yours to be."

She tossed her head back and laughed. "Goddamn, you don't say! What could be more natural than a man and a woman thrashin' all happy in a naked embrace? And what could be more unnatural than a man yankin' a lever and listenin' for another one's neck to pop?"

"I consider it far more natural for me to perform a professional execution on an already condemned man than for a woman to pretend that she's *all happy* while being taken by a man she cares nothing for."

"There are different kinds of happy, hangman. We sportin' ladies—including Iva Lockwood—are happy long enough to make good money. How else are we going to do it? Be lawyers, or marshals, or bankers, or railroad officials, or…professional executioners?!" She took a sip of whiskey, caught her breath. "You sound like a mealy-mouth preacher—all full of the spirit and empty of common sense."

"So, for you it is all biology—like glorified beasts in the barnyard—and practicality, gathering in all the pleasures and comforts that you can?"

Hattie's eyes radiated anger, and a cruel smile formed. "You're treadin' on my bare toes, hangman, and we need to stop, but I'll say this: you might consider me a sow, but you also might be surprised if you knew how many people in that shit hole of a town I offer a helpin' hand to in a steady way. You might be surprised to know that every single girl on The Row that gets the pox squirted in her by some filthy drifter gets seen by a real doctor—and sometimes sent away to be seen by higher docs in St. Louis, and I pay for it all. You might be surprised to know that when wagon load of grub or clothes gets delivered by the stores to some ramshackle home for the street waifs, it's me that sends it. I don't go, and I don't send Rufus because I'm afraid to be connected, for fear some idiot with a lethal dose of religion wouldn't take it." She drained the glass and banged it on the table.

"I…did not mean to call you…an animal…I…"

She cut him off with knife-like wave of her hand. "I don't really care what you meant, I don't even know why I got so riled. Silly." She waved her hand again, slowly and with her fingers spread. "Maybe I am a sow…with more teats than you can imagine."

She stood and turned to walk away, but before she took a step, she saw Iva standing at the top of the stairs. The women glanced at one another for only a moment before Hattie walked toward the kitchen and Iva came down the stairs.

Iva walked up to Graf, who now stood with a visage set in bewilderment. She said, "I imagine that didn't go well."

He nodded, said, "Let's go outside."

They walked out onto the porch, but Graf took her hand, continued to the buggy. He said, "Let's go into town, go to some stores, have some supper later."

She was dressed modestly in a quiet, white dress with no frills, buttoned to the neck. "I have a better idea. Let me go back and find some britches and a shirt and we'll buy some store food in town and then come back along the river and find a place for a picnic."

"I would like that."

"And I want to take Son along."

"I would like that too—very much."

Iva went to her room and changed clothes, and then went back downstairs and pushed open the kitchen door. Hattie was sitting at the table with Hector on her shoulder, a cigar clenched in her teeth. Dilla was puttering about in the pantry. "Miss Hattie, we're going into town for a while and…uh…would like to take Son along."

Hattie studied the smoke pattern curling up from the cigar ash. She flipped the hand holding the cigar and said, "Up to him." She drew on the cigar, spoke with the expelled smoke. "Just bring him back."

Iva found him on the porch of Rufus' cabin, both the man and the boy sitting at a little table. Son held a hickory-handled knife with an eight-inch blade and on the table was a whetting stone. They both looked up at Iva. She nodded, smiled, and said, "Hey there, Mr. Rufus…Son. That's a fine looking knife."

Son said, "Mr. Rufus says I can have it soon as I learn to sharpen it right."

"That is kind of him. A good knife is a very useful tool."

Rufus raised his eyes at her, but said nothing. She said, "I'm not as fragile as I look. I know knives and guns as well. Your shooting coming along too, Son?"

"Yes ma'am."

She said to Rufus, "Did you turn him around?"

"Couldn't. He's strong right-eyed."

Son held up his right hand and wiggled his middle finger. "This one works fine."

"Good for you, then. Listen, the reason I came is me and Mr. Graf are going into town, and we wondered if you might like to go along. Maybe shop a little, get some food… come back and eat down by the river. Miss Hattie says it's all right with her."

Son looked at Rufus, who shrugged his shoulders and got up. "You ain't tethered."

Hattie looked at Son and said, "Alright then?"

"Sure, when?"

"Right now, we'll be in front." He glanced down at his shirtsleeves and then his trousers. "Your clothes are just fine. Come on."

Graf was standing by the buggy and when they drew near, he stepped forward and extended his right hand and tapped it on the boy's shoulder. "It is good to see you, son." He laughed easily, said with emphasis, "I mean, *Son*. I understand you still go by that."

"It's still me."

Graf nodded toward Son's right hand. "The finger coming along?"

"What's left of it. Miss Dilla says the bandage comes off soon and then I need to toughen it up."

"I'm sure she knows what is best."

"I think she's a magic woman. She tells me about where she came from—New Orleans—and that there's good magic and bad magic down there, and she only took the good."

Iva said, "Shall we, gentlemen?"

Graf helped her onto the seat, and when she extended her hand to Son, Graf said, "No, why don't we let him drive. Come to the other side."

Son made a noise that was half surprise and half laugh. "Really?"

"Why not? I understand that you are learning to ride a horse now. This is far easier. She won't require much driving."

Graf unhitched the mare and took a seat beside Iva. "Just tell her giddy up and tug a little on the left rein and she'll head to town."

From the parlor window, Hattie and Sally watched

through the haze of cigar smoke. Sally said, "I don't know what to make of that."

Hattie said, "Not often—but every once in a great while—something happens that don't make any sense to me."

"I take it this is one of those times."

"It sure as hell is."

"Reckon she'll take up with him?"

"Seems determined…for now."

"What could change her mind?"

"Needs to see a hangin' soon. Maybe she sees him up there lookin' like some goddamn black angel of death, tuggin' the noose around a neck, it'll take hold—sensify her."

Sally looked sideways at Hattie. "Don't believe I ever heard that word."

"Can't recollect that I ever said it before, but you know what it means, don't you?"

"Yes I do, Miss Hattie. I do for sure."

An hour before sunset, Iva, Apsel, and Son stood at the edge of a steep slope leading down to the river. At the boy's feet were a small pile of stones that he had gathered, all with smooth surfaces and none larger than the palm of his hand. He picked up one of the smaller stones with his right hand, and then gave it a tentative overhand toss toward the water. The stone bounced halfway down the slope.

"I'm still shy of throwin' it real hard. But watch this."

He picked another one with his left hand and threw it all the way to the water's edge. "Mr. Rufus says it's a weakness to just lean on one hand to do something."

Iva said, "That's sound advice. I learned it early on the keyboard."

"But I've got to get tough with the sore one." He picked up another one with his right hand and threw it farther down the bank than the first.

Apsel said, "Give it time, there is no rush."

Iva and Apsel exchanged smiles and walked a few steps away before they stopped and turned back to watch Son. Their fingers brushed and Iva linked hers with Apsel's. She said, "What will become of him in time?"

"It is hard to say."

"I wonder how long he will stay around here."

"Hopefully, not long."

"Because of Hattie, or Rufus?"

"Both."

Fifty yards to the west, standing in a copse of cottonwoods, Hattie and Rufus watched the scene unfold. Hattie said, "To anybody who didn't know it all, it sort of looks like a nice little family—a hangman, a young whore, and a street waif." She snorted a little laugh. "But, look at us from a distance—an old whore and an Indian ex-outlaw."

"Just five people. You think too much."

"It's a habit of mine."

"You should break it."

"They can't have him."

Rufus looked at her. "What makes you think they want him?"

She shook her head. "Gawwd…blind men."

"He will soon grow into a man."

"And that's a damn shame, Rufus—a damn shame that boys have to grow into men."

"I did, and you don't seem to mind."

"I don't think you were ever a boy."

John Post Oak raised his head and flared his nostrils as he drew in the breeze that carried the perfumed scent of Hattie Wax. He had left his horse with the two men who had ridden with him to a point a half mile from her place, and from there he had traveled on moccasin-covered feet with the evanescent shadows of the trees lining the riverbank. He had intended to spy on Rufus and the boy, and maybe the woman if she came out, but it was a curiosity to him that he now watched Rufus and the fiery-haired whore as they watched the boy with another man and woman. He had crept as close as he dared with Rufus present. Absent him, Post Oak would have enjoyed slithering through the shade and then the long grass so close to any of them that he could have heard them breathe. But for now he was content just to watch the watchers, and farther away, the watched, and puzzle on what the silent drama might mean and what part Rufus played. Rufus was the only one of worth.

CHAPTER 15

Imprints on my soul

Judge Burleigh Plume sat stiffly in his favorite chair, which he had turned slightly to face the tall window of his study and the deep gloom of night beyond. The grandfather clock in the hallway sounded its soft melody and then the chime hammer sounded a single final note marking the hour. He was dressed in the formal attire that a few hours before he had worn under the judge's black robe that defined him as he sat perched high on the courtroom bench. He was within three months of attaining his sixtieth year, yet his well-trimmed hair was devoid of gray, his features angular and handsome except for his chin, which he had always considered weak. This he had corrected with a goatee, full and wide.

The faint creak of the door opening behind him broke his reverie, but he did not turn his head. The hallway lamp bled yellow into the room and against the window glass, and in the panes he watched his wife's gown materialize, white and ghostlike. Her scent—like lilacs on a faint breeze—wafted to his nostrils and he breathed it in, felt the small hand on his right shoulder, and he raised his hand to touch it for a moment.

She said, "Dearest, you need your rest. Come you to bed."

"In time."

"This mustn't become a habit."

"It will not; there are not that many sentencing days."

"Ah, yes…the sentencing days. And yet, you only do your duty as God leads you to do that duty. We both know this to be true. He was a sinful, despicable man if ever one lived, and he took life wantonly. How could you not send him to the gallows?"

"He is not the one upon whose memory I dwell."

"Hummm…so still the young cowboy you cannot let go. It has been months, Burleigh, he was found guilty by a jury that combed over every detail of the encounter, and the boy had decent counsel as well."

"But it was I who chose the death sentence rather than prison. It was I, Estelle."

"And God led you to that decision…as He always does."

"I agonized."

"Understandably. But it is finished. You were trusted and sent here to a harsh land by the highest authorities to restore civility…the rule of law. Harsh measures are required in a harsh land, sir, and there is no harsher land than The Indian Territory, in which shadow we reside."

"Well, there is little doubt that I am recognized as sufficiently harsh by the citizenry."

She lifted her hand from his shoulder and clenched her fist before replacing it, the memory of the episode with Hattie Wax flashing through her mind. "You must never confuse the citizenry with the rabble, and there is no greater rabble than that flamboyant harlot."

"It was a memorable scene, that."

"You should have had her held in contempt…or…or for disturbance of the peace. That was the third time, sir. The third time!"

"And if I had done that, perhaps she would have gotten what she wanted."

"More notoriety?"

"That was my first thought…and second and third, for that matter, and the reason for ignoring her…at least to this point."

"It would appear to me that she is hardly in need of more notoriety."

"Indeed." He reached up and gathered his goatee in the fingers of his right hand, stroked it like a man squeezing water from a cloth. "Then why?"

"She is simply a brazen hussy. Why wonder about why such a creature would make a public spectacle?"

"And yet I do."

"Husband, at times you worry me. A man of your intellect and morality wasting time and thought on such as this." She shook her head, looked down.

"Three times she has done this…the three most difficult cases in all these years for which I've handed down the death sentence."

"Coincidence. Probably a belly full of liquor…or God knows what else. Or she just wants to be seen, all gaudy, with her talking bird on her shoulder. Or they may have been regulars of hers—lost income."

"Not the young cowboy. He would have used The Row."

She flipped up her hands, shook her head again, then rested them on his shoulders, smoothed the cloth of his coat. "I seem to be making little progress here."

"Introspection is always beneficial, even if painful."

"I am not at all certain about that premise. Not when introspection becomes self-flagellation."

"This is beginning to feel like an exchange with a wily attorney."

"Should I take that as a compliment, or an admonishment?"

"I suppose both."

"With weight on the latter, no doubt." She waited for his response, but there was none. "I'll leave you be, husband. I am not in the habit of tilting at windmills."

She turned to leave, but he raised his right hand, said, "Stay...please." He waited until her image again filled the window. "Your literary metaphor intrigues me."

"How so? It seems straightforward enough to me."

He raised both hands, spread his fingers, and rotated them back and forth. "Don Quixote believes he sees giants to be slain, and he cannot discern the windmills that turn the millstone—necessary and useful tools."

"No, sir, I see clearly any windmills, and that noisy harlot is no useful windmill."

"So I am the useful tool of God, she, the tool of Satan... to be ignored. Simple as that?"

"That is an accurate and succinct summation in my view, except for the fact that she certainly cannot be ignored. Sooner or later, you will have to put her in her place."

"Would to God that anything were that simple, my

dear. We all are children of the Fall, imperfect beings in our respective ways."

"Some imperfections dwarf others."

"Yet, you know of the stories afloat about her…brighter side—goods and monies that appear at poor houses, orphanages."

"'Stories' indeed. You can't really believe all that."

"What if any of it is true, even a single time?"

"Even the vilest people sometimes do decent things to assuage their own self-loathing or to justify their…methods."

Estelle's image disappeared from the window pane, but she did not leave the study. She scooted a chair next to his, sat down and curled her legs under her, arranged her shawl around her shoulders. The minutes ticked by in silence until the hall clock chimed the quarter hour.

Plume said, "I'm not sure how much longer I want to do this."

"Our conversation, or holding your judgeship?"

"The latter, of course."

"I wasn't sure of that."

"Estelle, you are my only sounding board…my only true advocate. There is a great loneliness with this position; without you I don't think it would be bearable."

She reached over, laid her hand on his. "This I know, Burleigh: you…we…must strengthen our resolve to see this through, and it won't be forever. We will return East one day, leave this savage land and its rabble to their own devices and ends. You will have a highly-respected law practice and the place of honor that you deserve for sacrificing years of your life to a nearly impossible cause. And we won't be arguing— if this indeed is what we are doing presently—about a screeching, blasphemous harlot with a talking bird on her shoulder."

He puffed air through his nostrils, the trace of a rueful smile on his lips that she could not see. "That thought is of some comfort, but all of this—these years, the sentences, the agonizing—indelible imprints on my soul."

"Indelible imprints to be sure, but not on your soul, my dear. Rather, they are imprints on what will be your history; I would go so far as to say your essence…but no farther. There is nothing you have ever done on the bench, or will do, that stains your good and pure soul." She moved closer, placed both hands over his. "This is what bothers me the most about these incidents—the possibility that you would doubt your honor and goodness…and…I dare say, your *righteousness.*"

"Such a dangerous word, that."

"No, sir, it is not; the dangerous word is *unrighteous.* The Bible refers many times to righteous people—great leaders-- who are led by God's hand, as you know, and it refers to the unrighteous as well."

He lowered his head, pinched the bridge of his nose. "We seem to be moving slowly in a great circle here."

"It would seem so."

"Go to bed, my dear. I think that I require a short night stroll."

"You know how I despise your night strolls. I may as well sit in your chair until you return, then we will retire together."

"I will be just another shadow man moving quietly about in the darkness."

"With your revolver in your coat pocket."

"Only for your peace of mind."

She stood, waited for him to get up, watched as he arched his back against the stiffness, drew in a long breath. She said, "Don't you realize just who it is that is the real deliverer of final justice?"

Plume turned toward her, his head nodding steadily. "My deputies play a critical role, true enough, but…"

"It is not 'deputies', rather 'deputy'. It is your tall black Deputy Dak Hatch that is the real deliverer. Often he brings you bodies covered with blankets in the bed of his wagon, and for them, the final justice has been administered sans any jury, or deliberations, or lawyers, or your …agonizing. If anyone should be agonizing over his actions, it should be him, and I am not at all certain that even he should. But he is the one out there with the wild people and he shoots them down without much, if any, deliberation, on that I would wager greatly."

"I believe him to be an honorable man in every respect. He has my complete trust. He is a fearsome man, true enough, but he is unlike those whom he tracks down. He has a moral compass, they do not."

"It is none of them, nor Hatch, about whom I fret. Go you now and hurry with your walk in the dark and come back and rest."

Plume knew of his destination before he had taken a dozen steps away from his front door. He increased the length of his stride; it was not a short walk to National Cemetery. The air was cottony, the gentle night breeze caressing his face, the steady cadence of his footfalls the only sounds. A half moon cast light silvery and not exiguous, giving shape to houses and trees and fences, and after a thousand footfalls it was the white-washed boundary fence of the cemetery that the man's eyes locked onto in the distance. Once through the arched gateway, his gaze swept back and forth at the headstones and crosses, their pale reflections and shadows forming a latticework of past lives, now one with the earth, dust to dust. But some were not yet dust and it was one of these that the judge sought, and he knew that the grave would be in the far corner of the cemetery, where the paupers without families were granted their final fragment of the great earth.

His visual purple now active, beacon-like, Plume moved to the smallest of the headstones—all thin and boot-top high—until he spied the still rounded patch of ground with no sign of flower or remembrance. He squared himself in front of it, facing east, knew that the feet of the body also faced east, as was the custom of the church folks who had seen to the proper burial of the young cowboy, and who believed that anyone who came to read the inscription would also be in proper and respectful Resurrection Day position, looking in the direction of Jesus Christ's return —The Coming— that would empty the cemetery of all believers. Plume knelt, blinked into focus the shallow inscription.

DELBERT DILLINGHAM

BORN 1862—IT IS BELIEVED

DIED MARCH 27, 1886

IN HOPE OF RESURRECTION

Plume knelt on one knee, lowered his head as he placed his right hand on top of the headstone, and then he prayed aloud.

CHAPTER 16

I just look for rocks

The two men reined in their horses when the stooped and bedraggled shape of a man materialized one hundred feet ahead from the sparse saplings beside the road. He wore a misshapen broad brimmed hat, and curious to his watchers was a thin dark shawl—the color of his skin—wrapped about his shoulders and reaching to his waist. A wooden crutch was nestled in the pit of his left shoulder, and he hobbled forward to the middle of the road, the shawl flapping over his left hand resting on the crutch handle.

Instinctively, the men released their right hands from the reins and lowered them until they rested atop revolver holsters. The man slightly in the lead wore a droopy thick mustache below which was several day's growth of black whiskers like wire bristles on a brush. He squinted into the slanting rays of sunlight, reached up and tilted his hat downward but he could not completely shade his eyes, and a flicker of irritation passed through his brain. He returned his hand to the side of his holster. The man behind him was much younger, beardless, sandy hair spilling from under his hat, and he too tilted it downward. The man in front nudged the flanks of his horse first, moving forward slowly, and the other man followed suit.

The black man nodded deferentially, lifted his fingers from the crutch handle in greeting. "Howdy to you gentlemens dis fine aft'noon."

The bearded man squinted harder, said, "What you doin' out here in the middle of nowhere in the middle of the road, old nigger?"

"Well suh, truth is I's like a child wanderin'." His voice was high and squeaky. "Nigh on to seventy years I am, and some crazy too, 'cause when my wagon horse come up lame yonder ways ahead, 'stead of stayin' with it, I commenced to hobblin' on a bad gouty foot." He shook his head, laughed softly. "Damn my time...dats what my woman used to say back..."

"Ain't interested in your life story. Shut up and get your black ass out of the road 'fore we run you over."

"Yassir, yassir...don't mean t'be no bother." He crutched backward three steps.

When the riders were twenty feet from him, the black man hobbled back to the middle of the road, and as he raised his head the crutch fell to the ground. The steady, authoritative voice came from deep within the man's chest. "Name's Hatch, U. S. Deputy Marshal."

It was the younger man who drew first, but before he could fire, the bullet took him squarely in the cheek, an inch from his nose. The man in front had cleared his holster, but he did not raise his revolver, his eyes fixed on the dark hole of Hatch's gun muzzle. Hatch said, "Take it down real slow now and drop it, Crumpton. Don't matter to me how I take you back."

The man lowered the gun, released it to the road. Behind him he could hear the boot of the dying man scraping the packed earth, coming to his ears like the sound of a child casually playing with a stick. "Reckon he's good as dead?"

"He'll settle directly."

"He was my sister's boy, not a bad sort really. I thought he was quick is why I let him ride with me."

"A misjudgment."

"Be goddamned if that ain't the gospel truth."

"Want me to recite your arrest warrant?"

"Not in particular, bein' real familiar with what I done."

"Get down and step over here in front of that tree." Hatch motioned toward an elm about a foot in diameter. Crumpton slid from his saddle and walked to the tree, stopping a foot from it. Hatch moved behind him. "Nose and hands to the bark. I will pat you down and you will not move a muscle, else I will put a bullet through your knee and they will saw it off at the thigh in Fort Smith before your trial."

"Consider me like this here tree then."

Hatch pulled a long knife from the scabbard at Crumpton's waist and shoved it inside his own belt. He squatted and ran his fingers inside the man's boot tops, pulled a double-barreled derringer from the right boot, which he dropped into his own coat pocket. From the other pocket, Hatch took out a short length of chain with a padlock hooked to one end and two attached lengths, each with a wrist cuff attached.

"Put these cuffs on and chain yourself around the tree and latch the padlock." Crumpton did as he was ordered and when the padlock snapped Hatch checked it. "Gonna get the wagon, be back soon."

"Figured as much. Don't hurry on my part. I'd as soon starve out here chained to a tree than go in and prob'ly get hung by old Plume."

"Ain't no 'prob'ly' to it in your case."

"Reckon it does appear right ugly how it all went down, but they both deserved it."

"They deserved bein' bound and tied and carved up in their own house, you figure, huh?"

"Always told her she ever throw me over for another cock, there'd be hell to pay."

"Well, there sure enough was for them, and now there will be for you, but you'll get a lot less hell than they did, and that's a shame, 'cause it won't be the judge hangin' you, but Apsel Graf, and he ain't never failed to pop a neck in all these years."

"That ain't much of a comfort I'll say."

"It ought to be. Slow death by the blade next to a drop and a pop. Had my way, you types would go out the same way you done your killin'."

Crumpton craned his head around, glared at Hatch. "Tell you what, you big bad fuckin' nigger, all high and mighty with me chained to a tree…how's about you havin' it your way. You unchain me and toss me my knife and you take yours up and you can have your way…if you're man enough, which I don't think you are. Just me and you out here in nowhere. How 'bout it, you mouthy fuckin' nigger?"

"Nuthin' I'd enjoy more, but that ain't the way it works. I made a promise and swore an oath to the judge."

"You're a chickenshit fuckin' nigger is my own swore oath."

Hatch smiled, said, "I'll give you this, Crumpton, it was a good try on your part, but you ought to be glad I ain't takin' the bait."

"Had nuthin' to lose."

"That ain't exactly so."

"Full of bold talk, ain't you, nigger?"

Hatch walked behind Crumpton, reached around his body and clamped his hands around his wrists. He lifted them high, slammed them against the bark and began to slowly rake them up and down, each time increasing the pressure. Crumpton struggled at first but soon realized that he was helpless and he grunted and then began to scream as the skin was peeled from his palms. The pressure on his hands finally lessened and then he felt himself being lifted off the ground and the toes of his boots danced off of the trunk. Hatch released him and he slid down to his knees where Hatch was waiting in his own squat. He placed his lips close to Crumpton's right ear, sniffed the fear.

"Time to time, Crumpton, in special cases like yours, I allow myself to stray just a little from the judge's ways of justice. This case, I just wanted you to be sure that you knew you did have a lot to lose if Graf didn't hang you. We got us an understandin' now?"

Crumpton tried to catch his breath, his fingers coiling and uncoiling like the legs of great spiders. He nodded, but Hatch had already walked away.

Word filtered its way to Judge Plume that Deputy Dak Hatch was on the outskirts of town, and that he would soon reach the jail. The judge watched from his second story courthouse office window as Hatch's wagon rumbled to a halt in front of the hitching post. A chained man slumped against the sideboard of the wagon and a blanket-covered body lay against the opposite sideboard. The chained man's hands were wrapped in strips of cloth and he cradled them in his lap. Two saddled horses were tethered to the wagon. Hatch walked into the jail and returned with another deputy, to whom he gave brief instructions, and then Hatch walked to the front door of the courthouse building.

Plume waited for the knock on his door, then said. "Come in."

Hatch opened the door, removed his hat and nodded at Plume. "The Crumpton warrant was served, Judge, but there was some trouble."

"As I have seen, Dak. It appears that Crumpton is the one still among the quick. The body?"

"A young relative, sir, who Crumpton says he let ride with him as another gun."

"And that gun was raised first I take it."

"It was…about one eye blink after I identified myself."

Plume nodded, hooked his thumbs behind the lapels of his coat, and then walked to the window and looked down. "What happened to Crumpton's hands?"

"I had to chain him to a tree for a bit while I went back for my wagon, and he must'a took a fit of anger. I heard him yellin' and cursin', and when I come back he'd messed his hands up considerable on the bark."

"I see. No great surprise, that, given he is a man who would half-skin two fellow humans, then drunkenly boast of such a deed in a bar."

"We've seen a few like that in times past, Judge."

"Indeed, Dak…indeed we have." Plume turned away from the window, motioned to a chair for Hatch as he sat down behind his desk, and then he looked up at the ceiling. "When will it ever end?"

"Won't ever, Judge. It'll outlive me and you and those that come behind us."

"But it *will* be better, Dak…it surely will become better as time goes on and men like this are weeded from civilized society."

Hatch suppressed the doubt that sounded inside his head. "Surely will, Judge…as time goes on."

Plume brought his hands together, formed a bridge with his fingers. "Any word on the bad one, John Post Oak?"

Hatch slowly shook his head. "He's a slippery one. Reckon the slipperiest I've ever chased. Maybe the meanest too."

"That would be quite the title in this territory."

"Sooner or later, he'll make a mistake. They all do… even the slipperiest."

"Let us hope it comes sooner rather than later."

Hatch nodded, said, "Yes, but there's always this too: sometimes things just shake out in this here world like turnin' up a sack full of rocks and marbles. Sometimes a useless rock falls out, other times a nice pretty marble." He waved a hand in a wide arc. "All these lives bein' lived… good people, bad people, old, young…all comin' together with all their many wants and seekin's and such. Can't ever tell when the sack shakes just right and out falls a rock. And when it does, I'll there to pick it up."

"I have never thought of it quite like that, but it is an apt analogy indeed."

"After I've been with my wife and youngun's for a short spell, I'll go back out there and look for rocks again. That's all I've ever really studied, Judge."

"And for that I am ever thankful. I can't imagine having been without two lawmen in particular for all these years— you and Apsel Graf."

"That Aspel Graf, he's way more than a hangman to you, ain't he?"

"That is true."

Hatch stood, nodded, and turned to walk away. When he reached the door, he turned back toward Plume. "Who shakes the sack, Judge? The Almighty, I reckon?"

Plume stared at Hatch and arched his eyebrows for a moment. "I do not think that God, in the beginning, ever meant for the sack to contain what it contains." He arched his eyebrows again. "That is the only answer that I am able to come up with for so lofty a question, Dak."

Hatch put on his hat, adjusted the position to his liking. "Didn't mean to get lofty, Judge. I just look for rocks."

"Be careful out there. I cannot do without you…and neither can your family."

Hatch smiled. "I always try to keep the sun in their eyes, Judge."

CHAPTER 17

Unlucky breeze

Hattie's eyes opened, and she blinked the nightstand into shadowy focus, and then the chamber pot on the floor beside it. She pulled the sheet down, flipped it from her legs, and then sat on the edge of the bed. The rectangle of the window beckoned, pallid moonlight bleeding through like an apology from the sky. *Sorry to intrude, but it was you who opened your eyes.* She stepped to the chamber pot, lifted her white night gown and squatted, listened to the sing of her stream. She walked to the window, which was open a half foot, and she raised it so that she could bend down and lean on her hands as she peered out. It was then that the coyote howls came to her, faraway at first, then ever closer. It was unlike the usual coyote songs, which always seemed to be from faraway, and the fine hair at the base of her neck tingled. She heard the faint creak of the cabin door, and then watched Rufus walk a dozen steps from the door and stand silently. Although she could hear no sound of hooves, the rider and the horse appeared like phantoms who owned the night, and when the horse drew within a few feet of Rufus, it stopped, the rider slipping from its back in one fluid motion.

She quickly turned from the window and picked up a single match from the box on the nightstand and walked into her closet, closed the door behind her. She struck the match with her thumbnail and allowed the flame to settle before moving it along the garments at the near end of the rack. When the light revealed the black gown, she snatched it from the rack and blew out the match. Gathering the gown around her shoulders, she scampered on bare feet down the staircase, through the kitchen, and then inched open the back door. Once outside, she paused to allow her vision to adjust before gliding over the grass to a point behind the cabin. The voices were barely audible, but loud enough to allow her to determine the sidewall along which to advance. She gathered the loose cloth to the front of the gown and pulled it up over her cheek and nose with one hand, and with the other hand tugged at the curls and pulled her hair down over her forehead. Inches at a time, she slinked along the sidewall until she dared go no farther. The voice of the stranger became words, spoken solemnly, and in the sturdy voice was a timbre the mere sound of which chilled her to the core.

"Enough of old times, my friend. Let us talk of the future, as we did the last time."

"Nothing has changed since the last time."

"Things are always changing, it is the way of the world."

"In some ways, in other ways not."

The breeze freshened and when it puffed into Hattie's face the realization struck her like a fist in the stomach. *Goddamn, Hattie, but you're lucky the wind doesn't blow you toward them.* Her heart hammered as she drew in a long breath, and she steadied herself as the silence between the men grew into a half minute.

The stranger said, "Here is a way that it has changed. There are some good places an easy ride from here where we can take a train that carries Wells Fargo things—gold, silver, paper money—and the things that the passengers carry. The trick is to pick a train that they don't consider special, just an ordinary one with an ordinary amount of money—which is still a lot. The goddamn Pinkertons can't be on every train and I have whites who can find out such things. I always keep some whites that I can make happy with money, and they are useful eyes and ears. The rails a few miles west of the Clarksville station have good ambush spots. Clarksville is a rough town too—sorry law men, and full of hard-ass people left over from building the rails, and that is a good thing for my spy. And I have a good gang riding with me… one is too mouthy, but they all can shoot and ride well, and they like money and blood for fun. It will be an easy job."

The silence settled in and grew again, but as before, neither man seemed to mind. The stranger placed his head against his horse's jaw and stroked it with one hand. A minute passed, and the breeze freshened, swirled. Rufus said, "Why would you need another gun for such a job?"

"You're not just another gun, you are Rufus."

"What if the others don't want another split?'

"It doesn't matter what any of them want, and besides, the mouthy one…I have a feeling that something bad will happen to him soon."

"I don't need money."

"Now maybe, but who can know the future? A man can never have enough money."

"A man can never have enough peace."

The stranger snorted like a small horse. "'Peace you say. Yet I hear that the chores for your woman are sometimes not peaceful."

"They are still easy...peaceful, next to the past."

"But your blood still rises to the chore. You are a man again, if only against harmless cowardly whites. You need to remember how your blood once rose when we fought against more than that. Now your blood only rises to your cock for a few minutes and never gets to your heart, and it goes limp, and you're back to your chores...and your new pup."

Hattie could see Rufus' head as it slowly turned directly toward the stranger. "The boy is none of your concern."

"He seems to be a concern of many."

"What would you know of that?"

"Why do you teach him to shoot? A white pup will grow into white dog, and some dogs cannot be trusted."

"I asked you a question."

"The river bank on that fine afternoon when and you and your woman watched him and another man and woman...and a fine woman at that. Looked too good for a whore, but 'spect she was, and all snugly with the goddamn hangman himself." Post Oak paused, stroked the horse's jaw again. "Hard to figure."

"You have been in these parts for a while."

"Yes, and I told you that I have eyes and ears around. That is why I will always have a white or two ride with me. Useful servants that I send to places that I cannot go."

"But on riverbanks you do not need them."

"All I really need is you and one white man. Sooner or later, the others I would run off or kill." Post Oak stepped away from the horse, clamped his right hand on Rufus' right arm. "And all you really need is me and the one white servant. This you know in your heart."

Thunder rumbled from the west and the breeze swirled again, persistent now, and Hattie felt it push against her back and hair as it rushed past her, and with the unlucky breeze came the fear. She pressed her shoulder to the wall and retreated three steps, waiting for the gust to die down. But it only stiffened, and she cursed the scent of perfume infused in the gown. She heard Rufus's voice, but she could not discern the words, and she turned and crept, cat-like, back to the house. When she reached her bedroom window, she knelt and peered from over the sill. The stranger still held Rufus' arm and their faces were only inches apart. When the stranger finally released his arm, Rufus slowly took a step backward as the man sprang onto the back of his mount as if the wind had lifted him off his feet, but before he turned the horse away, he raised his head and glanced toward her window. Then he and the horse faded as one into the windswept gloom as silently as they had come.

She came to him in the cool pre-dawn, her nakedness wrapped in the black gown; she had not slept since the night rider had disappeared. She crept to the door of Son's quarters, listened intently until she was certain that the boy slept. At Rufus's door she tapped the code with two knuckles—one tap, then two, and finally three—before she turned the knob and pushed open the door, stepped inside, closed the door behind her. The buttery glow from an oil lamp bathed him as he stood peering—shirtless and in buckskin breeches—out the window. He did not turn toward her. His hair was tightly braided in two lengths that hung to his shoulder blades, his hands resting on the window sill.

Hattie moved to his side, and when her shoulder touched his she said, "You've braided your hair."

"Something to do while I thought."

"And you're still thinking."

He nodded, said, "You trusted the wind too long. Couldn't you smell the storm?"

"I wasn't thinking on nature at the time." She paused, took a breath. "I'm not like you...or him."

"How much did you hear?"

"More than I cared to...but I heard no answer from you." She waited until she knew he did not intend to reply. "Who is he?"

"A man from the past."

"What is his name?"

Rufus knew there was nothing to be gained by lies and procrastination. "John Post Oak."

"Sweet Jesus Christ!" She turned away from him and sat down on the edge of his bunk. "I should have brought a bottle and a smoke."

"I figured you would."

Hattie shook her head, as if trying to escape a nightmare, her hands clasped in her lap, fingers locked and writhing. "Why the hell did he have to come back to these parts... why didn't he just roam out in the Indian Territory where he belongs?" She drew a quick breath, posed an answer to her question with another question. "Because of you?"

"He has always roamed where he pleases and he never stays in the same places for very long."

"I reckon not, half the U. S. Deputies workin' for Plume after him for years."

"They waste their time. They catch stupid Indians and stupid whites…a stupid black here and there…drunk and mouthy, sloppy about their ways. He is like an animal with a man's brain."

"He can't've done all the things they say he's done."

"That may be, but it doesn't matter. He's done most."

"Word is that he was at the Little Big Horn slaughter."

Rufus turned toward her, and when Hattie looked into his eyes they appeared wolf's-eye yellow and they pierced her. "Why do you say 'slaughter' instead of 'battle'? The goddamn blue soldiers had guns and blades too, and they came to kill us."

"I…uh…but they were all killed, to the last man."

His voice took on an edge that she had never before heard. "That just means that we won the battle…to the last man."

Hattie heard nothing beyond *we*, and the tiny word hammered inside her head."

She swallowed, looked down, said, "Do you mean 'we'…as all Indians…or…were…" She could not finish the question.

"I was there."

"With him."

"Yes. At the Greasy Grass River. If you name the place, name it right."

"You'd never told me that."

"Never asked." He turned back away from her.

"I've never asked much about your past."

"And that is good. It has always been understood between us. I cannot change the past…even if I wanted to."

"And you don't?"

"Some things yes, some no. Same as you, huh? Same as anybody who ever passes through this life."

Hattie nodded, but Rufus was peering out the window, his arms at his sides. "Rufus, I don't care about the past, not a goddamn bit of it. But I do care about us living out the years together. We have a good thing, you and me. I ain't gonna get womanly sentimental on you and tell you how much I love you, because I don't know just what the hell 'love' really means. Never did, and I don't care anymore. But I have strong feelings…name them what you want, or name them nothing at all…but you know how I feel about you, and I think I know how you feel about me. We are an odd pair in the eyes of others, but neither one of us gives a shit about what others think. Maybe that's why we belong together…and should stay together."

"That was a long speech."

"I can be wordy, when it matters. Come here."

He turned from the window, moved in front of her and she placed her hands on his stomach, spread her fingers like flowers nudged by a puff of wind. She said, "You go back to him, sooner or later you end up on a wanted poster beside him, no matter how good at bein' bad he is."

"I think you worry about the boy as much as you do me."

"Am I less to you if I worry about you both now?"

"No."

"That's good to hear." She laid her head against his stomach, wrapped her arms around his waist, and like this they remained until dawn's light replaced the lamp glow, and then Hattie slipped away from him with a final stroke of her fingertips on his stomach.

CHAPTER 18

Peace by the waters

Iva and Apsel sat in two chairs pulled together so that they could link arms and look out the window into the gathering dusk. It was Saturday night, and the inexpert but inspired plunking of the piano arose from the parlor as several patrons were being entertained. Aspel said, "I don't think that Sally will ever master the keyboard despite your tutelage." He had been silent for nearly a quarter hour, content to allow Iva to rattle on about whatever popped into her mind. It had been five days since word had spread about the sentencing of five prisoners, all to be hung side by side, on the following Tuesday.

"No one ever masters any technique—on the keyboard or elsewhere in life, Apsel. And for purposes of this establishment, she's mastered it well enough."

"Quite true."

Since the sentencing, Apsel had been preoccupied. Iva had ignored it during his daily visits, but decided to not to ignore any longer. "Do you want to talk about it?"

He made a sound in his chest, a low rumble of contemplation. "I'm not sure."

"I said that no one ever mastered any technique, but that is not true in the case of your professional capabilities. Your responsibility to the condemned I cannot imagine, and although to most people it would seem simple enough, I know that it cannot be so simple."

"Death is never simple."

Iva allowed the hush to grow, and soon the door to the room beside theirs opened and closed with the mingled laughter of a man and a woman. Apsel said, "Let's go for a walk near the river."

She had brought a blanket, and when they drew close enough to hear the voice of the water, she spread it and they laid down facing each other. She said, "What is it about the sound of the river that is so peaceful?"

"Ah…'peaceful', yes, I need that, must seek it more often."

"I think it is because the flow of the water outlives us all. It flowed before any of us and it will long after we are gone from earth. That thought brings peace to me, Apsel. Wherever life leads us together, it must be near a river or the sea—and very far from here. Peace by the waters."

Apsel rolled onto his back, laced his fingers over his chest. "The trapdoor is twenty feet long and thirty inches wide. There is room for twelve men standing shoulder to shoulder. Years ago, someone named it *The Gates Of Hell*. He shook his head from side to side, raised his fingers for a moment. "From the ancient Hebrew, 'Apsel' means 'father of peace.' How inappropriate for me. To my parents, it was but merely a solid German name for a boy child. I grew up in Bavaria and within me grew rage, born of what I know not. My parents were ordinary, my three younger brothers were ordinary, but I was never like them. I fought—tooth and nail—anyone who crossed me and I came to enjoy the feeling of others cowing before me…even larger, stronger boys. They stood no chance, because I had the rage within me, then one day in my seventeenth year, the daughter of a farmer whose family had moved near us came into my life, and with her life touching mine, the rage waned and—I thought—finally left my soul. We married in our eighteenth year, and her father built us a little house on his land, and we made a child to grow in her womb."

Iva shifted her position so that she could steal a glance into his eyes, but he seemed to study the sky in the manner of a man attempting to divine the meaning of the swirling cloud formations. She would say no more until he emptied himself, if indeed that was what he wished to do. He said, "One night, at supper, I was weary from the fields, young and ignorant of the ways of a pregnant teenage mother, who was far wearier than I, and she…she spilled hot coffee on my hand. And the rage—the tiniest flicker—rose within me and I shoved her backward and she fell. Her head struck the corner of the stone hearth. She lived until morning and then she died, and in her womb a baby died. A baby that she had told me early on would be a girl." A single tear leaked from the corner of his eye nearest Iva and she watched as it meandered and disappeared into his ear. "That was in summer and I never saw another autumn in Bavaria, but I have dreams, visions… so real…I can never run far enough away. Sometimes, I don't know if I even *want* to run, but I do know that I deserve the haunting…'father of peace' that I am not."

Iva sat up, leaned on her arms toward Apsel, her eyes flashing, and she waited for him to turn his head and meet them. "You anger me, Apsel!" She got up, turned away from him and crossed her arms over her bosom, then quickly spun back around. Apsel, blinking in bewilderment, sat up and looked at her face. "You carry your sorrow...so long past, like a man carrying a bag of stones on his back. It is a sad story, but everybody has sad stories of their own—me included, as you know. But, damn...I refuse to carry stones and would hope that you dump yours."

"But I...uh...I did not mean to..."

Iva knifed her hand toward him. "We're planning a life together, and hopefully with Son as a part of it...and...and you're still haunted by something that happened a lifetime ago—no matter how terrible or sad—and it seems that he and I are not enough to bury it, Apsel. Is that what this means? Your ghosts will trail us forever?" Iva swept her arm in a wide arc before returning it to her bosom. "I wanted you to purge yourself, let it all go, but now I'm not so sure because it doesn't sound to me like you want to let it go. It doesn't sound like I'm woman enough to chase away ghosts...and maybe I'm not."

Apsel, jumped to his feet and reached for her, touched her shoulder, but she moved a step away. "That is not so, Iva. I swear to God that is not so."

She spun around, grasped his hands. "Then swear it to *me*, Apsel! God does not need your pledge, but I do. And Son does. I was resigned to lying with strange men for years, then....then after that, just what, I didn't know. I didn't even care. But I care now, and part of me is afraid. I'm not steel like Hattie. I'm like a thirsty flower in a summer draught,

Apsel, and you gave me water, but without the water, I will dry up again and die. This is my last chance."

From the riverbank and high in an ancient sycamore, a great horned owl hooted its forlorn melody, and Iva and Apsel were drawn to it—welcomed the owl song as a respite from the struggle of two souls. Suddenly wearied by the conflict, Iva leaned her forehead against his chest, slipped her hands to his back. She said, "I'm not certain just where all that came from. I had no right to say anything about… them."

"There is no 'them', rather their memory and my guilt that trails after me. Sometimes I imagine that it is my head going under the black hood, my boots that press against the trapdoor…waiting for what I deserve…waiting to solve the great mystery at the end of a well-oiled one-inch hemp rope."

"Surely you can't equate yourself with the killers and the mad dogs that roam this land."

"Ah…but the last one—the young cowboy, Dillingham, was neither a killer nor a mad dog. He was young and stupid, like I was. The man that he shot was a hundred times worse than him."

"Yet he was tried before the judge and a jury, and found guilty under the law."

"Plume did not have to sentence him to death." He looked toward the river, waited for the owl to hoot again, but it did not. "It is the only time that I believe Plume made a terrible misjudgment."

"From what the girls have told me, Hattie Wax believed as you do."

He nodded, said, "We agree on something at least." He

turned around to face her. "Did the girls tell you what she said to the boy at the end?"

"Yes, they did."

"The infamous madam of Fort Smith, parrot and all, had the last word."

"She always seems to have the last word."

Apsel held both of her hands, looked into green eyes that he hoped would read his. "She will not have the last word about us…or Son."

"So we have come back to my question."

"And my answer is that the ghosts will not trail us forever. My answer is that you *are* woman enough."

"That is easy to say, Apsel, here on the riverbank, with no others near us, the strange ways of the world seemingly far removed…but they are not far, will never be far."

"Words, yes, I know. I will have to show you, and I will."

"Let's walk nearer the water, Apsel, I want to hear it rush, fill me with the sound of forever."

Arm in arm, they walked toward the river and a great sycamore tree, and when they drew near, and mingled with the sound of the water, they heard the whoosh of massive wings as the owl flew away. They looked up, caught but a glimpse as the bird melted into the gathering darkness.

Iva said, "To soar above it all like that…that would be freedom."

"We will find it down here, Iva. We will find our freedom despite the strange ways of the world."

They both listened in silence as the night gathered about them, and after a quarter hour, made their way back to Hattie's house. When they were fifty yards away, Apsel looked up at Hattie's bedroom window and in the center of the dark rectangle he saw the tiny glow of her cigar as she drew on it, and then it disappeared.

Hattie turned from the window and stubbed out the cigar before walking to Hector's cage. It was uncovered and had been since she had brought the colorful bird home eleven years past. She had discovered early on that there was no need to ever close the cage door. His habit was to perch in the door opening rather than inside the cage. He was a late-night bird, and although Hattie believed that she had taught him the habit through her own ways, Rufus had told her that birds, like people, had their own particulars and nothing could change them. She looked at him now, the stunning plumage now muted in the darkening room.

"My boy…my boy."

"Hattie wants to talk Hattie wants to talk."

"And do you want to talk?"

"Hector likes to talk Hector likes to talk."

"That's a damn good thing, my boy. Afraid it won't be long before you're the only one with sense enough to listen to old Hattie."

CHAPTER 19

❖◆❖

Like a man tryin' to act

After a week spent with his family on twenty acres and their modest cabin, Dak Hatch packed his saddle bags and rode into Fort Smith to pick up the warrants for six men who were believed to be within an approximate fifty-mile radius of the city, but his mind dwelled mainly on the warrant for John Post Oak that he had carried far too long by his reckoning. Hatch's wagon, its driver, and a newly-sworn deputy marshal with his mount tied to the wagon would never be more than a mile or two distant, and when the situation dictated, brought into service. Hatch rode his favorite horse—a brown and white mustang mare he called Shadow that possessed intelligence the like of which Hatch had never noted in any other animal on which he had ridden. He could sense what the mare felt, whether it was from underneath him—mysteriously released upward through the horse's hooves and bones and sinew—or from urgent signals from its ears. On two occasions when Hatch had been surprised by men intent on his death—and with the sun in his eyes—the mare had slowed for no apparent reason, the long ears suddenly alert and pointing forward like curved knives set for battle. Both times, Hatch had snatched his Winchester rifle from its leather scabbard and flung himself from the saddle as the first bullets whined past his head. Then Dak Hatch became one with the trees and brushy tangles and shadows beside the road as the death game began for the doomed men who would perish in the untamed domain, preempting their meetings with Judge Burleigh Plume and the man in black, Apsel Graf.

So it was that with dawn's first offering, the tall, black deputy and his horse began their rounds down the first of many dusty, narrow roads that connected the little towns east of Fort Smith. But the rail lines that also connected the towns were of even greater interest to Hatch. In addition to Post Oak's, three of the warrants he carried in one of his saddlebags contained the names of men who had been drawn to the rails and the trains that carried Wells Fargo riches.

At high noon, Hatch rode into Clarksville along the main street through town as it paralleled the railroad tracks. He looked down the street, dusty and hard-packed, the hoof and boot prints and the wagon wheel imprints barely visible. The scorching summer had arrived, and it had not rained in nearly three weeks. He looked up, saw the depot a hundred yards ahead, the edges of its slanted tin roof aglow, seared by the harsh rays of the sun. As he grew near, most of the people on the depot platform turned their heads to watch him with cold, hard eyes, but there were children too, and their eyes were only curious at the sight of a huge black man riding a mustang mare that appeared to be too small for him.

The men wore wide-brimmed hats over grim visages and stained heavy work shirts from which hung quadrangular hands, appearing more as tools than flesh and bone, and it was the eyes of these men that were the coldest. Hatch's mind drifted back to his youth as a slave in Texas—a time when he dared not meet such eyes. But now, he looked squarely into the eyes of the men, smiled thinly and touched the brim of his hat with the fingers of his right hand. The children—scruffy and wide-eyed—were clumped together beside two women as Hatch reined in the mare in front of them. He reached behind him into a saddlebag, fished around for a moment, and withdrew a handful of horehound candy, which he extended toward the oldest child, a boy of eight or nine.

"Always keep some candy around for little ones I see along the way."

The boy pilfered a glance at one of the women, and after she made a tiny nod, he reached up and took the candy in both of his hands. Hatch said, "Plenty to go round, you give some to the littlest ones, alright?"

The boy nodded, said, "I will."

The men turned away, as did the women, but the children cackled with glee as they gathered around the boy with the candy.

Hatch nudged Shadow and she nimbly crossed the tracks and walked to the side of the depot where the hitching post stood. Hatch dismounted but did not tie the reins to the post, rather, just wrapped them loosely around the saddle horn. The boy with the candy now held only a couple of pieces in one hand, and he trotted over to Hatch, looked at the mare. He said, "You ain't gonna use the post? What if the horse runs away?"

"Oh, my Shadow ain't the runnin'-away kinda horse,

son. She knows I want her to stay right here…keep an eye on things for me." He winked at the boy.

The boy popped a piece of candy into his mouth, his cheeks collapsing as he sucked the morsel. With his tongue, he shoved it to the side of his mouth. "You look too big for this horse, mister. My daddy says you're the biggest nigger he ever laid eyes on."

"Well, I 'spect your daddy is right. I am the biggest one I ever saw too. But not too big for Shadow, she's a strong little mare, don't pay no mind even to the likes of me."

"Why you name her 'Shadow'?"

"Oh, reckon 'cause she's kinda like one…when I want her to be—watchful and quiet like."

"Why would you want one like that?"

Hatch took off his hat, wiped his brow with the back of his hand, and then put it back on as he took a step toward the door. He said over his shoulder, "Comes in handy now and then, son."

Hatch entered the depot and closed the door behind him. There were three long benches, like church pews secured to the floor, and in these were scattered a few travelers waiting for the 1:15 for Little Rock. At one end of the room was a raised counter and behind it stood the station master, his gray hair poking out around the black visor on his head. He wore wire-rimmed spectacles that appeared to rest more on his fleshy, red cheeks than his nose, under which stretched a wooly white mustache. The seated passengers glanced up at Hatch as he walked toward the counter, and three of them stared. The station master had been watching Hatch since he had opened the door, and he nodded as the tall man approached.

The man poked at his spectacles with a finger and said, "Deputy."

Hatch nodded, said, "Milo, how are you?"

"Older and fatter."

Hatch smiled. "Just as watchful though, I hope."

"I am that. We need to go back in my office and talk." He turned toward a seated clerk and said, "You're up here 'til I get back."

"Yes, sir."

Milo led the way to his office and after he closed the door behind him, he motioned toward a chair for Hatch. "Let's rest my fat and your muscle, deputy." He plopped down in his desk chair with a long sigh, laid his forearms on his desk.

"What you got, Milo. Ain't often we come in here to talk."

Milo pointed toward the door. "That boy I called up out there told me somethin' a few days ago that led to what I'm about to tell you. When he first started jawin' about it, didn't seem to amount to much at all. But the more he talked, the more I cogitated on it, and it was like chewin' on cold collard greens…the wad just didn't want to go away, you understand?"

"Yes I do."

"Anyhow, the boy—Hiram, brighter than I thought when I hired him—mentioned to me that a feller was in here who was a little mouthy…not bad mouthy, mind you, but the kinda mouthy that asks sideways questions in a laughin' sorta way." Milo shook his head, tilted his visor back. "Anyhow, he walks up to Hiram at the counter and commences to shoot the general breeze about how he used to work on the crew that laid the last of the line up to Fort Smith. Been what…thirteen, fourteen years ago? Whatever, anyhow, he jabbers and jabbers and finally tells Hiram he's got an old aunt he wants to take his mother to see, and if he was to buy tickets anytime soon, she wants him not to schedule a train carryin' some really big Wells load…her bein' skittish and all about the ruffians roamin' about. So Hiram—from instinct he tells me, but he did not use that word, but I deducted it myself—so he tells me he commences to studyin' the man real close, without lettin' on he was doin' so, and all because the man won't look him square in the eye, and, too, because he acts like a man who's tryin' to act, but ain't worth a damn at it. Young Hiram falls in with him, all jabbery himself, which ain't like him at all, and he acts like he knows everything in the world about the Wells money that rides the rails regular…about which of course he don't know shit."

Milo pulled his visor down and leaned forward, his cheeks rising with his smile, pushing up his spectacles. "And then, United States Deputy Dak Hatch, he had one of those things I think they call 'epifomy'—where a great piece a thinkin' comes unawares to a man—and Hiram tells the man to wait a minute while he goes to the office to check on the Wells train schedules." Milo pointed to Hatch. "And, sittin' right there in that same chair you're in, he tells me what I just told you. And then I had my own epifomy. I left Hiram in here and went out there myself and confirmed that the boy's instincts were sound, and immediately thereafter says to the man—word for word I am here— 'Sir, I'm the station master and my helper tells me of your momma's concern, which I can certainly understand, because I got one of my own and she tends to worry too much, just like yours.' Then I leaned in real close, winked at him and then I continued. 'I checked the schedules and if you folks ride out on the three-twenty to Fort Smith three weeks from Thursday, there won't be no more than around fifteen thousand in gold and silver in the little safe—which is way below the big runs, which they keep in the big time lock safe anyways.' He thanks me kindly, says he'll pass the word on to his momma, and out the door he goes."

Hatch stared into Milo's eyes until Milo couldn't hold the gaze, and when he looked down, Hatch said, "What did this man look like?"

"He was big…not as big as you, but big and long-armed. He was clean-shaved, 'cept for a mustache trimmed short, but he was nicked up like he done the shavin' hisself. Wasn't no barber job, that's for sure. Same for his hair—black as two foot up a cow's ass—but bad cut. He was ordinary-faced enough and dressed decent, but not fancy. Never saw his boots."

"What did his hands look like?"

Milo closed his eyes for a moment. "Hummm…he did set 'em down on the counter once or twice, but I don't remember what they looked like."

"Reckon Hiram would remember?"

"We'll see." Milo hopped up and opened the door, motioned with a wave of his hand. "Trade places with me for a minute. The deputy wants to ask you about the mouthy Wells man."

They passed each other, and as Hiram approached, Hatch stood and extended his hand, which Hiram shook. Hatch said, "Want you to know, Hiram, you did a fine piece of work on this thing by telling Milo about him. Not just anybody can read people."

"Well…well, I 'preciate that, comin' from you 'specially." He was tall and thin, narrow-faced, and when he spoke, his Adam's apple rose and fell like a mouse was trying to escape from his throat.

"I was wondering about his description, which Milo filled in good except that he couldn't remember what his hands looked like. Do you?"

"Oh, I do and I'll tell you why. He said he was from back East—said he went there for a softer job after he worked layin' the rails years ago—but his hands warn't a match. Big and dirty-nailed, damn near to claws, and about half of his left first finger was gone missin'. Didn't look like no back-East hands to me. No sir, I seen that right off, I did."

"Anything else?"

"Well, he wouldn't look me in the eye, and he talked sorta strained—like he was tryin' to sound citified, but it didn't fool me, no siree."

"There's just one more thing you need to do for me, Hiram."

"What's that?"

"Just be real quite about it, just like it never happened. There may come a day soon when you can talk about it, and if that day comes, I promise you, people will know who started things off. Will you do that for me? I'm counting on you."

Hiram's Adam's apple slowly rose and fell as he swallowed. He said, "I promise", then turned away and opened the door, and within seconds, Milo closed the door behind him as he entered the office. Hatch sat back down and waited for Milo to get situated in his desk chair. "Milo, I'll be around for at least a day, maybe two. I got some thinkin' to do, but I'll lay it out for you now straight up. The jabbery man was almost without a doubt one of John Post Oak's men. I was told a while back that one of the big whites in his gang was missin' a finger. Turns out it was just a part, according to Hiram, but it has to be the same man. Which means that I'm gonna board the train over in Russellville three weeks from Thursday along with four or five other deputies, and I 'magine that within a few miles either way of here they'll try to take the train…if what we're thinkin' is a fact."

"But you all ain't gonna look like deputies are you?"

"Anything but."

"Damned if you don't look like the hardest lawman on earth to disguise."

"Just takes some imagination, Milo. I've stayed alive a long time with imagination…and instinct, and a lot of that, I'll admit, was my horse's."

"Your horse won't be with you on that train."

"That's a fact. So I'm left with my imagination, which will have to do."

"Well, you're sittin' here, can't argue that. They've tried to get you a time or two I've heard."

Hatch nodded, said, "More'n a time or two." He paused, looked up at the ceiling for a moment, then back down. "How many coach cars will there be?"

"Pretty sure two, three at most, and I'd bet just the two for that run."

"So, five more deputies will work for me. I'll be in the

safe car with one man, and the other four can be in the two coaches—two by two."

Milo drummed his fingertips on his desk. "Likely be lead a flyin' around inside them cars." He shook his head. "You, I know, can shoot straight, but the others won't be as good."

"They'll be handpicked…and good. I ain't the only one who can handle a gun."

"At five-thousand wanted, that injun Post Oak must be a bad sonofabitch. All he's done over the years…goddamn… the woman from Little Rock getting' a finger hacked off for a ring…goddamn him to hell…and reckon she was lucky at that."

"Nobody wants him more than me, Milo. Nobody in the whole Indian Territory."

"I hope you gut shoot him."

"I hope I don't have to shoot him. I want to chain him to my wagon and walk him back to Fort Smith and stand him in front of Judge Plume, and then watch the hangman drop him through The Gates of Hell."

"Wonder if you could talk the hangman into short-droppin' the heathen?"

Hatch slowly shook his head, said, "No…not Apsel Graf. Not that hangman."

"Shame, that."

"No argument on that."

Hatch stood, said, "Got things to tend to, Milo. He ain't the only bad one out there."

Milo pushed his chair back and stood with a grunt of effort. "Can't help but wonder how that five-thousand might come into play here."

"If it does, I'll do all I can to see that it comes back here." He paused, smiled. "And Hiram?"

"It ought to be halves, I know, and fine by me. I ain't a pig, though I'm getting' closer every day to lookin' like one."

"Get out and stretch your legs for a mile or two once in a while and eat along the spine of the beeves and hogs instead of the bellies…skip the pies and cakes now and then. Some things a man can control…some he can't."

"That's hard advice, deputy."

"My momma, before our master worked her to death in Texas, used to say, 'Hard advice is the only kind that means anything'."

Milo scrunched his mouth and cheeks together, as if he had just tasted bad food. "You was…a slave family? You'd never mentioned that before."

"Never felt like mentionin' it before."

"Well, sir…I uh…well, bless her soul."

"If her's ain't blessed, Milo, ain't none of the rest of us stands a chance to be blessed across the river."

Milo tried with all his might to say something, but he couldn't, but it would not have mattered. Hatch left quickly, closed the door quietly behind him.

CHAPTER 20

Can't stop the wind in March

When Hattie heard the soft knock on the door to her bedroom just after dawn, she knew who it was and what was about to happen. There was no dread, nor much irritation remaining regarding the situation; the worst of it had been spread over the course of the previous month. She said, "Come in."

Iva opened the door and slipped in on bare feet, softly closed the door behind her. She wore a long white flannel gown, her hair wild and loose over the collar. Hattie sat in bed, two pillows propped up behind her, her silk nightgown enwrapping her from neck to ankles.

Iva said, "Can we talk."

Hattie pointed to a high-backed chair. "We already are."

Iva sat down, curled her legs under her. She looked up at Hector, stirring in his cage and he hopped to the edge of the door and said, "Miss Hattie get up Miss Hattie get up."

Hattie said, "Hector quiet now." The bird's feathers

stirred, its wings fluttering slightly, and it made a few tiny croaks as the feathers smoothed down. She said, "That's a good boy."

Iva said, "Why doesn't he ever fly out?"

"That sounds like a leading question."

Iva blushed, said, "No…I…uh…just wondered. I always thought birds had to be cooped up."

"We had us an understanding early on. Big, smart bird like Hector—you can train him like you would a dog, and he's a hell of a lot less trouble." She paused, looked at Iva. "But you're not here to talk about my bird flyin' away, are you?"

Iva shook her head, the fingers of one hand absently trailing through her hair. "We've decided to make a life together, and it makes no sense for me to stay here…for either you or me, and especially you, with me taking up a worthless room."

"Worthless." Hattie turned her head toward Hector, allowed the word to hover in the room for several seconds. "That's a word that's trailed me my whole damn life, one way or the other. Little lost girl raised by half-monsters, young girl sellin' her ass and tits to scrape by until…until the young girl started to use her female brain—which is always way better than a brain with a hard cock hooked to it—and before long, I ain't worthless anymore." She looked back at Iva. "So I'll decide what's a worthless room or not."

"I appreciate what you've done for me, Miss Hattie, I truly do."

"I hear he lives in a boardin' house in town. He goin' to buy you a house and some ground, a nice piano, some horses to play with?"

"Maybe in time, but for a while, I'm fine with wherever we live."

"Where will 'wherever' be? I know you won't stay around here for long."

"We're not sure, but probably west, clear to San Francisco is where I'd like to go."

"Never figured he'd get tired of bein' Plume's hangman."

"He's a lot more than the executioner to the court. He's more of a law officer for the judge than anything else, and that part he's not tired of, but…the other part, he wants to be done with."

Hattie got off the bed and sat down opposite Iva at the little table, on which was a wooden cigar box. She picked one out, lit it with a Lucifer match, and then drew in the first taste. She sprayed the smoke downward in her lap. "I'm fightin' the urge here to form the first decent thought I've ever entertained about your hangman, Iva."

"I don't understand why you hold his job against him so much. If it wasn't him, it would just be somebody else who might not do the job right…and he always does it right, from what he's told me."

"No denyin' that." Hattie drew on the cigar exhaled through her nostrils. "Maybe it's because I see him as a part of old Plume—sorta like a second pair of arms. Him and old God Hisownself…givin' the death sentence out more often than not." She smiled crookedly, bitterly. "The one that got to me the worst—nothin' close—was the young cowboy a while back that I made such a ruckus over."

"But it was Plume that sentenced him…Apsel just…I don't see…"

"What you don't see is that the hangman and Plume

have worked together so damn long, have had each other's ear so damn long, that I guarantee your man is bound to have some sway when Plume is deciding between life and death."

"I doubt that. I doubt that a lot."

"You can doubt it a lot all you want, but I have my feelings and my eyes and ears around town, and they don't often turn out wrong."

Iva got up from the chair, walked to the window. "There's no use in talking about him…us…any longer. You've made your mind up, and so have I."

The tense silence gathered, broken only by an occasional, tiny croak from Hector. A half minute passed, before Hattie said, "Well that part of it is settled it appears. I never really figured I could talk you out of it anyhow. The hell with it."

Iva waited for her to continue, but she just puffed on the cigar. Iva said, "The *other* part isn't up to you or me."

"So you reckon a twelve or thirteen-year-old boy can make a decision like that himself, do you?"

"Yes I certainly do. He's made some harder decisions before in his young life. In reality, he's lived a lot more than a dozen years on this sorry earth, and he's survived pretty well, I'd say."

"And he's damn lucky to make it this far. Lucky somebody didn't cave his head in or stick him with a blade back in New York, or in town here for that matter."

"Well, don't forget who it was that rescued him here."

"And what did he do with him? He gave him to the sheriff, who gave him me. Your man had his chance, by God, and he gave him up."

"That's hardly fair. It's not just Apsel now…it's Apsel and me, Hattie. We're a couple."

"And you don't consider me and Rufus as a couple?"

Iva heard it in Hattie's voice—clearly, as distinctly as a bell pealing from nearby—and she knew what was about to happen, but did not care. "It's hard…uh…to see it that way. I know you care about Son, but Apsel says that Rufus has a…history."

"Ah, so Apsel Graf, the high moral man, says so, huh?" She signed, stubbed out the cigar with an angry twist. "You remember that urge I said I was fightin' a couple minutes ago about your hangman? Well, lady, the urge is gone… to-tal-ly-god-damn gone. I can stand a son-of-a-bitch, but I cannot stand a sanctimonious son-of-a-bitch." Iva began to walk toward the door, but Hattie stopped her with a raised hand and the shake of her head. "Hear me out, it ain't likely we'll ever have another polite conversation." Iva stopped, turned to face her.

"I reckon you think it's nigh on to impossible that an old whore like me could have a real lover…like you—a young beautiful whore could. Well, there's a hell of a lot more to bein' a lover than spreadin' your legs…as you might or might not come to understand down the long road. In my case, it means helping a man—and, yes, a red one—live past what he did in years gone by. It means being one with him and giving him a place where he can find some peace for the most part. And now, the boy is a part of that peace—and mine too, I don't deny—and if you manage to steal him away, I'll not be surprised, but I'll despise you for it as long as I live."

"I didn't know you and him…"

"It's not common knowledge around here, mainly because it's nobody's damn business, not because I feel the need to hide it. I'm sure Dilla knows, and probably Sally, long as she's been here." She stood up, walked to the window and looked out for a few seconds, and then turned around. "The first time I slipped down there to his cabin, I swear I can't say just why I did, but when he opened the door, he didn't act the least bit surprised, and when he stepped back to let me in he said, 'What took you so long?' And then I told him I didn't know, but that we'd make up for it. And we have. We like to go down by the river and screw like the coyotes, and maybe it's because the whole goddamn world considers us more like coyotes than people—a whore with a past and a red nigger with a past—but I'll tell you true, when we're together down there in each other's arms, after the passion, we feel more in common with the coyotes than the people, and it doesn't feel like a bad thing. Not a bad thing at all."

Hattie walked back to the table and fingered another cigar, but she did not pick it up. She thought back on the night of John Post Oak's visit, and a great sadness filled her—quick and hot, like stepping out into a July sun—and then it was gone, as if she had returned to a cool refuge. "Sooner or later, everything in life will make you sad, so you damn well better make the best of the good times, Iva. They blow away like the March wind."

"I am sorry it had to end like this…between us."

"It didn't *have* to, but it did. Can't stop the wind in March."

Hattie picked up the cigar, struck a match, and then turned away to light it. She waited for the door to close behind her, and then she walked back the window, looked down at the cabin, and waited. Within a few minutes, Rufus walked out of the main door, tilted his head back, lifted his arms in a great stretch that reminded her of an eagle spreading its wings, and then he regained his posture—tall and straight—and stood like the statue of a man touched by the first light of morning. The second door swung inward, and Son stepped out and walked to the man, and for a few seconds, the sunlight touched them both as they talked, then the light was taken by the cloud shadows of dawn.

CHAPTER 21

A little island in the middle of a wild country

Apsel hopped down from the buggy and tied the reins of the horse to the hitching post in front of Hattie's house just after ten o'clock on Sunday morning, and then he climbed the porch steps and sat down in the swing to wait for Iva. A couple of minutes passed, the tiny creak of the swing chains the only sound, and then Iva opened the front door and stepped out, sat two large travel bags down at her boots. Apsel stood and said, "Good morning," and then he picked up her bags and put them in the buggy. He returned to the porch and took both of her hands in his.

She smiled, tilted her head as a preface to her question. "Are you alright, Apsel? Your face is drawn."

"My mind is too full—thoughts moving about like marbles on a wood floor." He looked at the front door. "At least this is the last time I have to come here."

"There may be one more time. Come, let's sit. It's time to sort some of the marbles."

"I'm not sure what you mean."

"I think you do, Apsel. The boy has become a part of my life that I don't want to give up...and for his sake as much as mine."

"I don't think Hattie Wax and her Indian see it that way."

"I know that they don't, and I don't care. The boy is incredibly bright despite the pitiful schooling he got from the city orphanages. I have him reading and writing at a level well beyond his years...and arithmetic as well. I know that the skills he learns from Rufus are useful too, but..." her voice trailed off and she shook her head.

"The rest of your thought is, 'but'...only in this setting, in this place of lawlessness and violence. Judge Plume believes that one day it will all get cleaned up, made decent for people who just want decency and a peaceful place to make a life. I am not certain that I share that outlook, at least during the years to come when Son develops into a man."

"Exactly—that is how I feel too." She drew him close, locked her arms around his back. "So, are you as committed as I am to this? Are you willing to share our new life for four or five years until he's on his own feet, pointed in a good direction? This is no small thing, Apsel."

He nodded, did not look away. "There is room in both of our lives for the boy."

She laid her head on his chest. "Good...it is good to hear you say that."

"When the room came open next to mine at the boarding house, I told the landlady to hold it for me until

I was sure I wanted it." He smiled. "She would be very surprised to learn just who the new boarder is…if he comes."

Iva said, "Oh my, but wouldn't she? The street waif thief."

"He has come a long way in a short time, to be sure."

"Come, let's go find him and take a walk down by the river. It's time."

They walked around the side of the house to the cabin and found him behind it, sitting on a small stool beside a tree stump that served as a work surface. He was honing a knife, carefully stroking the blade along the whet stone. He looked up as they approached, said, "Hey."

Iva said, "Hey to you, Son."

Apsel looked past Son, into the barnyard, where Rufus was kneeling beside the hind leg of a horse, his fingers probing the long tendons below the knee. Their eyes met for a second, and then Rufus stood and walked the horse into the barn. From the corner of her eye, Iva saw him too, but she ignored him, looked only at Son. She said, "Son, Apsel and I…well, we'd like for you to take a walk with us down to the river. We need to talk."

Son looked up from the knife, his face open, expressionless. "About what?"

"Oh, it's a pretty big thing—the sort of thing people talk about best on a walk off by themselves. Alright?"

"Sure, Miss Iva, it's alright with me." He stood and slid the knife in the sheath he wore on his belt.

From her open bedroom window, Hattie—Hector perched on her shoulder—watched as Iva, Apsel, and Son began the walk to the river. She drew on her cigar and released a cloud of smoke that was caught up in the gentle wind and swept away.

When they drew even with the barn, Son glanced at it, said, "Should I tell Rufus where we're goin'?"

Both Iva and Apsel took note of the dropped "Mister." It was the first time either had heard him address Rufus in that manner. Iva said, "No, he saw us when we talked back there. He knows you're with us."

Son walked between Iva and Apsel, and above them, the soothing hiss of the breeze pushing through the canopy of leaves was welcomed, each person lost in thoughts revolving around words that would soon be spoken. Soon the trouble-free mutter of the river filled their ears, and they stopped in the shade of two tall birch trees.

Iva placed an arm around Son's shoulders, said, "I know it's no secret that I will soon leave and make my life with Apsel."

Son said, "Yeah…secrets don't keep so good around here. I figured you'd tell me sometime." There was a hint of regret in his voice, and it cut her like a razor.

"I…uh…I know that I should have talked to you before now…but…I…"

"It's alright, Miss Iva. Some things ain't easy to talk about. You said 'soon'. What does that mean?"

"It means today, Son."

Son looked up at her face, then quickly away, toward the sound of the water. He nodded in the manner of grown man. "Where will you go?"

"After we're married, I'll move into Apsel's room in town, but it won't be for long. We want to go west, all the way to San Francisco and start all over with our lives."

Son said, "I'll miss our lessons. You were a good teacher, and I thank you for that."

Iva said, "It doesn't have to be 'were', Son."

The boy looked up at her, then at Apsel. "So I can come to town now and then for lessons?"

Iva said, "Much more than that. We want you to come with us…be a part of our lives for as long as you want."

Son blinked, and then quickly again, his face a mask of wide-eyed bewilderment. "I don't rightly know what to say."

Apsel said, "We don't expect you to say anything just now. Just think long and hard about it. We know that others besides Iva have been good to you around here, but there are other things to think over about your future."

Iva said, "You live here on sort of a little island in the middle of a wild country…so wild you can't imagine, Son."

Apsel said, "The Indian Territory is full of men who live only for doing bad things, and through my job, I have seen many fall to their just deaths from the gallows, but there are always more out there, and will be for a very long time. We know that the skills Rufus has taught you are fun and interesting to you, and they are useful skills when used in the right manner, but we hope that you are never put in a…situation…where they are a matter of life or death, and not fun."

Son's mind drifted back to the night of the stranger's visit to Rufus, and the chilling feeling that enwrapped him as he stared in wonder at the Indian and his horse, the sound of his voice, so heavy, so foreboding. *He is more horse than man.* Rufus's words lingered inside of his head for a moment, and then they were gone, but not the image of man and horse. That, he had to blink away.

Iva said, "Son, a boy your age doesn't think too far ahead, we know. We didn't either when we were young, but it's a good thing to do. And be sure of this: the four or five years before you become a man of your own will fly by so fast you'll look back and be amazed. And we intend to help you find your way in a civilized world…not at the edge of a violent wilderness that might well drag you into it."

Apsel said, "We do not desire any hold on you, Son. The opposite really. You have the makings of a fine man. We just want for you to have a decent chance at becoming one."

Son squatted down, and then sat, his back to a tree. He looked straight ahead, and neither Iva nor Apsel could discern any idea of what was going through his mind. They sat down on either side of him, waited.

"If I went with you…well, it was the sheriff sent me here to start with for my stealin'."

Apsel said, "The sheriff and I know each other well. What's more is the fact that Judge Plume is the most important man in Fort Smith, and I've worked hand in hand with him for many years. The matter of your custody is not a consideration. Trust me on that."

Iva said, "We have a room beside ours at the boarding house that would become yours until we leave town."

"I have to talk to Miss Hattie…and Rufus."

Iva said, "We understand."

"What if they talk me out of it."

She said, "Then so be it, Son. We can't drag you away. If you don't want to come, you don't have to."

"They've been awful good to me."

"Yes they have. All Apsel and I ask is that you think it through for yourself, think of the time soon when you will be a man and what will become of you."

They sat in silence in the tree shade, the sounds of the leaves and the running water all about them, and after a few minutes, they all got up and walked away from the river.

CHAPTER 22

Just spit it out

When they reached the barn door, Son stopped, but Iva and Apsel continued to walk, neither looking back. He looked in the open door, saw Rufus still working on the mare's hind leg. The horse was a gentle red dun named Rosie, and she was Hattie's favorite. Rufus didn't acknowledge the boy, even after he walked up to the horse. Son reached up and stroked the long nose, allowed the horse to nuzzle his hand, then he said, "Sorry, girl, I got nothing to give you right now." He looked down at Rufus and asked, "What's wrong with her?"

"Stockin' up in the legs. Water building up. Ought to be run more than she is."

Son fidgeted, shuffled his boots on the straw-covered soil. "I was wonderin' if you and me and Miss Hattie could talk…about something."

"About what?"

"Well…I was hopin' that we could all be together when we did."

"I'm right here, start with me."

"I'd still like…"

Rufus looked up at him, said, "It ain't like when you and Iva and the hangman go off to the river—all family-like and all, now is it? So just start with me, and you can talk to Hattie whenever you want."

Son wanted to say something in reply, but his mind whirred emptily, clearly dazed by how quickly the conversation had gone in the wrong direction.

Rufus said, "Just spit it out."

"They want me to leave here and throw in with them. They're gonna get married." He paused, formed his thoughts. "I like it here. I like the things you've taught me…the things we've done."

"But they warned you about being around a red nigger too long."

"They never called you any such a name. They…"

"Don't matter what they called me or didn't call me. I know what they think."

Son reached up and fingered the brim of his hat, tugging and twisting to no purpose. "It don't seem fair for you to…"

Rufus cut him off with a glare as he stood and laid his hands on the back of the horse, then he looked straight ahead as he stroked the smooth hair. "When I was about your age, we lived up near Fort Laramie in the Dakota Territory. My father was a fine warrior among many such. One summer, some white settlers passin' through blamed us for a killed cow, and they went to the fort and the blue army sent a shave-tail little spearhead named Gratton with about thirty men and two cannons to our camp. Said he aimed to leave with whichever savage bastard killed the cow. He was loud and stupid and got so worked up, the warriors figured he was about to commence firing." He looked back at Son and then quickly away. "My father and the warriors killed every damn one of 'em before they knew what happened. And things ain't got any better since then…which is to say, that between us and the whites, there is a wide gap and it won't ever be closed."

"But I…Miss Hattie…we're white."

"Every once in a while…a really long while…one comes along that's worth a damn. You and her are among 'em."

"Well then…I thank you for sayin' that."

"It ain't something you need to thank anybody for sayin'. You're either worth a damn or you're not."

"Still glad you think I am."

Rufus walked to the far side of the mare, slapped the muscular shoulder a few times, and looked over her back at Son. "You want me to tell you to stay? I will not. You want me to tell you to leave. I will not. Like I told you the first time they wanted to walk you to the river, you ain't tethered. Do as you please."

Son took off his hat, looked down at it, and then jammed it back on his head. "This didn't turn out like I thought it would."

"Damn little does, boy. So, if you learnin' that is just one more lesson in living, it will be the most useful."

As Rufus walked past him, he said, "Tell her she needs to ride Rosie more. No sense in a good horse stockin' up."

Son tapped on the back kitchen door and waited for Dilla. She opened the door, smiled, and said, "I know you're hungry, Son, and I got a pot of beans and fat back just about simmered proper."

"It ain't that, Dilla. I was wonderin' if you'd go see if Miss Hattie would come talk to me…about somethin'."

Dilla's eyes widened a bit, and she looked Son over, head to boots. "Somethin' wrong with you? I can fix it."

"No, it ain't like that. I just need to talk to her."

"Alright then, you wait here."

Dilla returned within a couple of minutes, opened the door, and said, "Come on in, Miss Hattie says you're to go up to her room."

At her bedroom door, Son lightly knocked on the door, and he heard Hattie say, "Come on in, little man."

Hattie was sitting at the table near the window, unlit cigar in hand. She motioned for him to join her, pointed to the other chair. Son took off his hat, hooked it on a chair post, and sat down. Hector stirred on his perch, but only croaked a time or two. She looked at the cigar, then said, "I'm pretty sure I was eight when I started smokin', and I'm pretty sure you got a hold of smokin' tobacco back in the big city…so have a smoke with me while we talk." She pushed the cigar box in front of him, waited until he took one out, and she struck a match with her thumbnail and watched as he puffed the dark tobacco to life.

"It's been a while."

"Don't lung much of it then or you'll go green on me and I don't want to talk to a dizzy little man."

Son nodded, puffed the smoke from his mouth. "Alright."

"So what are we gonna talk about that's so terrible urgent?"

He studied the smoke rising from his cigar for a moment. "Think I'll just spit it out."

"So spit."

"Well…Miss Iva and Mister Apsel…uh…they want me to leave here and throw in with them after they get married."

Hattie snorted, the smoke jetting from her nostrils. "Married, huh? I'll be goddamned and do tell."

"Yes, ma'am, that's what Miss Iva said."

"She do all the talkin'?"

"Most, but Mister Apsel talked to."

"I'll bet he did…but not about me I'd bet too."

Son fought the urge to draw a long pull deep into his lungs, feel the buzz in his forehead, but he only puffed. "I don't remember Mr. Apsel even sayin' his name, but that's what Rufus thinks too."

"So you and Rufus already talked?"

He nodded. "I asked him if we all three could talk, but he wouldn't have none of it."

"Despite bein' Indian, Rufus ain't any good at powwows, even little ones. Two is all he can generally tolerate." She drew on her cigar, her bosom rising and falling, and she tilted her head upward, shot the smoke stream to the ceiling. "When did you drop the 'Mister Rufus?'"

"Oh, maybe a week or so. He told me he was gettin' tired of it…sounded too much like a white man's title."

She smiled, but with only half of her mouth. "So just how did Rufus Not Mister advise you to proceed?"

"Wouldn't tell me one way or the other. Just told me I wasn't tethered."

"You think I want to tether you?"

"Don't know…I don't know what to think right now. I'm dizzier than a drunk in an alley and I ain't sucked the least bit of this smoke down inside of me. It's just from stewin' on things."

"Oh what the hell, little man, suck that sumbitch as deep as you want. It's a dizzy damn world anyhow."

Son drug deep on his cigar, released the smoke slowly through loose lips. "This is way better than the stuff I could get a hold of in the city. The passed out drunks that we took stuff off of never had a decent smoke."

"Well you won't get any smokes of any kind from your new keepers…if that's the way you decide."

"That's for damn sure."

"No cussin' allowed either."

Son looked at her, took another draw. "That's for goddamn sure."

Hattie laughed, full and deep. "Feels good, doesn't it, little man…just to cut loose with some necessary vices now and then when you're with people who enjoy it like you do."

"I ain't gonna argue that."

She waved her empty hand through the air. "Ah…we ain't gonna argue anything, you and me. No use in that. Miss Iva sure enough took a strong likin' to you, that's plain to anybody payin' half attention, and I always pay full attention to everything." She paused long enough for a thoughtful puff on her cigar. "She's a good woman, I came to like her a lot, and I told her herself—like I do all my girls—this was just a stop-over to somethin' better down the road. Same for you. She ain't an ordinary woman…so damn smart and talented. If she just hadn't fallen for that damn quirky hangman, I'd feel better about it all."

"He's never been but nice to me. And in the beginning, he could've went hard with me, but he didn't."

"Yes…yes…I get that. But it just sticks in my craw that he does what he does, and has for so long."

"He don't plan to do it much longer. They want to head off to San Francisco for a new life."

"Well, I'll tell you, my reckon is that old Judge Plume will make that hard for him. He can't order him to stay, but they've worked so close together for so long…" She shook her head, waved her hand again. "Nah…even Iva will have trouble with that. I'll bet they stay in Fort Smith for a good long time." She looked at him, let it soak in. "You need to consider that in your dizzy mind, little man."

"That part don't mean shit to me. If I went with them, where wouldn't matter."

Hattie stood and walked to the window, her thoughts forming clearly now, like stacking stones so that they wouldn't topple over. She felt no compunction about what she was about to do. She truly cared for the boy, would do nothing to jeopardize his future, and one way or the other, she considered him already gone, knew that it was a fight she could never win. Iva Lockwood was not an ordinary woman.

Hattie said, "I want for you to consider doin' me a favor." She turned around, sat back down at the table. "I figure you'll decide to go live with them somewhere down the road…and that's probably a good thing for you, I have to admit. But I'd like for you to stay with me and Rufus here for just a while longer…say, two or three weeks, maybe a month."

"Sure, Miss Hattie, I'd do that for you, but it don't seem to matter much to Rufus."

"It does, trust me. That's just Rufus bein' Rufus. He'd never admit his attachment to you, just ain't his way." She placed the cigar in the ashtray and put both of her hands over her nose and cheeks before pulling them slowly down. "Son, I'm gonna tell you something you probably already figured out on your own—you being advanced beyond your years and all. Rufus is a lot more to me than a ranch hand, has been for many years."

Son looked at her, said, "Figured somethin' like that."

"I'm worried about him. He's had a hard past…done some things he ought not a done, but he's made a clean start with me here and I don't want it to end bad." The words came to the boy as clearly as the peeling of a bell inside of his head: *He is more horse than man.* He knew what Hattie was about to say. "There's a bad man showed up at Rufus's cabin not long ago in the middle of the night…a part of that hard past. But he's the type that never stays in one place for long. He's a wanted man, name of John Post Oak, an Indian. So, I'm thinkin' that if you can see fit to stay here with us just a while longer, he'll drift away."

Son put his cigar in the ashtray and watched the thin trail of smoke waft upward. "So you figure I'm pullin' on the good part of Rufus and this man is pullin' on the bad part."

"I truly do."

"I saw him."

A shudder passed through Hattie, cold and tingly. "When was that?"

"A good while back, maybe two or three weeks, deep in the night. Not sure what woke me, but I could hear low voices and I peeked out the door and there he was, on his horse, and he and Rufus were talkin'."

"Did you hear what they said?"

"No, ma'am, I couldn't make out what they said."

"How did they sound toward each other...I mean... uh, were they havin' fun like old friends, or were they... serious like?"

"Serious like, and Rufus didn't say much, the other one did most of the talkin'."

"Did Rufus know you saw him."

"I didn't try to hide it from him. He saw me right after the Indian left and asked if I heard what they said. I thought he might be mad at first, but when I told him I hadn't heard words, he was alright."

"Were there other riders with him, farther back?"

"Didn't see any, and the moon was good." Hattie reached down to pick up the cigar, but she just rolled it back and forth on the edge of the ashtray. Son said, "I ain't seen all that many riders sit a horse, I know, but there was somethin' about that man and his horse...like magic... it was somethin' to see, and when I told Rufus that, he said words that seemed strange then. He said, 'He's more horse than man.'" Son hesitated, then said, "Don't seem so strange now."

"That's because it isn't."

CHAPTER 23

I wish it was you layin' there, hangman

The portly, gray-haired reverend's name was Uriah Hudspeth. He stood beside the parlor window, his wife standing on the opposite side, as the couple peeked through the slivers of space between the curtain and the edges of the window pane at Apsel and Iva, arm in arm, strolling down the narrow rock walkway leading away from the front door of the house.

Uriah, mouth half open, shook his head in wonderment, his fleshy, red cheeks jiggling. "I will declare that I never figured the hangman to be the marrying kind."

His wife was lean and tall for a woman, and her hair—still more dark than grey—was pulled back into a tight bun. Her eyes narrowed as she cast Uriah a quick glance, and then she resumed her watch through the window. "I must say he did himself proud with that one…at least based on her exterior."

Uriah nodded thoughtfully as his brain processed

several suitable replies, but he could not decide on one that did not risk overstatement, so he only said, "True."

"That's all you have to say about the likes of her, Uriah?" She waited for several seconds for a response, but none came. "You've never had much trouble coming up with words suitable to the occasion."

"I'm not behind the pulpit, dear."

"Indeed, you're peeking out of your own window, and I am sure that your eyes aren't on the hangman. In fact, I don't have memory of your eyes being on him for more than one second during the entire ceremony."

"Wasn't much of a ceremony."

"Well, sir, it got the job done and it got us a twenty-dollar gold piece…which is a sight more than the ham supper you usually get…or a skinny pig…or a cow that needed to be culled before it was gifted to you."

"True." Uriah released the curtain, turned and walked to an armchair in the parlor and sat down.

His wife followed him and sat down in her own chair, and crossed her arms over her bosom. "There was something about that woman that doesn't square with being in these parts. She was…cultivated…the way that she spoke, carried herself, and so beautiful without a touch of paint on her face, her hair pulled back and under that gaudy old hat, clothes decent, but far from fine. And did you hear the notes when she passed by the piano? Four heavenly notes, above middle C, and with her *left* hand." She made a humming sound in her throat. "It was like she was trying to hide who she really was."

"True."

"Uriah, if you say that solitary word again with nothing behind it, I will become fully agitated."

Uriah's brain was whirring for all it was worth—comprehending what his wife was saying, and yet on a deeper plane, remembering the rumors that had sprang up in certain manly church circles around the striking beauty about whom it was said, had ridden away from town in a buggy driven by the Indian who worked for Hattie Wax. He despised rumors—had despised them long before he entered the clergy—and yet he knew that he was as powerless at ignoring them as any man, and especially concerning a woman of dazzling beauty. He said, "Fort Smith is a pretty good-sized city, dear. People come and go for a number of reasons…and meet each other in many different sets of circumstances."

She arched her eyebrows, brought her fingertips together forming a little steeple. "Apsel Graf, chief executioner for Judge Burleigh Plume. The hangman that people cross the street to avoid walking past…he's the man who weds the mysterious beauty from somewhere, who ends up in raw and rowdy Fort Smith." She huffed. "I do declare."

"Signs and wonders, dear. Signs and wonders."

"Oh, come now, Uriah. Let's not bring the apostles, much less the Lord Jesus himself, into this. I'm not at all sure your reference is appropriate."

Careful not to mouth the word, Uriah said it to himself, "*True.*"

Apsel sat Iva's bags down and opened the door to his room. "Home, but just for now." He led her inside. "I have about finalized the rent of a house and five acres a mile outside of town. It will give us some elbow room."

Iva knew precisely what he meant. "That sounds very nice, but I'm not concerned about...what shall we call it? Prying eyes? Yesterday, the thought came to me that I should cut my hair, like I did when I escaped my situation years ago, but that thought passed somewhere during my last night at Hattie's place. This is only a temporary condition, in this room or at a house, but the house would be much better if Son decides to let us take him."

He pulled her close, kissed her forehead. "I was thinking of that too...hoping." He stroked her hair with his fingers. "And perish the hair thought forever."

"When will you talk to the judge about our plans?"

"Very soon. I don't consider myself irreplaceable by any means, but we have worked together for so long that I doubt if he's ever considered my giving up the job before he is through himself. He will need a reasonable time to find someone else. I certainly owe him that."

"Agreed." She looked quickly around at the room, clean and sparsely furnished. "I intended to spend tomorrow cleaning up around here, but there appears to be little to be done. That doesn't surprise me."

"I am of the orderly sort...for a man, I suppose."

She smiled impishly. "First domestic admission: I'm not...for a woman."

"We'll learn each other's ways." He kissed her again. "We already have about the things that matter."

"Yes, Apsel...yes we have."

At seven o'clock the next evening, Apsel tapped on the door and said, "It's me." Iva flipped the inside latch and opened it, kissed Apsel as he hurried into the room. He said, "Long day, and it's not over."

"How is that?"

"It doesn't happen often, but the judge granted a favor for a convicted murderer's lawyer—a very vocal and demanding sort—who asked, if one can call it that, for a night sentencing hearing. I have to be back at the courthouse in forty-five minutes."

"Are you always at sentencings?"

"Yes, it is one of my duties to the court. Being a presence, the judge likes to say. I usually have a calming effect on prisoners, although it would seem the opposite would be more likely."

Iva pilfered a quick glance at the two revolvers worn cross-draw style on his hips, but he saw her and said, "I've never actually fired one of these other than practice since the war. I have drawn them on several occasions and that proved sufficiently…calming." He smiled at her in assurance. "A presence is all that is required of me, trust me." He looked over her shoulder at the small counter under the cabinet. "I'm hungry."

"Dilla stuffed so much food in one of my bags that your landlady won't have to feed us for another couple of days at least. Jerky, dried apples—with some sort of cinnamon crust on them that is wondrous—fresh bread, two jars of preserves, a bag of horehound candy, and pickled pig's feet that I won't fight you for."

"Ha…good, I love them."

She put some of the food on the table and they sat and ate, the conversation light and exuberant, as if they were eighteen with no pasts. Apsel got up, dropped three pieces of the horehound candy in his coat pocket, and pecked Iva on the cheek. "Shouldn't be more than an hour or so."

Darkness would come early; low, scudding clouds had drizzled intermittently all afternoon, and now the rain fell again, airy and balmy and gentle against his face. Apsel walked briskly past the courthouse door and stopped in front of the main door to the basement prison cells, and rapped on it. The door creaked open and a deputy stood aside and let him pass, said, "Evening, Apsel."

Apsel said, "Evening to you, George, are we ready?"

"Now that you're here, reckon we are."

Both men walked to the door of a large cell containing four men, one of them named Tildon Butler, the convicted murderer. He was twenty-seven years old, not a large man, but sturdily built, and his thick wrists poked from ill-fitted coat sleeves, his hands wide and square, fingernails thick and grimy.

Apsel said, "Butler, we've come to take you to your sentencing. Step to the front, the rest of you step to the back of the cell."

The three prisoners complied, shuffled to the back wall, and Butler walked to the door and said, "Don't see much use in all this. Everybody knows Plume is gonna lay a hangin' on me sure."

"Your lawyer requested this, it's not my idea of a good way to spend an evening."

"Ma and Pa here?"

"I have no idea, but the court is open for sentencing hearings. I'm sure your lawyer told them, so I would think that they'd be there." Apsel motioned for the deputy to unlock the cell door.

Before he could turn the latch, Butler held up his right hand, like a man trying to stop an approaching horse. "Wait.

Tell you what, hangman, I got a deal for you. If'n you was to take these three boys outta here with youun's, and if'n you was to slide one of your pistols over to me just before you shut the big door, I could save a lot of folks a lot of trouble."

Apsel shook his head. "Doesn't work like that, Butler."

Butler grunted a sound that was part laugh and part grumble. "Well, what the hell, hangman, wouldn't want to cheat you and all the gawkers outta so much fun on hangin' day, would we?" Butler looked squarely into Apsel's eyes, and it was Apsel who looked away first, and as he did, a mental shiver darted through his brain that he would regret ignoring for the remainder of his life. With a detached calm, Butler said, "Aw, shit…let's go ahead with it then, all proper like."

He held out both hands together, lowered his head in acquiesce and waited for the manacles. The latch turned with a metallic clack and the door groaned open. When the deputy raised the manacles, Butler took a step forward and swung both fists upward, one at each man. His right fist caught the deputy full in the Adam's apple and he toppled to his knees. His left fist struck Apsel at the juncture of his neck and jaw and he staggered backward and went down to one knee. In a blur, Butler ran toward the main door. Apsel staggered to his feet, blinked away the bright stars in his eyes and drew the revolver from his left holster, pointed it at the three prisoners who stood wide-eyed, their backs pinned to the stone wall. He grabbed the cell door, swung it shut, and turned the latch, removed the key and tossed it toward the deputy without looking at him. Had Apsel looked down, he would have seen that George was on his hands and knees, wheezing and blowing bloody spittle on the floor, his larynx fractured.

When Apsel cleared the basement steps, he stopped and squinted into the gathering gloom, spied the running man, arms and legs flailing toward the east wall of the compound. Apsel fired when Butler was forty yards away, but the bullet missed. He cocked the hammer, held the front sight a half foot over the man's head and squeezed the trigger. Butler crumpled face down, as if struck by a lightning bolt, and when Apsel reached the body, the blood was already pooling under the head, seeping from both sides like oil from a cracked lamp.

The sound of hurried footfalls caused Apsel to reflexively raise his gun, but he saw Judge Plume leading the half dozen people toward him. Plume held a derringer in his right hand and when he reached Apsel and the body, he dropped it into the front pocket of his black robe. Plume said, "What in God's name happened?"

"Butler…he jumped us when George reached out with the manacles. Got us both solid with each fist."

Plume looked toward the prison door. "Is he covering the other prisoners?"

"I shut the door and locked it, tossed the keys to him before I took after this one."

A woman with a shawl pulled over her head and shoulders began to weep quietly over the body, and beside her, a man knelt down and placed his hand over the head. The woman said, "Sweet Lord Jesus…oh, sweet Lord Jesus…"

The man suppressed a sob, then said, "A youngun don't always turn out like you want. This'n wasn't all that bad really…just never could get a hold on his temper…never knew how strong he was."

The woman knelt beside her husband, pulled an

embroidered white hankie from her dress pocket and held it against her nose. She sniffled, looked up at Plume and said, "I want to take him home now. Is that alright with you?"

"Why…yes…yes, ma'am. I am so sorry that this happened the way it did. I will send for men to help you get him home."

Their lawyer, a well-dressed man, stepped forward with an air of authority, and said, "No need for that, Judge. I will tend to this."

The woman said, "It's better this way. Tildon knew I couldn't bear to see him hang…and he knew that I couldn't bear not to watch it." She began to weep again, pressed the hankie to her mouth, and then said, "Sweet Lord Jesus… it's all such a shame."

From the prison, the shouting voice of a man pierced the darkness, and Apsel turned away and trotted toward the sound. When he reached the cells, he saw the still form of the deputy curled on the floor, hands clamped around his throat. He was stone dead.

One of the prisoners, hands clamped tightly around the bars, said, "I swear to God, I would've tried to help him if I coulda got to him…swear to God."

Apsel was on his knees, his right hand on the shoulder of the body. "I believe you."

Another prisoner walked slowly to the cell door. "I swear to God I would not have. And what's more, I wish it was you layin' there, hangman, God damn you."

CHAPTER 24

•◆•◆◆◆•◆•

We are finished with ghosts

Iva looked at the clock sitting on the bed nightstand. It read half past nine and she began to pace. She chastised herself for being silly, but to no avail and she continued to pace in the fifteen-foot square that defined the room. The footsteps on the stairs came ten minutes later and she unlatched the lock and swung the door open before Apsel identified himself. He said, "Always be sure you know it is me before you open it." He did not look at her as he walked to the table chair, took off his coat, then his gun belt, and hung them on a corner post of the chair. He sat down in the chair and laid his forearms across the table and for the first time since entering the room, looked at Iva's face, but only for a moment before looking down at his hands.

She sat down opposite him, reached across the table and covered his hands with her own. His features were devoid of expression. She said, "Apsel, what is wrong?"

"I have just shot a prisoner to death, and I have lost a

good and faithful deputy friend…all in the span of a few minutes."

Iva forced herself to take a breath before she spoke and she relaxed her grip on his hands, which had instantly tightened with the death pronouncements. "Do you…want to talk about it? You do not have to. I only want to help you."

"It was all my fault…all mine. As long as I have been at this job, dealing with condemned prisoners…" His voice trailed off as he slowly shook his head. "There is no such thing as 'routine', I know that, have preached it to younger lawmen, and still!"

He pulled his hands from hers, stood and began to walk aimlessly around the room, and Iva thought of her own pacing only moments before. She said, "Tell me what happened. I can't help you unless you tell me."

"I missed a clear sign from the prisoner. His name was Tildon Butler, and he gave me a clear sign…and I sensed it, then, damn me, I just let it go."

"Maybe it was not as clear as you think, Apsel. What did he do?"

"Not what he did, it was what he said. He made what I thought was a crude and stupid joke…about me giving him one of my guns so that he could kill himself and save people much trouble. And then…for just an instant when he looked at me, I felt something dark pass through me…the clear sign that I ignored. Just as George was about to manacle his hands, he struck at us with his fists, one for me, the other for George. Down we went. It was like a rattlesnake striking. I don't even remember seeing his hands move. And then he was gone—out the main door. I locked the cell so the other three prisoners couldn't escape, and tossed the key ring at

George…didn't even look at him. Butler was most of the way across the courtyard before my second shot struck him in the back of the head."

"But the deputy…I don't understand how he died from just a single blow."

"His windpipe must have been crushed. Another prisoner shouted for someone to come back, and when I got there and found George dead, he said that he would have tried to help him if he could have. Strange as it may sound, I believed him."

"I do not think it strange at all. They are just men when all is said and done, and none of them are totally evil. Some just refuse to listen to their better angels…as we all have done from time to time." She stopped his pacing, took his hands and led him to the bedside and they sat down. "As far as your actions in stopping a convicted murderer, you simply did your duty. What if he had rushed into the courtroom… or the street, and harmed innocent people, Apsel? Such a wild and desperate man that had just overpowered two men. You did your sworn duty, you must let that part go. And the part about your…missed sign, as you say. Ah… Apsel, I think that you grant yourself too great a power of perception. We will never know what went through the man's mind when he made his crude joke, or at the instant when he decided to strike out at you and the deputy, or if those thoughts were even related."

Apsel passed his tongue over dry, parted lips, realized that he was powerfully thirsty, and he got up and walked over to the cabinet counter and drank from a water jug. He wiped his mouth with the back of his hand as he returned to the bedside. "What you say may be true, but I know what I felt…and it was a sign that I ignored."

"Well then, Apsel, that is something you…and I…will just have to live with, and we will. We have figured out how to live with a dreadful death in your far past, and now we must figure out how to live with one that is in your near past. No more ghosts, love. We are finished with ghosts."

She knelt in front of him and pulled off his boots, lifted his legs onto the bed, and then she snuggled against his side, laid her hand on his chest. The oil lamp cast an amber glow about the room, and after a time, it soothed them, bathed them inside of their tiny peaceful refuge.

Apsel said, "It will not be as difficult as I had imagined when I tell Judge Plume of our intentions."

For the next two days, the deadly, failed jail break was the talk of the town. On Thursday morning, Apsel hurried toward the courthouse complex, head down, half trotting, his boot heels hammering away at the boardwalk as he tried to sort the thoughts zinging around in his head. For two days, he had heard snippets of the rumors floating about, like little balloons tossed by a capricious breeze. He had heard reports that he had fired anywhere from three to all six rounds from his revolver, that the range was from point-blank, or from one hundred yards, as Butler had attempted to scale the compound wall. At first, he paid them no mind, but as they grew in their inaccuracy, even downright silliness, he began to care. He also admitted to himself that he was irritated with the Fort Smith Daily Tribune for apparently ignoring the story, much less having come to him for the facts. Such was his mindset when he looked up to stare at a chubby-cheeked man in a bowler hat half trotting toward him, note pad and pencil in hand. Apsel held up a hand and waited for the man to stop.

The man adjusted his spectacles as he tried to regain his breath, smiled apologetically, and said, "Beg pardon, Deputy Graf, I'm Sheldon Lipskey of the Tribune, and I wonder if I might have a word with you about the...uh... incident Monday night."

"You may. In fact, it is a curiosity to me that someone from the paper has not contacted me until now for the facts."

"Well, sir, may I offer my profound apologies for the delay. I am yours, sir. Please proceed with your account." He touched the pencil lead to the tip of his tongue and raised his note pad.

"The deceased convicted murdered, Tildon Butler, was being brought to Judge Plume's court for a night sentencing hearing. Myself, and...the late Deputy George Miller were in the process of removing him from the holding cell, at which point, as Miller was about to put his hands in manacles, Butler struck each of us with a fist, knocking us to the floor, and dashing away. I shut the cell door, locked it, and ran after him. At about forty yards, I fired one shot and missed. I took more careful aim, and at about seventy-five yards, my second and final shot struck him in the back of the head. He was dead when I reached him."

"So...it was then when you returned to the cell and found Deputy Miller?"

"Yes."

"And he was dead?"

"He was."

The reporter touched the pencil lead to the tip of his tongue again and furrowed his wooly brows. "It seems very strange…and of course incredibly unfortunate…that a single, quick blow could strike a man dead. He must have struck his head on the floor, one would surmise."

"My belief is that his windpipe was crushed from the fist blow."

"Then it would have taken…what? A few minutes for him to die?"

"Likely, yes."

The bowler hat rocked from side to side, stopping at a tilt. "I can't help but wonder about the other prisoners in the cell…the men who actually witnessed the entire escape event. Might I…uh…query them?"

"To what purpose?" Apsel paused, glanced away for a moment. "I spoke with them. None of them have anything of consequence to add to what happened. All that matters is that a good man was killed by a man who had already wantonly killed, and who was about to be sentenced to death for his crime."

"Just so…indeed, sir." He looked down at his notes and said, "Well, I see a blank page, so I'd better proceed with my scribbling, lest I record an inaccuracy. However, I do tend to remember short conversations verbatim."

"I would appreciate that."

"Just one more question, if I may. The irony of the Chief Executioner of the Western District of Arkansas…uh… dispatching a murderer in such spectacular fashion, can't be overlooked." He attempted a weak smile, but it never formed. "At least, that is what my editor will no doubt… uh…desire to see appear in the story. Readership numbers and all that, don't you see? Do you have a comment on that?"

Apsel stared into the man's eyes until he was certain

that a sufficient level of discomfort had registered. "My only comment on that—now and forever—is that I greatly regret the lack of an orderly and normal progression for this court-related incident."

Apsel nodded curtly, turned and walked directly into the courthouse, climbed the stairs, and at Judge Plume's chambers, rapped lightly on the door.

"Come in."

Apsel opened the door and closed it behind him, and Plume looked up from his desk chair and said, "Sit, my friend. I see that you are still ill at ease." Plume shuffled a stack of papers to the corner of the desk, locked his fingers and placed his hands in the center of the desk. "Apsel, you must put this behind you. It is a great wonder to me that it hasn't happened before, and as we have discussed, it will never happen again with the new protocol." He tilted his head forward. "A third deputy, or just a guard, with a shotgun at the prison door, will see to that. Further, as I have told you twice in the last two days, no one is at fault here. If anything, I am closer to fault than you. You know full well how I am about detailed protocol; I should have instigated this long ago." He flapped his hands up and down, opened his mouth as he tried to form further comments, but Apsel raised his right hand and stopped him.

"Judge, I didn't come here to talk about that anymore."

Plume registered a flicker of foreboding, but refused to allow it to grow. He pushed away from the desk and leaned back in his chair. "Very well, Apsel, the floor is yours."

"Judge, there is no use in beating around the bush about this. I knew the time would come that…I would grow weary of this position. I just didn't realize that it would come quite this soon."

"You force me to take back the floor, sir. You said that you did not come here to talk about the Monday incident anymore, but it appears to me that that is precisely what you are talking about."

"I don't claim that it had nothing to do with my decision. It is fair to call it a...meaningful incident, but I have placed the oiled, hempen rope around the necks of seventy-eight men over the course of my tenure here, and I remember each one in precise detail...the weeping, the pleas for forgiveness, the curses, the anger, the trembling, and at times, the stench of men fouling themselves...and always, Judge, always, I remember the silence following the banging of the trap door. It all has had a cumulative effect over the years."

Plume lowered his head, then said, "I am all too familiar with the cumulative effect of the executions, since after all, it is I who send them to you up there on the gallows." He pointed to the window. "I stand there and make myself watch every execution...every one that has taken place... because I need the reminder of the gravity of my sentences. I have always considered the burden to be shared with you... the far greater portion lying with me to be sure, but... shared, knowing that you would carry out your duties with honor and precision."

"I realize that, sir, I truly do, and that is what makes this decision so difficult for me." He paused for a moment, then said, "I was married—albeit quietly and privately—Sunday last, and my bride shares my wish to travel far and make a new life. So it is no longer just me involved in momentous decisions."

Plume brought his hands together, rubbed them like a man trying to sooth aching fingers. "Apsel, there is no such thing in this town as 'quietly private', especially when Reverend Uriah Hudspeth's wife is involved. She and my wife are friends."

Apsel was taken aback, felt the hot rush to his cheeks. He drew a long and thoughtful breath. "Ah...so it is. I should have known better. About some things, I am thick-headed."

"Apsel, I am a judge in profession only. I do not judge otherwise, believing since I was a boy, the words of admonishment from the Bible: 'Judge not, lest ye be judged.'"

"I...uh...I appreciate that—more than you will ever know."

"Let us step back here for a moment of reflection, but be assured that I will not attempt to dissuade you from your—and your new bride's—dreams of new lives. My wife and I as well have intentions of going back East when this is over, and perhaps not as distant in the future as you might imagine."

Apsel shook his head. "This is violent land filled with violent men, and when one dies, another takes his place. I fear it will be so for many, many years to come."

"You are aware that the powers in Washington have shrunk my jurisdiction very substantially, and this irritates me. Several more courts have been given authority over parts of Indian Territory. An element of vanity there? Perhaps, but I have put my heart and soul into this endeavor, and I am not at all certain that others would see this as the mission that I consider it. But far more important is the fact that the Supreme Court of the United States has made it nearly routine to reverse my decisions in capital crimes sentences and send them back here for re-trial. And each time that it happens, I pore over every detail of the trials, and yet I cannot—and, yes, I can be extremely objective about intricacies of law—I cannot find one single detail that would warrant these reversals." He tapped both forefingers on his desk. "One can only conclude that they have an aversion to the death sentence…sitting back there in the safety and comfort of Washington, while you and I live in the midst of the wild men that I was sent by former President Grant himself to tame, and if warranted by law, eliminate. So you see, Apsel, this has also had a great cumulative effect with me. Arguably, I have already been rendered ineffective in some measure. Inarguably, I will eventually be made impotent, and this eventuality is fast approaching."

"'Fast' is a relative term. I know that you cannot be precise, but it seems that you wish for me to make some sort of joint commitment with you regarding the end of our tenures."

"The year is about half gone. Could you see your way clear to the end of the year?"

"I will discuss it with Iva, but we have our eyes set on San Francisco, and, although I have some faith in the Central Pacific Railroad, I would prefer not to travel across the mountains in the dead of winter."

"Then if you would give me just another four months, I would be forever grateful."

Apsel nodded his head in agreement. "I have rented a house and a few acres outside of town—mostly for Iva's refuge—until we make longer term arrangements. I will stay until then. She will be fine with that, I am sure."

"Thank you, Apsel. I have no wish to end the affairs of this court in haphazard fashion, and absent you, that looms as a distinct possibility."

Apsel stood, approached Plume's desk as he too stood, and they shook hands. Apsel turned to leave, but when he reached the door, Plume said, "What will you both do in your new life?"

"I would like to run a small business…sell groceries, dry goods…it doesn't really matter. What matters more is that I want to set Iva up so that she can use her musical talents—which are extraordinary—to full measure. We think more along the lines of teacher rather than performer, but we will see." He studied Plume for signs of disbelief, but none appeared. "Have you heard of the great tenor, Granville Pollard, in Baltimore?"

"Indeed, I have."

"In another life, Iva came very near to accompanying him at the piano."

Plume's eyes widened for a moment, and Apsel knew that his brain was abuzz attempting to fathom such a declaration about such a woman. Plume said, "Well…I must say, that is quite…amazing."

"We both have past lives that we wish to bury, but part of Iva's should be resurrected, and I aim to see to that."

"I have no doubt that you will, sir. No doubt whatsoever."

CHAPTER 25

As iron sharpens iron, so one man sharpens another

Hattie and Dilla watched from the kitchen window as Son and Rufus walked toward the cabin. Dangling from Rufus's right hand were three squirrels that he held by the tails. Son carried a double-barreled shotgun, broken open, in the crook of his right elbow. A week had passed since Son had spoken with Hattie about her wish for him to stay until the trouble with John Post Oak had passed.

Dilla made a dismissive sound in her throat, scrunched her nose and mouth. "Just smell that stew pot simmerin' now, like heaven's kitchen come down, and that fresh bread in the stove, and them two sure as the world gonna skin those tree rats out and make a fire over yonder." She shook her head. "Nigh on to insultin' it is."

"It's no such thing, Dilla. It's just a big hunter and a little hunter, doin' what they naturally do, which in this

163

particular case is eat stringy squirrel meat over your fine stew with tender beef and fresh bread. No use stewin' over your stew. The boy eats with us often enough."

"Ah…reckon so. Least you and the gals appreciate my cookin' regular."

"Oh yes, Dilla. Sometimes too much."

"Ha…I have let out a dress seam or two, now and again."

They watched as Son and Rufus disappeared from view behind the cabin. Dilla stole a sidelong glance at Hattie before she said, "I sure do think the world of that boy. He gonna stay with us, Miss Hattie?"

"For a time, but probably not a long time."

Dilla waited, hoped for more, but Hattie turned from the window and walked from the kitchen.

Rufus flopped the squirrels on the tree stump and said, "You want to skin and gut or make the fire?"

Son said, "Don't matter, you pick."

"Clean 'em then, you need more practice on that. I don't want to bite down on a damn lead shot."

"I'll find 'em all."

They both set about their tasks in the silence that they had grown comfortable with over the months. What needed to be said was said, and only that. Rufus had the fire going hot before Son had the carcasses ready, but it would take time for the good cooking embers to form, so he sat back on his haunches and watched Son carefully work the pointed knife. The unspoken question had hung over them like a spell—shadowy in its own way—but not burdensome to the man or the boy. But now, Rufus felt the urging, would put it off no longer.

"When will you leave with them?"

Son was poking with the knife point into the meaty back strap and before he replied, he pinched out a lead shot and tossed it away. "Ain't sure I am."

Rufus looked up too quickly and instantly regretted it. He stood, walked over to Son and feigned inspection of the two finished carcasses. "These will do. You're gettin' decent at this."

"I'm gettin' decent at a lot of things."

"That why you ain't sure?"

"Partly."

Rufus went back to the fire, poked absently at the wood with a stick. He despised being lead in any conversation, much less one with a sprout, so he waited for a full minute before he was certain that he would have to speak next if he wanted to extend the talking. "What is the other part?"

"I like being with you."

"It cost you half a finger so far."

"I learned what not to do around beeves."

"That is true." He turned and walked toward the cabin. He returned with two pipes and a tobacco pouch in one hand and the bird pipe in the other. He laid the tobacco pipes on the stump, said, "Made one for you, it's time you tasted tobacco."

"Miss Hattie already saw to that with a cigar."

"The hell."

"Yep, it was pretty strong, but I liked it. Used to steal 'em off of drunks in the city."

"She can have her cigars, this is the way to smoke like a man."

"Sounds good to me." He looked at the bird pipe. "You think you can ever teach me to blow that right?"

"Besides the finger, you ain't fucked up anything so bad it couldn't be fixed."

"That's my recollection too."

Son smiled. Rufus grunted and began to fill the pipe bowls.

Three hours past midnight, Rufus woke with the sound of Post Oak's coyote call from the river drifting toward him. He sat up on the edge of his bed, waited for his eyes to adjust to the meager offerings from the window. He stood, snatched a shirt from the bed post, and then pulled on buckskin britches, and finally slipped his feet into moccasins. When he was a hundred yards from the cabin, Post Oak stepped out from behind a cedar and said, "How was the squirrel?"

"Squirrel is squirrel."

"Yes it is, for damn sure. Looks to me like you would eat the fat beef loin, or high off the nice hogs."

"I do now and then, when it suits me."

"Yes, but you never go long before you—or your pup— kill something wild and skin it and cook it and eat it like a man."

"You didn't come to talk about meat."

"No, but I did come to talk about the old ways, and it pleases me that you always return to the old ways...even if just for squirrels." He smiled, said, "Walk with me for a while, old friend, and let me tell you of more than squirrel meat."

At first, Son thought he was in the midst of a nightmare, but when the earthy smell of the big hand covering his mouth came to his nostrils, he knew it was a living nightmare. The voice was low and growly, just above a whisper. "Be quiet, else I will gut you like a river catfish. Understand?"

Son nodded against the hand, felt a stabbing in his

bowels but he willed himself to ignore it. Slowly, the hand slid down his face and he blinked wildly as he tried to focus on the shadowy features of the man, who sat down on the edge of the bed. "I ride with John Post Oak, who sent me to visit you while he talks with his friend, Rufus. Do you know why he sent me?"

Son decided to lie, saw no good that could come from a true answer. He shook his head, tried to quiet the hammering in his chest and merely breathe. The man said, "They call me Smoker, and that is because when I cook a white man—or sometimes a white boy—I like to smell the smoke that comes off the skin when it begins to burn. But that does not have to be the way that you die, if you do what John Post Oak wants you to do. Do you want to know this?"

Son struggled to control the trembling, and when the realization struck him that if Post Oak had wanted him dead, he would already be, and the trembling subsided. He found his voice. "Yes…just tell me."

"He wants for you to go away…far away, and very soon. He gives you one week."

"I'll be gone. I…I…promise."

The Indian leaned over and sniffed at Son's neck. "It don't matter to me one way or the other. I like the smell of your tender hide. It would make a fine smoke."

Then he was gone, shadows to shadows, and after a minute, Son ran out the door toward the outhouse.

Rufus and Post Oak walked slowly, and a few yards behind them Rufus heard the steady movement of a heavy animal and he knew it was Post Oak's horse trailing after his rider. Post Oak said, "I have a man that has been snooping in the Clarksville train station, and he tells me of a perfect run for us…not really a big enough payload to cause heavy guarding, but big enough to satisfy us. And there are two or three places where it flattens out after a long uphill climb. Hell, we could probably jump the fucking train afoot if we wanted." He laughed. "But we don't do we, Rufus? We need our mounts under us, the wind in our faces, the power of it all, the feel of it all. You remember, don't you?"

"I do."

"And you do not want it anymore?"

"I told you that before."

"That was before, this is now. I cannot believe that you want to grow old without riding with me again. Just one more time, Rufus. If you ride with me just one more time and you still want to go back to your woman and your chores, then I swear that I will not bother you again." Rufus stopped, looked up at the dark sky, but said nothing. "When we are gone from this earth into the spirit world, all that will matter is the fame, Rufus. To be remembered, our stories passed down from generation to generation. It is only the fame that is lasting."

"The whites have a word for us called 'infamous'."

Post Oak reached out and took Rufus's right forearm in his and pulled him close. "I know of the word, and I laugh at it. The dumb sons-of-bitches do not know that when they call us that, they lift us higher yet. Don't you see, Rufus, the more infamous they make us, the more true fame they give us. They think they are shitting on us, and they are lifting us higher. It is too perfect, don't you see?"

Rufus felt the swell in his chest, the spurt of adrenaline from just listening to Post Oak. He waited for it to subside, but it did not. "If I was to ride one more time, when would it be?"

"Soon, I've been in these parts a good while, and I like to keep on the move. It will be within two weeks." He firmed his grip on Rufus's arm and laughed when he felt his friend's steely hand squeeze his arm like a vise. "I knew it would be so. I was saving a story for you if you still faltered, but I want to tell you anyway, if you care to hear it. It was from long ago." They relaxed their grips and began to walk again.

Rufus said, "I want to hear it."

"Good, I want to tell it. When I was a pup—about the time I started to wake up with a stiff cock and wonder what was wrong with me—one day a wagon with a man and a woman in it just rode into our camp with no fear. The man was white-haired and bearded and wore a black frock coat and a top hat, but his face wasn't as old as his hair…eyes dark like rain clouds, and the woman must have been his daughter, and she did a fair job with speaking our tongue. Our chief and the main warriors came up to him and he told them he meant only goodwill and wanted to tell us about Jesus, and he held up a big black Bible…held it out at the chief like a weapon, and I figured he did not have long to live, acting like such a fool, but the chief just nodded. The rest of us gathered around and he got into it…his daughter had a hell of a time keeping up with him and she was as worked up as he was…fire in their eyes, both of them. He went on for a good while, and I mostly just watched the old man's eyes and the way he worked his mouth and head…all snake-like…I didn't give a shit about the words…but then he said something that stuck in my ears and will forever. He said, 'As iron sharpens iron, so one man sharpens another.' I remember the chief grunted and nodded his head and so did a few of the warriors. And then he rambled on for a while longer and they climbed back up in the wagon and rode off. Some of the warriors still thought they should go bring them back and burn them in our fires and that they spoke craziness, but our chief said no, they were just confused about the Great Spirit, but they had the part about men and iron right, so they should live." He paused, clapped Rufus on the shoulder. "Don't you see, my friend? Those words were about men like us. We have always sharpened each other's iron. I cannot believe that we have been parted so long. Damn me for that, I should have come for you sooner."

"How could you? You did not know where I had gone."

"That is true, but it is also true that I did not try hard enough. And when I did, I found you. I always knew that I would."

"But you found others who could sharpen your iron."

"Only stand-ins for you. They were never worthy. They could never be you."

"What if my edge has been dulled?"

"We will sharpen it again. It will not take long."

CHAPTER 26

❖❖❖❖❖

You'll see the fire from a long way

Rufus eased open the door to his cabin, but as he was about to go inside, he stopped and walked to Son's door. He pushed it open a few inches and peered inside at the dark shapes—the small table and chair, the hides and furs hanging on the wall, an open chest with tangled forms protruding upward, and the bed with its occupant lying on his shoulder, facing away. Rufus studied the boy for signs of wakefulness, but there were none, and after a half minute, Rufus drew the door shut and slipped away.

Son's eyes were wide open, as they had been since he had laid down a half hour before. Clutched in his right hand was his skinning knife, held close to his face, with its sharp tip pointing upward in a position he imagined would have been directly under the chin of Smoker as he leaned close when he began the living nightmare less than an hour past. It was a span of time that seemed to exist in the far past, and yet it was ongoing—a scene played out in his mind by two actors, and even though one of them was him, he could see himself, feel himself trembling, as he uttered his one line perfectly. Now he had much to think on, much to consider, and only after another hour had crept past did the boy fall asleep. When he awoke, it was still dark and the first sensation that came to him was the feel of the flat side of the knife blade against his cheek, cool and deadly, and in his fingers was a new and certain power as they tightened around the grip. Yes, he thought to himself…yes, I will go away. But only for a while.

He got out of bed, struck a match and lit the oil lamp on his table, turned the light low. From the drawer, he took a sheet of paper and a pencil, and then he sat down and began to write.

Miss Hattie & Rufus

I have thout this out as best I can & I need to go away by mysef for a while. Part of me wants to go with Miss Iva and part of me wants to stay here with you and Rufus. For now, I feel like I am to close to everthing to decid the right way. Plese do not worry about me as I have took care of mysef before I came here and I am good at doing that & Rufus has made me better even. I will hop a train and go somewhere and be lost but alrite trust me and do not come after me as I can hide like a mouse in a haystak when I want. I will come back when I have made my mind up. If Miss Iva ask after me it would be kind of you to show her this leter. So long for now.

Your friend Son

He folded the paper in half and left it on the table under the pencil. Within minutes, he put on his clothes and boots and gathered in a knapsack a spare shirt, two pairs of socks, the deer hide moccasins he had made with Rufus, a pocket knife, a whetstone, a tin of matches, and a fistful of deer jerky wrapped in oil cloth. He slid the skinning knife into his belt sheath, and then turned off the lamp as he stuffed on his hat. He inched open the door, closed it behind him quickly, and became one with the darkness. He judged the time to be around four o'clock. He would have ample time to reach the depot, find the tinder car on the morning train, and hide himself in the jumble of wood on the back side. He walked briskly, but did not run, and he wondered if sharp eyes followed him as he walked away.

An hour past dawn, Rufus banged his fist on Son's door and said, "Roll out, chores to start." He walked back inside his cabin. After several minutes of silence from the other side of the partition wall, Rufus stopped his puttering and stood still, listened intently. Total silence. He went to Son's door and banged again, louder than before, and when there was no response, he opened the door, looked inside. He walked around the cabin to the outhouse and tapped on the door, said, "You in there?" He returned to Son's room, where nothing appeared to be amiss, and then he looked down at the table and saw the folded sheet of paper under the pencil. He picked it up, unfolded it, knowing what he was about to read. He read the note, and then sat down in the chair and read it again.

From the kitchen window, Dilla saw Rufus approach the back door. Her brow furrowed for a moment; it was a most unusual time for the man to approach the house. She opened the door before he could knock. "Mornin', Mister Rufus, can I get you somethin'?"

"Need to go get Hattie and tell her to come to my cabin."

"I sure will, Mister Rufus, right this minute."

Five minutes later, Hattie opened the cabin door and walked in. Her hair was a wild tangle and she was wrapped in a long, plain gown. "What's this all about, Rufus? You know I like my beauty rest in the early day."

He held out the note, said, "Sit down."

She pulled the chair from the table, sat down, and read the note. Her features betrayed no emotion, but after she glanced up at Rufus, she looked back down at the note, and he knew she read it again. She inhaled deeply through her nostrils and released the air through parted lips. "Should've brought a smoke."

"If I go after him, I need to leave now."

She shook her head. "No, Rufus...ain't nobody goin' after him."

"He'd be damn hard to find, like he said."

"I wouldn't send you after him if I knew exactly where to find him. Me....mainly, and you and the other two...we all put him between that good old rock and hard place, and that ain't no place for a young'un. Goddammit anyhow...us grown-ups and our selfish wants." She got up from the chair. "I need some air, let's go out back."

Rufus followed her as she picked her way over the uneven ground on bare feet. She sat down on the edge of the work stump, facing the rising sun, its light filtering through the trees like blinking yellow stars, hung low and misplaced.

Rufus stood beside her and he too looked at the sun stars. Hattie said, "Yes, me mainly. It's mostly on me."

"I don't figure it that way."

"I know he ought to go with Iva and the hangman. It's his best chance for a good future, but…but I asked him to stay for a while. Stay until your wild Indian friend got tired of waiting for you and rode off somewhere else. I didn't think that I was enough to hold you by myself. But how long is 'a while' to a boy? I asked for 'a while' from him, and now he writes he's going away for 'a while.'" She uttered a guttural sound from her throat. "I heaped a burden on a burden that he already carried. It was too much."

Rufus squatted, rested his back against the stump. He reached out and wrapped his hand around Hattie's foot, brushed the sandy soil from her toes. "If I was to be held, you would have been enough."

"Would have been…would have been…" The words whispered in her head, as if spoken from a previous lifetime, or one yet to come. Bile rose in her throat and she spoke the words quietly, fervently, like a prayer instead of a curse. "Goddamn John Post Oak. Goddamn him to hell."

"I will not stay with him after this one last ride. I will come back, but only if you want me to. He would never leave me be until I rode with him one last time. He thinks that my fire will be rekindled, but it will not."

"How can you say that? It was rekindled enough for you to decide to ride with the most wanted man in Indian Territory… one time or a hundred times…I think it's all the same."

"It is not the same. I will not lie to you about the old part of me wanting this, but I want to come back here too. I will leave no ties with him, take no money, just ride away, and hold him to his promise to leave me be after that. I will be masked—just another faceless rider—and it is not an important train. He has spies that have learned this. I will be back before the next dawn, and that will be the end of it."

"Why can't you just let the old part of you die, Rufus? It makes no sense to me and I'm a far cry from a church lady, that's for damn sure. You've drawn your blood, done your killin'…and till now, you've let it go. We have something between us—call it what you want—I call it love…yes, by God, love, I'll say it out loud, and I know you never will, but I don't care. Just let us keep what we have. I don't understand!"

He bowed his head, closed his eyes. "What you don't understand is that I am proud of my red skin like him. We battled and drew our blood, done our killin' together as red men, proud warriors, brothers. Red is the color of my spirit. I cannot change it."

Hattie stood, looked down at him. "Go on then, proud red man. I don't fight battles I can't win, and I've never begged for anything in my life and I ain't gonna start now." She took several steps, then turned around and walked back to him. "When will this ride happen?"

"Soon. One night I will ride away and the next night I will ride back here. And if I see that a board has been nailed over my door, I will ride away, and I will not blame you."

"If I decide I don't want you back, you won't have to ride up close. You'll see the fire from a long way." She reached down and placed a hand on the top of his head for a few seconds, and then she walked away.

CHAPTER 27

I'll be here come sunrise

Son stayed hidden in the tinder car of the train until nightfall. He had done his best to arrange the wood chunks in a fashion that provided him a flat space on which to lie, but it was an impossible chore, and he was sore from the constant need to shift his body to seek relief from the cruel edges. But now, with the darkness as a shield, he sat up and took his time in forming the semblance of a seat with a back to lean on and a place to stretch his legs. He had counted nine short stops at little towns, and knew that the train must be nearing Little Rock. He picked his way across the wood pile until he could grasp the side of the car, and there he cobbled together a seat facing forward, and twenty minutes later he could see the vast twinkle of lights at the edge of Little Rock. His belly growled and he fished around in his knapsack for the last of the jerky. There were two pieces and he ate them both as the tinder car creaked and groaned its way down the rails. He looked up at the smoke trail hurtling past like ghostly clouds in the moon glow, and when the great engine throttled back, he looked ahead with hawk's eyes as he moved to the back wall of the car, near the steel ladder that would mark his first steps into the city, and he was not fearful, but mystified by the ever-changing ways of life.

He looped his knapsack over his head and pushed it behind him, jammed down his hat, and descended the ladder to the bottom rung. He flexed his legs and with one hand, hung onto a rung near his head until the train slowed to the pace of a fast-walking man, and then he jumped clear of the cross tie ends and landed on both feet. He staggered only for a moment, and then he slipped away into the deep shadows at the edge of a storage building near the main station. He hurried behind the building and waited for several minutes until he was certain that he had not been seen. The voices from the station were low and without urgency, mostly from men, an occasional woman, the tired whine of a child. When the last of the voices had died away, he cleared the spot where he would sleep with a few sweeps of his boots. He took off his hat and then his knapsack, tucked them under his head as he lay down, careful to face the east, where the sunlight would touch his face and wake him if he slept too long. He pulled the knife from its sheath, wrapped the fingers of his right hand around the handle, and tucked his fist against his neck, with the blade pointing upward. The weariness swept over his body, as if his muscles and bones were moaning inside the shell of his skin, and after a time, he fell asleep.

He awoke in gray light with a gnawing in his empty stomach. He sheathed his knife and took the water jar from his knapsack, screwed off the lid, and drank what remained. He was not worried about water, which was easy to come by, but food was another matter, and not just for a next meal, but for days to come. He stretched, urinated at the base of the building wall, and then began to walk. When he reached what appeared to be a busy street, he looked ahead and saw a barn-like building with a sloped awning over wide doors, swung open, and a loft above. He walked closer so that he could read the lettering painted on the sign over the doors.

D. L. TOOMER

LIVERY & SALE STABLE

HORSES & MULES WANTED

He watched for a few minutes, and finally spied a man just inside of the opening, moving purposefully back and forth. As Son neared the opening, the man glanced toward him, but quickly looked back to his chores, and it was only when the boy edged his boots into the opening that the man stopped and lowered a feed bucket to the ground. He was maybe forty, lean-faced, and his upper lip was hidden under a black mustache as thick as a paintbrush and droopy at the ends. His forearms were corded and brown and the fingers of his square hands were curled, as if—even empty— they held heavy phantom burdens. His features were not unfriendly, just curious.

Son said, "Mornin', sir."

The man tilted his hat back, and Son watched his eyes as they swept over him, calculating with little movements.

After several seconds, he said, "Mornin' to you. Whatcha need?"

"I was hopin' you might have some work for me. I'm hungry."

"A traveler it appears. Young to be a lone traveler."

"I'm near to sixteen."

The man grunted. "The hell you are. You look sturdy enough but you ain't no sixteen." He grunted again, said, "Train?"

"Yes, sir."

"And no ticket?"

Son shook his head, but did not look away. "Tinder pile."

"Bet you're beat all to shit."

"Fairly so."

"Must be in some kinda trouble I'd think."

"No, sir. I ain't done a thing wrong, ain't runnin' from a thing. Just like to move around, and I'm good with horses and there ain't a chore I can't do proper."

"That so, is it?"

"Yes, sir."

"Hummm…" The man looked Son up and down again, and he reached up and smoothed down his mustache with a thumb and forefinger. "Hummm. You look too old to be a street waif—damn, I despise those thievin' little bastards— so tell you what. Let's see what you can get done before noon, and if you get that far along, I've got a couple extra boiled hen's eggs I can spare. Best I can offer for now. I don't mind strangers, I just don't naturally trust 'em, you understand?"

"I understand. You won't be sorry."

"We'll see about that. You say you know horses, whatchu know about mules?"

"Not as much as I do horses."

"Which means damn little. Myself, I like mules a damn sight more than horses. Most people think horses are smarter than mules, but it ain't so. I tell you this 'cause I don't want to feel obliged to carry your broke ass to a doctor and pay for it, should he require me to. Thing is about a mule—male or female, don't make no difference—is that they either take a likin' to you or they don't, and if they don't, sooner more likely than later, they'll find a way to hurt you. I got several in there and they all like me. You, who the hell knows? So mind yourself around the mules, you understand?"

"Yes, sir, I will."

"What's your name?"

"Floyd.

"I go by Dabo, same as my daddy's, 'cept he goes by D. L." He pointed over his head at the sign over the door. "He built this business mainly, but he worked my ass off with him since I was about your size. He's all broke down now, my wife tends him like a baby. Cryin' shame." He shook his head, as if to clear it of a puzzlement. "Ain't like me to give into a thin whim about a stranger." He stared at Son for just a second, then said. "Time's a wastin'. Pick up this here feed bucket and let's see if you last to noon. And if you do, we'll see if you last to supper, and if you do, you can bed down in the straw, and if you're still here come sunrise, we'll try another day. Best I can promise."

"I'll be here come sunrise…Dabo."

Son thought for a second that the man smiled, but he was not certain. The mustache hid much. Dabo said, "Well, that sounds a damn sight better than 'sir.' I was tirin' of that pretty quick."

The tall grandfather clock chimed twelve times. It was midnight in Hattie's house and Sally walked the final customer down the stairs as they chatted amiably. He was a well-dressed man who carried a shiny walking stick with a gold knob and he tapped the point once on each tread as they descended, and when they reached the front door, Sally opened it and they exchanged final pleasantries, in the manner of a couple parting from a formal function. She stood in the open doorway for a few moments, waved a final goodbye, and went back inside, quietly closed the door behind her. At the piano bench, she tested a few notes, barely touching the keys, tried to remember the way that Iva's fingers looked on the keyboard when she tutored her inept pupil. The parlor was empty, but upstairs she could hear the other girls puttering about, quiet footfalls, low voices. She was certain that she would bother no one, so she sat down and began to play slowly and deliberately, the only way that she could.

Above her, in her room, Hattie sat at her table in an evening gown, a black cigar locked between two fingers of her right hand as it encircled the glass half full of whiskey. The simple melody drifted to her and she recognized Sally's notes—so eager, so inexpert, so beautiful. Hattie, stood, poured the glass full, and walked toward the music. From the corner of her eye, Sally saw her approach and redoubled her efforts on the keys, but she hurried her fingers, lost her rhythm, and stopped.

Hattie said, "You were doin' fine, girl, 'til you got ahead of yourself."

"I'm doomed to be a plodder on this thing, safe to say. Probably wouldn't have made any difference if she'd stayed and worked with me for a year."

"Who can say, Sally…don't matter now, she's gone."

Sally stared wistfully at the keyboard, held her fingers above the keys, but did not touch them. "I think I'd be better off just sitting here pretending…pretending and remembering what it sounded like when she played." She hesitated, touched her fingertips to the keys. "My God, but she was something, wasn't she? I miss her already." She played a couple of notes with one finger. "That day she played for Son…good God…Dilla choppin' off his mangled finger and all, us all joining in. Reckon that was as close as I've ever come to feeling like I was part of a big family. She was something, that Iva."

"That she was…and I miss her too. But you'll have to play your own notes now. You'll get better…as long as you don't get ahead of yourself." She drew deeply on the cigar and sprayed the smoke in a wide arc as if she were trying to paint the air above her, and then she drank the whiskey glass half empty. "While we're studyin' on things gone away, you just as well know that Son is gone too. I know you were partial to him too…hell, weren't we all."

Sally turned to face her, eyebrows crinkled at the pronouncement. "I don't…I mean…why in the world…"

"If I could explain the total *why* of it all, Sally girl, I'd make old Confucius seem ignorant. But the little part of *why,* I'll take a pitiful stab at…mainly 'cause I'm half-drunk I reckon, but some 'cause I need to talk to somebody, and your playin' drew me down here." She swept her hand theatrically through the air. "The moth to the flame…and all that shit, don't you know." She puffed on the cigar, took another sip of whiskey. "Iva wants the boy to go with them, figurin'—and rightly so, bad as I hate to admit it—he can have a brighter future with them than at this establishment. But I want him to stay...for a 'while' I told him...but the rank truth is that I want him to stay, with no particular 'while' hooked to it. Too damn much, it was...too damn much for just a boy, and so he up and wrote a note and left in the night. Said he needed to go off and be by himself to think it all through."

"That is worrisome, the Territory being what it is and all."

"Right now, I'd say that damn near everything in my life is worrisome to one degree or another. But I brought some of it on myself...by bein' selfish, so I'll just have to by God deal with it. That's the way of the world."

"You intend to let Iva know?"

"Yes. I sealed his note in an envelope with the hangman's name on it. Rufus will take it to town and tack it to the courthouse door before first light."

"What does Rufus make of all this?"

Hattie shrugged, took another sip from the glass. "Rufus is Rufus, and that's mostly a closed book." She looked at Sally, locked eyes with her for a long moment. "Even for me, Sally girl...even for me." She laughed softly, swirled the remaining whiskey in the glass, and then gulped it down. "As far as openin' up to me, Hector is a hell of a lot more reliable, and he makes more sense to boot."

"Closed is the way of most men worth a damn. The whiney tongue-waggers ain't worth piss in a bucket far as I'm concerned."

"If I was stone cold sober, I'd prob'ly agree with that. As it is, I'm undecided."

At noon the next day, Apsel tapped the little code that they had created on the rooming house door, and Iva opened the door with mild surprise. She smiled and said, "If I'd known you were coming back to have dinner with me, I'd have fixed us a bite."

He walked to the table and pulled out a chair for her, then one for himself, and they both sat down. He placed the envelope on the table. "Disturbing news, but not altogether surprising to me."

Iva took the note out of the envelope and read it, re-folded it and held it in her hands. "Yes, disturbing, but for me, surprising too."

"I figure Hattie Wax put too much pressure on him. You read what he said about being pulled in different directions. He just reacted like anyone would in those circumstances."

"He's just a boy, Apsel. Boys that age just don't leave the security they have and go off alone in this…this harsh land. My God, this isn't right at all."

"He has never had the chance to be just a boy. The first conversation we had in this very room told me that very quickly, and he managed to make it here and survive…in his own rough way. He is a survivor. Some are and some are not."

"That doesn't make me feel much better." She looked out the window. "Where would he go?"

"He came on a train, and I suspect he left on one. If I had to guess, I'd say Little Rock—a big city to get lost in."

"I was selfish. It almost seems like I…I coveted him."

"That is not so, Iva. Just not so. We both saw a life

for him, and if we hadn't thought so much of him—and what he could become—we wouldn't have made the offer. Covetousness has nothing to do with any of this."

"Will he come back as he claims?"

"I truly believe that he will, and I'm not saying that to make you feel better."

Iva looked around the room, as if for the first time. "I'm beginning to feel boxed up in here, Apsel. How long until we can move to the rented place outside of town?"

"Monday next, the arrangements have been made, the first month's rent paid."

"That's good. I need some space and air."

"I have a surprise for you. I have bought a piano for you, and it will be brought to the house a day or so after we arrive." Iva's eyes brightened. "It is very small and not in the best of shape, but we will have it tuned, and I will restore the finish. The merchant assured me it is of quality. He said it was a genuine Cristofori…whatever that means. I hope it is good."

She reached across the table and took his hands. "It is good, Apsel…very good. Thank you. It will be a balm to my soul, and I need one very much."

CHAPTER 28

✦✦✦✦

This world ain't big enough for the runners

Son awoke to the heavy odors of animals and dusty straw, but they were not unpleasant, merely essentials of his life over the previous three days. He slowly opened and closed his hands, working life back into his sore fingers. He studied the jagged corner of a thumbnail, dried blood down to the quick, and he thoughtfully chewed off the useless portion of the nail and spit it out. He stood and stretched before sitting down and putting on his boots. He walked along the row of stalls and looked in on several of the horses and mules as he passed, content that all was in order. Behind the stable, he urinated, walked to the pump handle and gathered water in both hands, washed his face and neck, and then he cupped his hands and drank. The first edge of sunlight crept around the corner of the building, and he took a few steps toward it, breathed deeply as a cottony puff of warm air touched his face. He heard the rumble of

Dabo's wagon wheels, growing ever closer, and he walked toward them.

Dabo reined in the horse and Son stepped up to the gelding Dabo called Big Luther and stroked his nose. It was the biggest horse Son had ever seen, and with its light chestnut coat and flaxen mane and tail, one of the most eye-catching as well. Son judged that one of its hooves would mostly fill a water bucket. The peach-sized eyes were docile, windows to the soul of the prodigious beast. Dabo said, "Right loveable for a monster, ain't he?"

"Never seen nothing like him…not even close."

Dabo puffed his chest, said, "He'll weigh outright a ton if he weighs a pound, by God. I don't think he even knows he's pullin' this here wagon. If a man could calculate how to rig enough ropes around this here livery, he could pull the sumbitch down—look like a cyclone piled it up, it would." He looked down at the horse's back. "Every horse or mule I got is for sale, 'cept for Big Luther."

"Ain't hard to see why."

"Near to irritatin' to me, it was…back when I bought him, how much I got to likin' the critter. Ain't like me, not a'tall, but I got over bein' irritated real quick."

Son grinned, clapped his palm against the long jawbone. It was like touching the handle of an axe. "Hard to believe anybody would sell him."

"Nah…man gets in deep enough shit, he'll do what he has to do to climb out. Feller I bought him off of fell into a Faro game at a roadhouse and lost half his crop money. Said if he didn't raise some money mighty quick, it wouldn't be safe to sleep if his wife was in the house. Hell, way I see it, I done the feller a favor…damn near to stealin' Big Luther, though it was." Dabo twitched his mustache a single time, like he was throwing a lever. "Supper time, I'm takin' you to the house and you'll sit with me and the wife and Pap and eat proper. You need to meet them two."

Son looked up at Dabo, tried his best to mask the incredulity that flooded his brain, but he knew that he could not. Dabo's mustache moved, like a snake quickly slithering across the middle of his face. He said, "Ain't like me to switch smooth between my thoughts neither." He jerked his thumb backwards toward the bed of the wagon. "Don't reckon them feed bags are gonna unload theirselves. Let's get on with it."

Dabo and Son ended the work day at the water pump, splashing rowdily like tall ducks, Dabo chattering, Son listening. Dabo used both hands to smooth down his face and hair, and then with his thumbs, wrung out the mustache, settled the hat back on his head. He said, "Go get your knapsack, Floyd, you'll be stayin' in the house with us from here on…that is, if you care to. I ain't no kidnapper."

"I'd like that, Dabo, and I thank you."

"No thanks necessary, way I figure it, I been comin' out on the long side of this deal. I ain't to the point of payin' a wage yet, but it ain't far off from what I've seen. Appears that you're gonna free me up from so many chores that I can spend more time buyin' and sellin' and tradin'—which means more profit—which will figure into your wage. And in the meantime, you'll grow to likin' the wife's table…hell of a cook…hell of a woman. I married up so damn far it's near to mysterious to me." He shook his head, lowered his chin, and Son saw a sadness pass through him—knifelike, but it vanished as quickly as it had come. "We lost a baby boy long ago…doc said he had no idea just what happened, but she blamed herself for years—some sorta woman thing I reckon—then it finally passed. Mostly."

"I'm sorry."

"Oh, sorry days are passed on that, son. Just a hard piece of life."

Son. The word hung in the boy's brain like the sound of a bell pealing, fading away in the distance, ever softer, and then it was silent.

Dabo clapped him on the shoulder, nearly knocking him off balance. "I'm hungry enough to chase a possum off his supper pile. Let's go on."

Nadine Toomer heard the familiar rumble and creak of Dabo's wagon, and she only peeked out the kitchen window as it passed. She turned toward the stove, but quickly returned to the window to confirm that there were two riders in the seat. As the wagon drew near, she studied the smaller form sitting beside her husband. She smiled, shook her head, thought back on the breakfast conversation about Dabo's intentions. She went back to the stove, lifted the lid on the stew pot, sniffed the rich, meaty aroma, and walked to the back door.

Son trailed behind Dabo a couple of steps and when he looked up at the woman, he snatched off his hat, tested a tiny smile. Her face was apple-shaped and sturdy, with roseate cheeks and wide-set, friendly eyes, and a yellow bonnet with frilly edges sat atop her head. She returned the smile, said, "So this is Floyd."

Dabo said, "A sound hand for his size, I'll tell you, wife, and we're both hungry as spring bears."

She walked up to Son and wrapped an arm around his

shoulders for a second, then stepped back. "Welcome to our house, Floyd. Got a place set for you at the table. Pretty plain for supper—beef stew and biscuits, and if Pap hasn't raided my kitchen, the best part of an apple pie."

Son swallowed at the saliva already gathering in his mouth. "Can't tell you how good that sounds to me, ma'am."

Her features scrunched into a mock scowl. "Just Nadine—though I do appreciate your manners. Come in and sit down."

The table was set for four, and Dabo walked to a room off the kitchen, where Son heard him talking with another man. He stood behind his chair, as did Nadine, waiting for the men to join them. Pap leaned on a cane with one hand, but most of his weight was supported by Dabo, who had one arm on his shoulder and the other firmly wrapped around the old man's back. He appeared to Son like a man with too many moving parts—disjointed and fighting one another— and his breathing was labored. His face was red and wide, his beard long and white, but above it, his eyes were lively and inquisitive, and they homed in on Son. After Dabo got him situated in his chair and scooted in to the table, the old man sighed and extended his hand toward Son, who quickly moved to his side and shook it. "D. L. Toomer, young'un. Pleasure mine."

"Thank you. How are you, Mr. Toomer?"

D. L. grumbled with a low laugh. "Don't ever ask an old man how he is, just say howdy." Before Son could think of a reply, D. L. said, "Just messin' with you, boy. I know you're already used to it, being around my ornery offspring." He wheezed a laugh.

Nadine said, "You two don't get started on this boy at

least until he's had something to eat." She motioned for Son to take his seat, and then took up his plate and filled it with the steaming stew. Son kept his hands in his lap as he waited until all the plates had been filled. When she finished, she sat down, served herself and bowed her head. Son looked quickly at Dabo and Pap, who lowered their heads, and he followed suit.

She prayed. "For thy bounty, oh Lord, we are thankful and mindful from whence it all comes. The Lord giveth and the Lord taketh away. Blessed be the name of the Lord. Amen." She looked at Son and said, "And now, let's see if this is any better than the hard-boiled eggs and apples that Dabo feeds you."

Son picked up his fork and held it the way Iva had taught him, then said, "I'll say I'm sorry right up front for anything sloppy I'm about to do."

They all laughed, and Dabo said, "Just you hit your mouth at least half the time, and that'll do. That's my regular aim."

Nadine waved a hand at Dabo as he forked the first huge bite into his mouth. "Floyd, take your time and remember to save room for some apple pie."

Son's cheeks bulged like a squirrel's foundering on acorns, and he could only nod his thanks.

When they had all finished with supper, Son started to help with the dishes, but Nadine shooed him away. "Go with the men and try not to laugh when they fib too big."

"I thank you again…Nadine. That stew and biscuits, and that pie…it was like I was seein' stars when that was goin' down."

"I suspect you being half-starved and overworked

had something to do with that, but I appreciate your compliments, Floyd." She nodded her head toward Dabo and Pap. "Now when they run out of wind, I've got a pallet made up in my sewing room, right next to Pap's room. Put your things in there, and let me wash up your clothes. I've put some of Dabo's old trousers and shirts on your pallet. I'll have a towel and some water heated up in the kitchen for to you wash proper with after me and Dabo go upstairs. There's a Castile bar beside the kitchen pump too. And…" she paused for effect, "I'll fry up bacon and eggs for breakfast to go with the rest of the biscuits. How does that sound?"

"Sounds like I might just stay awake 'til breakfast comes."

"Ha…I doubt that, knowing Dabo's work habits."

Son finished washing in the kitchen, and as he passed in front of Pap's open door, he looked in and from his bed, Pap raised a hand, gestured for him to come to him. Son walked barefoot to the opening, and Pap said, "Come sit with an old man, son. I ain't had anybody new to talk with in quite a spell."

Son entered the sparse room and Pap pointed to a chair beside his nightstand. "Sit yourself down, I won't keep you up long, know you need your rest."

Son sat down, did not know what to say. The oil lamp burned low, and its light made Pap appear so old that the word "ancient" popped into Son's head, and he remembered that it was from a story that Iva had read to him. But Dabo wasn't all that old by Son's reckoning—maybe forty or forty-five—so the old man was likely only middle sixties.

Pap turned his head toward Son and smiled through the white beard. "How old are you, boy, fifteen or so?"

"Not quite…but close."

He laughed with a soft wheeze. "That Dabo…started him out in the livery when he was 'bout your size and I worked him hard. So hard I feel bad about it now, so you can blame me, not him."

"Don't need to blame anybody, Mister Toomer. I ain't afraid of hard work. I just wanted a chance to be useful."

"Well, I'll tell you true, you passed that test on the second day as I remember…him all a crowin' about this tough little sprout that knowed horses to boot. I can't tell you how many stable hands he's run off…most grown men, and here you are…a sprout."

Son thought it sounded more like a question than a declaration, so he said, "I ain't had much practice bein' young, but a good bit actin' like I was old."

"Ha…the hell you say. I like that. 'Bout the same way with me, and then Dabo…and now you. The hell…I like that."

The old man turned his head back toward the ceiling, and through the half-open window, the friendly sounds of the night creatures chirped and chanted on the breeze as it whooshed into the little room. A minute passed, and then another. Pap said, "How'd you come to know horses so young?"

"I had a good teacher."

"Kin?"

"No, but he sorta feels like it sometimes."

"Couldn't a been that long ago, huh?"

"It wasn't."

The old man could hear it in his voice—the reticence, and yet the hint of longing to tell his story. He decided to dig a little deeper, but not too deep. "Dabo says you rode here in a tinder pile."

"Yes, sir."

"Runnin'…or just driftin', son?"

The specter of Smoker hovering over him, sniffing at his neck, came and went with another puff of the night breeze. "More driftin', I'd say. I've run far enough."

"That's good to know. Nobody…old or young…can live worth a damn runnin'. This world ain't big enough for the runners."

"That sounds like good advice."

Pap pointed a bony finger at Son's right hand. "How'd you get that one stubbed off?"

Son looked down, rubbed his thumb over the stub. "Surprised you saw it."

"I study a man's hands 'afore anything else…even his face. Guarantee Dabo saw it too."

"Didn't say nothin' about it."

"No he wouldn't…ain't his way. All he cared about was if you could grab hold of heavy loads." He paused, said, "Ain't many young'uns your age with stubs."

"I was tryin' to push a bull calf through an open gate with my hand on his head. He mashed it against the corner post."

"Get it clean off?"

"Mangled."

"Who took it off for you?"

"Women friends…not kin."

"Looks to be a tolerable job of it."

"Yeah…they can deal with most anything."

"But you left 'em."

"It wasn't because of them."

Pap sighed, flopped his hands in the air. "Well, young'un, I'm done diggin' here. Didn't mean no harm, hope you know. I'll be dead inside a year or so. You won't. Just wanted to talk some with you, maybe stumble on a notion that might help you along the way."

"You did."

"Good…good. Tell you one thing ain't no doubt about. When you leave here, you won't be bouncin' around in no damn tinder pile. You'll be on a fine horse or else back in a coach car."

"I sure hope so."

"No doubt of it. Knew it when Dabo told me the mules took up with you right off."

Son stood to leave, and when he looked down at Pap, the old man said, "I said 'when you leave here'…maybe oughter said, 'if you leave here.'"

Son let the words sink in, but could not think of a suitable reply, so he simply smiled and walked out of the room.

CHAPTER 29

A quarter-hour-chime in the night

Hattie sat in her room in a chair positioned in front of the open window as she watched the ominous space—barely visible—in front of Rufus' cabin. The night was cool, the air laden with the portent of rain, and a capricious breeze teased the leaves of oaks and elms into a serpent's hiss. She pulled the shawl tightly around her shoulders with one hand, and with the other she raised the cigar to her mouth, drew on it until the tip glowed orange for two seconds and then faded into the darkness. She had attempted to sleep but had grown weary of futile tossing and turning. This was the night, of this there was no doubt in her mind. It swirled in the dense air—a certainty equal to the promise of the rain that would follow the wind. From the sitting room below, the grandfather clock chimed three times, and to the woman it came as a faraway sound—dreamy and meaningless.

Through a drawn burlap curtain, a faint rectangle of weak light grew from the side window of the cabin, and as it grew brighter, the pace of Hattie's heartbeat quickened. The minutes oozed past, but now time had boundless meaning and she wanted it to stop, frozen forever inside of the clock. But it would not, and the quarter-hour-chime sounded loudly in her head. She groped for the ash tray and put the cigar in it, and then knelt at the window, her hands grasping the wood sill. The light in the cabin faded, and then vanished. The form of man moved from the doorway, stood still for a moment, and then it too vanished. She stared until her eyes burned and when she finally blinked, she saw another form—large and tall— moving steadily away like a ghost rider in the dark, and she felt the tears run warm down her cheeks, and suddenly she felt her bare feet pounding on the floor, then down the stairs, and through the kitchen toward the back door. She jerked open the door and dashed out into the yard, running wildly into the first raindrops. She ran for a hundred feet, raised her arms and shouted into the wind. "Ruu fuuusss!" But the rider and his horse were gone.

When she walked back to the house, Dilla was standing in the doorway, and Hattie nearly bumped into her. Dilla wrapped a wiry arm around her, pulled her into the kitchen and closed the door. "Miss Hattie…what in the world is goin' on here?" Hattie looked into her face, but could only shake her head, and shivers passed through her shoulders. "Let's get you up to your room, get you dried off. Come on with me now, Miss Hattie. This won't do, no ma'am, you come with Dilla right now."

When they reached Hattie's room, Dilla lit the lamp, pulled the wet shawl from Hattie, and then went to the closet and got a towel, and with it she dabbed at Hattie's wet hair and face, then her arms and legs. She tossed the towel on the floor, and turned down the bed cover. "You need to lay down now…lay on down for Dilla." She brought the cover up to Hattie's shoulders, and then smoothed the damp ringlets from her forehead. She hurried to the open window and shut it, then returned to the bed, sat down on the edge. "There now, that's better. Let's get calmed down."

Hattie pulled a hand from under the cover, and Dilla took it with both of hers, held it firmly, gently rocking to and fro. Hattie's features were blank, her eyes focused on Hector's cage, where the bird shuffled on its perch. Hattie said, "You ain't goin' away, are you, my pretty bird?"

"Pretty bird pretty bird pretty bird."

"That's right, my boy. My pretty bird…cage door open, and you're here with me."

Dilla listened to the exchange, but in her head remained the sound of Hattie's voice screaming her lover's name into the wind and rain. "Mister Rufus, he'll come back…don't you worry none."

"You don't know what he's gone off to do."

"No I don't, and it ain't none of my business, but Mister Rufus…I just know he'll come back. Whatever you two are mad about will pass, just like everything else in this world."

"We're not mad at each other—not really. Don't ever remember us bein' mad with each other for more'n a minute or so."

Dilla squinted, and her brow furrowed for a moment and then smoothed out. "Men folk…ain't but so much women can do with 'em when they get ill-minded about somethin'. Just the way with men folk."

"You ever had one that you loved, Dilla. I've never asked you, but I'd like to know."

Dilla stopped rocking, looked down at Hattie, thought about simply telling the white lie. *Oh, no, Miss Hattie, never had one of those kind.* But the thought passed quickly, and she peeled away the years. "I did, long time ago down near New Orleans. Fine-lookin' devil, that boy Silas, he was." She smiled. "You know I didn't always look like I do now. I could turn a head—high-ridin' titties like ripe apples, round tail all tight. He was mulatto like me, lighter even, and when I took hold of his arm, it was like holdin' a tree limb."

Dilla fell silent, and Hattie knew that the woman could see him now, feel him, smell the sweat that gathered in the hollow of his neck when they laid together in the thick Louisiana night. Hattie said, "No need to tell me more if you don't want to."

"I do and I don't, but reckon I do more."

"How long did you hold him?"

"Near to three year. Strange…we never made no babies… the master and his wife, they couldn't figure it, counted on us for solid stock. Tell you the truth, Miss Hattie, it always pleased us not to please them. Then one day, Silas—he never came back from the cane field. I run around half crazy that evenin' til somebody told me he got sold. About a week later, they tried to put me with another man, but I wouldn't have none of it. Told him he laid a finger on me, I'd slit his throat the first time he went to sleep. Then I ran off and made it to New Orleans…livin' like an animal hidin' along the way, but I doubt they even cared I ran off…not makin' any babies, and when I got to the city, those high titties and tight tail stood me well 'till I was on my own, then I shucked that life away, went to driftin'…learnin' all the way…got good at many things…drifted all the way to you, Miss Hattie. Don't want to drift ever again."

"Please, don't think about driftin' anymore, Dilla. I'd be lost without you…especially now."

Dilla reached down and smoothed Hattie's hair again. "Why you so worried about Mr. Rufus? What you think he's gone off to do?"

"I know what he's gone off to do, and who with."

"'Another Indian, reckon?"

"Not just another one. He rode off to meet up with John Post Oak. They rode together back in Rufus's bad days, and he came back for him and…and Rufus gave in. Says just this one time. I think he believes that, but I ain't sure about that at all.'"

"What trouble they gone off after?"

"A train. Don't know where exactly. Doesn't matter."

"Well, scoundrel beast…don't like the sound of dat."

"Said he'd be back tomorrow night…if I wanted him to come back."

"You do don't you, Miss Hattie? Surely you do."

"I can't say right now, Dilla. Just can't say for sure."

Dilla made a throaty noise, half sigh, half moan. "All this here talk is makin' me near to dizzy, I'll swear…the boy runnin' off and now this…one on top the other. Near to dizzy, I'll swear."

"That's a good word for it. Dizzy." She looked toward the window, pointed at it. "If his cabin was to burn, you don't think the house would catch fire, do you?"

Dilla nearly jumped from the bed, stood straight up, put

her hands on her cheeks. "Miss Hattie, you got to get hold of yourself! You're talkin' crazy!"

"No, Dilla...I'm talkin' dizzy. Hell of a difference. I asked you a direct question."

"Don't know anything about any big fires...never saw one."

"Still, you got sense about everything I've ever asked you to consider. So why not this?"

Dilla took her hands from her face, sucked in a long breath, thought for a moment. "Ain't no big trees between here and there, and after this rain storm, the house is gonna be good and wet for a long while, so...no...I don't think it would."

"Me neither."

Dilla plopped back down on the bedside. "Ain't this but a night to beat all?"

"If you would be so kind as to go fetch a bottle of our best, I'd be beholdin', Dilla, and even more beholdin' if you'd bring two glasses back with you."

Dilla stood, looked at the ceiling and said, "Finally, Lord God have mercy if you're really up there...finally, this woman says somethin' undizzy, and for that I give thanks."

Dilla left the room, and while she was gone, Hattie looked at the window and listened to the storm wind buffet the glass panes, the intermittent sounds not unlike distant, muffled gunfire.

CHAPTER 30

I just want to feel it all rise up again in my chest

There were five men with Hatch at the Russellville depot. Two were dressed in the manner of merchants or lawyers on a trip—dark coats over clean shirts, quality hats with silk bands, and in each coat pocket was a Colt .44-40 revolver with a barrel sawed off to three inches. Two more were dressed like tradesmen, or farmers—men of the rough earth—with clothing to match. They wore thin dusters with big pockets and they were filled with either sawed-off revolvers or derringers, according to their preferences. All of these men were of average height and build, and would blend in with any group of passengers riding in the coach cars.

The man standing beside his chestnut stud was named Ora Lee Tygart. He was twenty-three years old, appeared more like eighteen, weighed barely one-hundred-forty lean pounds, and yet Hatch often wondered if he could take him in either a wrestling or shooting match. He was clean-shaven, except for a wisp of a mustache that matched his light brown hair, which was tucked neatly behind his ears under a black bowler hat. He wore a white shirt and trousers with suspenders, but both pockets of his trousers had leather-lined pockets, and in each was a .41 caliber Merrimac Arms derringer with a three-inch barrel. Inside his right boot was a sheath holding a razor-sharp knife with an eight-inch blade.

Hatch said, "I'll declare, Ora Lee, but you do look like an express car clerk sure enough." The other men chuckled and Ora Lee—having heard it before—chuckled with them, nodded his head. Hatch waited until the laughter faded. "All of you'uns, like I said before, I have a strong feeling this is the train they'll try to take, and I can't tell you how bad this gang is, especially John Post Oak. He's like a mean ghost… until he shows up somewhere to do harm. I am hopin' today is to be our time with him."

The men muttered their agreement, and Hatch said, "Solly and Hub, you got the first coach car, and Elmer and Paden, the coach behind that one. Be sure to take an aisle seat, one toward the middle, the other toward the back. Don't get near any young'uns or women if you can help it. It's not a full load, so that ought not to be a problem. No use lettin' things get bad in there. There'll be two of you in each car and there won't likely be more than that of the gang, which means that I expect them all to die with a slug in the head each, if they come in with guns drawn among innocents and don't drop the guns the instant that you identify yourselves—in which case, they've sealed their own fates. You'll have each other's eye, so you can move and shoot in tandem." He lifted both hands and shook his head in resignation. "We all know there ain't no way to predict things once they get goin', but I'd be bad surprised if Post Oak himself don't go after the express car. I don't know exactly what he looks like any more than any of you, but we know he's Indian, and many accounts have him wearing an Army hat…which I consider a personal insult, seein' as how I rode with that Army in the war." He paused, looked at each of the men, said, "Questions?"

Solly said, "Where you gonna be up there with Ora Lee, seein' as how you don't look much like an express car clerk?"

Hatch smiled, said, "Well, they loaded two new-made coffins behind the safe. The bottom one is empty, but the top one won't be." He smiled again. "They made it longer than most."

"You'll still be scrunched up in there like a nut in a squirrel's mouth."

"But not for long, Solly. Not for long."

"Think I'd find another hidin' place, Dak. That one's too much like the truth for a place of close violence and the possible result."

"I'm not a superstitious sort, Solly."

"Evidently not, I'd say, and I'd say this too: reckon even you never thought he might be in a gunfight from his coffin."

"It'll just be borrowed. Don't aim to be in my own any time soon." Hatch reached up to the largest of his saddle bags and his knuckles rapped against something hard inside. "Steel plate goin' in there with me, even got a handle on the back of it. When I rise up most of me will be behind it. Blacksmith and me are good friends."

Solly said, "Well I'll be damned if we ain't led by a knight in armor."

"I'd feel better if I was to be in a full suit of it, but behind it is the best I can do."

He waited to see if anyone else had something to say, but they did not. "Let's tend to the horses and shade them up until the train gets here, and when we load them up, we'll make sure ours are nearest the door. There's a slide-down ramp racked on the wall beside the door."

Ora Lee walked beside Hatch, their horses' reins held loosely behind them. "Now comes the waiting. I don't like the waiting."

"I don't mind it so much anymore, Ora Lee. Did when I was your age though. You'll get to where I am before you know it. The waitin' is really the only easy part of this business."

Ora Lee stole a sideways glance at Hatch, and then looked back straight ahead. "Lord knows, I'm not one to question anybody, and surely you of all lawmen...but... can't help but wonder, if we know they're all coming with bad intent, why don't we just lay for them with Winchesters and shoot them before they even get on the train?"

Hatch took off his hat with his right hand, ran his left hand over short-cropped wiry hair, and then replaced his hat. "We've touched on this before, Ora Lee. You know that is not Plume's way...or mine either for that matter. He believes that he was sent by two gods—one in Heaven and the other'n down here named President U.S. Grant back in seventy-five—to tame this land, and if we act like them... killin' before we give them a chance to surrender...well, Ora Lee, reckon that might make us more alike than I care to be. And there's this: gunfight starts with them outside those train cars, their slugs start pokin' holes through that wood skin, some innocents are likely to bleed."

"Well then, that's that."

John Post Oak smiled when he heard the great steam engine chugging up the long grade toward him and his men, who now stood beside their mounts. They waited in the forest shadows of early afternoon, and before them to the west lay a long open field on which the tracks stretched into the distance on level ground for a quarter mile, and Post Oak knew that long before the train reached the next downgrade, Smoker would be inside the engine cabin with a Colt revolver under the engineer's chin, and he knew that the brakes would cause the iron wheels to scream against the rails and the train would stop in the correct location. He had scouted the approaching train from a mile east as it approached the long gentle hill on which it now travelled.

Post Oak laughed, said, "Mount up, you hard-ass sonsabitches. She's three minutes down the track. It's time to have some fun and make some money." With a shuffle of hooves and creaks of leather from the saddles of the white men, the gang mounted up. "Smoker, the engineer is yours. If he wants to be a hero about the brakes, spread his brains and brake it yourself quick. A quarter mile goes away fast."

Smoker wore his hair in a single braid, greased and shiny black, with an owl feather tied to the base, and under each of his eyes were three finger marks in white paint that reached to his ears. He looked at Post Oak and nodded.

Post Oak said, "Rufus rides with me and we take the safe car and the rest of you take the coach cars. There ain't but two, so a pair of you to each car."

Smoker nudged his tall dun gelding to the front of the group and looked down the tracks, saw the first puffs of smoke billowing from the black hulk.

Post Oak looked at Rufus, who looked straight ahead, his visage a brown study. Post Oak said, "Do not worry, my friend. Once we get started, the rush will take you to the old times, and it will only grow inside you and you will wonder why you ever thought you might not come with me."

Rufus looked at him, said, "I don't give a damn about the money, never really did. I just want to feel it all rise up again in my chest. I told you—all I want is one last good ride…like the warrior I once was."

Post Oak chuckled. "That's a hell of a long speech for you." He reached forward with his right hand and stroked the muscular neck of his horse. "We'll see if just one will do you. I doubt it, my friend. You'll remember that it is a thousand times better than fucking a woman…any woman."

Rufus turned his head, looked straight between the ears of his horse, listened to the approaching engine as the thud of his heart rose inside of his head. His right hand slid down to his holster and covered the bone handle of his revolver.

Post Oak saw what he did, and said, "Been meaning to ask—where the hell did you get such a fine Schofield revolver and holster?"

"I took it from dandy after I bit one of his teats off for roughing up one of Hattie's whores."

Post Oak threw back his head and laughed. "That is funny." He stopped laughing, said, "I have the feeling that it was the yellow-haired one with the hangman that I spied down by the river."

"You have accurate feelings."

"I always do. Did you swallow it or give it to her?"

"I left it on Hattie's night table."

"Did she thank you?"

"Never mentioned it."

"That ain't no surprise. Just like a goddamned woman, wantin' an enemy hurt, but not wantin' to get her hands bloody."

The churning engine was a hundred yards down the track when Post Oak said, "Go, Smoker."

Rufus said, "I hope you have accurate feelings today, John Post Oak," but his voice was lost to the engine. He reached down to the mask gathered around his neck, pulled it up over his head, and then adjusted it so that the eye-holes were properly aligned.

Smoker led the gang out of the woods at an easy lope as they fell in behind the train, and then Smoker nudged his horse and it leapt forward, streaking past the coach cars and quickly drawing even with the engine. Even before Hatch and Ora Lee in the express car saw the rider, the deputies in both coach cars were giving instructions to the alarmed passengers—"Heads to your knees, folks, U. S. Deputies on board, just stay down!"

Ora Lee saw the rider first and darted to the half-open window of the express car, stuck his head out so he could see forward. He watched in amazement as within the space of three seconds, the Indian swung his left leg over the back of his mount and with a push from his arms, launched his body from the horse toward the rear of the engine cabin, wrapped both arms around the back of the frame and disappeared inside the cab. When Ora Lee turned around, Hatch already had the lid to the coffin off and was tossing his hat inside, his revolver in his right hand. After he had climbed in, with his left hand he tucked the metal plate over his chest, rested the revolver on the plate, and then watched light turn to dark as Ora Lee placed the lid on the coffin. The snick of his gun hammer being cocked was eerily loud to Hatch—a sound more inside of his head than inside the coffin. He drew a deep calming breath through his nostrils, and the scent of pine came to him and he allowed himself a few precious seconds of sensory pleasure before he gathered all of his senses and concentrated them on the fifty square feet of the cabin where violence would soon visit. The slowing of the car and the squeal of braking wheels on the tracks came simultaneously, and within a quarter of a minute, Hatch felt the coffin slide an inch before coming to a stop. Hurried footfalls clambering up the three steps and then inside the car, and finally, the voice, deep from the man's chest.

"Mister express man, you got five seconds to live unless you start spinnin' the lock to that safe, and be damn careful about it. You got one chance to get it right."

Ora Lee altered his voice—high and strained. "Yes sir, yes sir…gonna get it right first time, but I'm plumb nervous you might understand…but…I…I'm gonna get it right, yes sir."

"Be goddamned, Rufus, but I think I like this white boy, callin' a red man 'sir'." He cackled. "Bet that's the first time in his life he's done such a thing."

Hatch raised his left forearm from his chest and slammed the armor plate into the coffin lid, which flew four feet in the air, and for a frozen moment that Hatch would remember precisely for the rest of his life, he popped up and stared into the wide, amazed eyes of John Post Oak. In the same moment, he raised and pointed his revolver at Post Oak's head. And then the head disappeared when the Indian simply dropped to his knees and fired his revolver. The bullet ricocheted off of

Hatch's armor plate with a zing. Although Hatch would have no memory of it, another shot sounded and from the corner of his eye he saw the other Indian spin around as Ora Lee followed up his shot by flinging his body toward the man. Hatch fired again reflexively, but Post Oak was a blur of motion and he vanished from the car. He turned toward the struggle on the floor to see Ora Lee use his gun butt to club the other Indian in the head until he lay still. When Ora Lee rolled over, Hatch saw the knife fall to the floor and he rushed to his side.

"He cut you?"

Ora Lee shouted. "Shoot him before he gets away!"

Hatch jumped up to the doorway, leaned out and fired at Post Oak as the Indian kicked the sides of his horse. Hatch saw his body jerk with the impact of the first bullet, and then lunge low and to the right but he stayed on the horse. The second shot struck the horse high in its rear, near the tail, and the horse slowed, favoring its left rear leg. Horse and rider reached the edge of the woods, and Hatch marked the entry point in his mind as he hurried back to Ora Lee.

"Is it deep?"

"I fear it is. I was worried about his pistol, but he didn't shoot…never saw the knife." He glanced at Rufus, saw his bloodied left shoulder. "Damn, I can't believe I made such a poor shot point blank."

Hatch jerked the mask from Rufus's head, and then took out his own knife and with several long swipes cut the back of the unconscious Indian's shirt into strips and then inspected Ora Lee's wound. It was near the bottom of his rib cage, with two splinters of bone about an inch-long poking upward. Hatch plucked them away and stuffed a wad of the cloth over the jagged hole before wrapping the tails around Ora Lee's body and tying a knot. Ora Lee said, "You get him?"

"Hit him pretty good, I'm sure. Shot the horse too, but they made the woods."

"Don't wait…it'll be hard enough in the woods. I can tie this one up, and the boys…"

They heard the two gunshots from the first coach, and then, five seconds later, two more from farther away. Hatch said, "Sounds like you'll have plenty of help here real soon, but keep your gun in hand 'till you're sure."

"I will."

Hatch jumped down to the ground, ran to the first coach, where a deputy emerged and shouted, "Both dead in this one."

At the second coach, he saw gun smoke drifting from the open doorway, but when he saw the face of the deputy, he knew there would be bad news. "We lost Solly. He was in front of me and after I shot mine, a young'un popped up between Solly and his man and he had to wait a fraction…" His voice faded away.

"But I heard just two shots from that coach."

"Shot each other in the face at the same time. I saw it."

Hatch clenched his jaws and a red blotch of anger grew in his brain, as if paint had been spilled inside of his head. You boys get up there to the safe car and tend to Ora Lee. He's been cut deep. After that stop the bleedin' on the Indian. It's just a shoulder wound. I aim to see him hang with Post Oak. Get that train back up to speed and get 'em both to Fort Smith to a doctor."

After a final jerk of his head and shoulders back toward the safe car, he turned around and ran toward the stock car for his horse Shadow.

CHAPTER 31

Through a glass darkly

Three minutes into the woods, Hatch spotted Post Oak's horse a hundred yards away. It was down on its stomach in the middle of a little glade, but Post Oak was nowhere to be seen. Hatch dismounted, drew the Winchester from its scabbard, drew the hammer back to half-cock, and then patted Shadow's head and neck. He moved on foot like a stalking lion—from tree to tree, bush to bush, his vision acute, missing nothing. When he was certain that no ambush had been laid, he walked up to the wounded horse. Blood seeped from the entry wound two inches left of the base of its tail, and with the man's approach, it had begun to struggle, it's hind legs useless from the bullet that had apparently struck its spine. Hatch saw with dread the severed rope that had served as the rifle tether. A man with a sidearm was one thing, a man with a rifle was a horror, and an Indian leaving a blood trail, more than a horror. He moved quickly down the blood trail and away from the wounded horse, hoping that it would soon cease its thrashing, and he regretted mightily that he could not risk a loud gunshot to end its misery.

At first, the blood trail was hard to follow; Post Oak was moving swiftly, the red splotches no more than droplets—like colored dew drops dripping from the tip of a leaf—and sometimes they were fifteen or twenty apart. But soon the pattern changed; the droplets became splotches that appeared every eight or ten feet, and then every four or five. Surely, Hatch thought, the man was badly wounded and slowing down, and Hatch crept again like the stalking lion. He came to a little creek, fifteen feet across, with the water running steadily over rocks just underneath the surface and he felt the first pangs of dread. He waded in, carefully made his way to the far edge and stopped to survey the grassy slope for the first blood sign. There was none, and this did not surprise him. He walked up the slope, and spent twenty minutes making ever wider concentric half-circles from the starting point, but he could find no blood. There was a fifty-fifty chance of following the creek in the correct direction, but a greater consideration was the likelihood of guessing his quarry's exit point from the water. Now convinced beyond doubt that the wounded man had become the equal of a gut shot deer that would eventually bleed out, Hatch decided to wait until morning and begin the search for his body. There would be no double hanging in Fort Smith.

As Hatch trudged back over his route, he paid scant attention to the blood trail until he realized that he should be covering ground where the blood was only drops, and yet...and yet, the large blotches staining the grass and overgrowth were still there, and he dropped to his knees and closely inspected the trail, saw tiny drops and great spots side by side. A sickening feeling grew in his gut and rose to his throat, and he whispered to himself, *You got one foot in your grave, Hatch.* He rolled over in the grass, flat on his belly, and he cradled his rifle in the crooks of his elbows. He crawled a couple of yards away from the trail, but he could still see the blood, and he began to inch forward, elbows and knees, head low. He crawled in this manner for a quarter of an hour, and then—like a sure sign of his doom—a red splash the size of his hand loomed a foot in front of his face, and farther to his left, another, and another. He knew that Post Oak had left the main trail and had sought a hiding place from which to shoot him as he walked by.

Hatch lowered his head, pulled off his hat and placed it over the muzzle of his rifle. He extended the hat through the long grass as far as he could reach then he raised it very slowly, in the manner of a man peeking up. But only silence filled his head, and he blinked against the sweat stinging his eyes. *What now, lawman? Jump and run zig zag and hope he misses? Lay here like a trapped rabbit? Crawl backwards and try to circle him?* As the thoughts raced back and forth in his brain, he felt something on the top of his head, as if a squirrel had dropped a fragment of an acorn, and he reached up with two fingers, felt the moisture and when he looked at the blood on his fingers he whirled to his back and raised his rifle, but he did not fire. In the fork of an oak limb he saw the form of a body, and then he stared into the dead, open eyes of John Post Oak, his arms hanging down like the clothed tree branches of a scarecrow. He sat up, caught his breath, and said aloud, "Lord God a mercy."

When he looked into the long grass under the body,

he saw the Indian's rifle, and near it, a United States Army hat with an eagle feather in its band. He stood, steadied himself, and then began to trot, rifle in hand, toward the pitiful sound of the dying horse in the glade, eager to end the misery.

He returned to the death tree riding Shadow. He dismounted, and took the rope from his saddle, and with this he formed a lasso that he tossed upward several times until the loop settled around the head and he drew it tight. On the second tug, the body crashed to the ground, and then he lifted it and tied it behind his saddle. After he had ridden a mile it occurred to him that John Post Oak had in fact hung after all, if only in death.

When Hatch saw the first twinkles of night lights in Clarksville, he eased Shadow to a stop and dismounted. He struck a match and held the flame near his pocket watch. It was a quarter after four in the morning, and he decided to take down his bed roll and sleep until morning. He led Shadow off the road and into a little clearing behind a copse of cedars, and then he untied Post Oak's body and laid it on the ground. When he had taken the saddle off of Shadow, the mare lowered its head and began to munch on the grass. "Early breakfast, girl. Get you watered good in town." He positioned his bed roll so that he could use his saddle for a head and shoulder rest, and after he had taken his rifle from the scabbard and laid it beside him, he closed his eyes and fell asleep.

He awoke an hour and a half past first light, and he stood, stretched, and urinated before saddling Shadow. The corpse had stiffened and he had to tug on the head and legs for it to drape properly over the horse. This accomplished, he mounted and with his knees nudged the horse toward the road.

By the time he had reached the railroad station, a dozen townsfolk had fallen in behind him and he could hear the excited chatter, but paid it no mind. He dismounted at the hitching post, then turned to face the little gathering. "Look all you want from a distance. Anybody touches the body answers to me."

He walked into the station, past three waiting passengers, glanced and nodded toward Hiram, then tapped the door to Milo's office before opening it and entering. Milo was at the window, peering out. He said, "Is it Post Oak?"

"It was."

"I hate to be the one tells you, but I knew you'd ask, so here goes… I telegraphed Fort Smith about your wounded deputy. He went out on yesterday's last run up there. Died before he got there. The doc here couldn't do nuthin' for him. Said the bleedin' was too deep."

Hatch walked to a chair and sat down, took off his hat. "That boy told me in the beginning that all he ever wanted to be was a lawman…since he was little."

"Well, sir, he got his wish. Damn shame he wasn't one longer."

"Yes…that is true."

Milo walked to his chair, sat down, propped his forearms on the desk. "By God, Dak, you boys got 'em all…every goddamn one of 'em, that's something." He pointed toward the window. "And the head of the snake, the worst of the worst. Didn't figure he'd be a match for you."

Hatch shook his head, released a long breath. "One got away, and the truth about Post Oak is that he was more than a match for me, even gut shot. He had me cold. He was better than me."

Milo scrunched features, shoved at the bridge piece of his spectacles. "How's that?"

"He doubled-back over his blood trail after he hit a little creek, and like a fool, I followed it until I got close enough for him to hit me with a rock."

"But…?"

"But…he was already dead, laid out over me on a big forked tree limb with his rifle. Reckon the climb took too much out of him, and he bled out before he saw me."

Milo exhaled with a whoosh between his lips. "Be damned if that ain't a shivery thought, I'll say. Makes my skin move around like a sheddin' snake."

Hatch nodded, said, "Yeah…somethin' like that." He stood, put on his hat. "When's the next train?"

Milo pulled out his watch, said, "Two hours ten minutes."

"I'm headed to the livery to tend Shadow. Reckon you can round me up an old mail bag or something like it?"

"To stuff him in for the ride?"

"Yeah."

"I'll come up with somethin' suitable. You gonna take the next train back to Fort Smith or ride your horse?"

"Me and Shadow goin' to deliver him back in Fort Smith. Besides, I need a ride to clear my head some."

"Damn sure can understand that, I can. I'll go find you a bag."

"Thanks." Hatch shifted his eyes toward the office door, tilted his head. "You gonna split the reward with Hiram?"

"No I ain't. I'm gonna let him have it all. He's got three youngun's…two still on the teat, and lives in damn near to a shack. Me…I aim to work at this 'til they shovel clay over my fat ass. I like it, don't need nuthin' else."

"You're a good man, Milo."

"That opinion would be widely disputed by many."

Hatch touched his hat brim, turned and walked to the door.

Judge Plume sat at his desk, the top of which was strewn with several stacks of paper—all of which required his attention, and none of which he could bring himself to care about, given the lethal circumstances of the day nearly past. Dusk was fast approaching, and he placed his Waterman fountain pen on the nearest stack, pushed back from the desk, stood and stretched his back. He opened the top drawer and took a match from a small metal tray, but as he turned toward the oil lamp, he paused, raised his head and listened. From the street below him arose the sound of muted voices, perhaps a hundred yards distant, and as the seconds passed, the voices grew louder, their tone rising to an excited pitch. Plume stepped quickly to the tall window and tilted his head near the edge so that he could look down the street. Leading the motley, tangled procession was Dak Hatch, astride his horse. Behind his saddle was a large canvas bag that drooped from one of the horse's flanks to the other, and Plume knew that it contained the body of John Post Oak. The train had arrived three hours earlier, and with it, the deputies—hovering over their pale and fading comrade—the four other outlaw bodies, and the wounded Rufus. Within an hour, the details of the failed train robbery near Clarksville had fanned out like a wind-blown grass fire, and within another half hour, the news grew calamitous with the pronouncement that Deputy Ora

Lee Tygart could not be saved on the table of Doctor Finley Gibbs, who had thereafter dutifully patched up the killer Indian, now locked in his cell below the courthouse.

He walked slowly from his office and then descended the flight of stairs. When he reached the bottom, he tightened his tie knot, and for a moment considered going back to his office and retrieving his coat, but he decided that the tie and the white shirt were sufficiently formal. He stepped from the courthouse and stopped at the edge of the porch, but did not descend the front staircase. When Hatch drew within a few yards, he looked up at Plume and touched the brim of his hat with his right forefinger and thumb. Plume acknowledged him with a solemn, deliberate nod. Hatch dismounted in front of the staircase and looped the reins around the saddle horn, and then stroked a hand along the side of Shadow's neck. He looked back at the gathering and waited for the silence that he knew would quickly come with the presence of Plume looking down from the porch. Hatch said, to no one in particular, "If one of you men would go fetch the undertaker, I'd appreciate it, and then when he's carried away the body, if another of you would take my mare over to the livery for tendin', I'd appreciate that even more."

Several men stepped forward, looked at one another for a few seconds, and then one said, "I'll go get him," and he turned and strode briskly away. Another man said, "I'll see to your mare."

Hatch touched his hat brim again, said, "Much obliged," and then looked up at Plume. "Judge, this here is the body of John Post Oak, killed in the mortal combat that I know you've done been wired about. I regret the way he died, but he left me no choice."

Plume's voice carried more weariness than forcefulness. "It is often the way with such men, Deputy Hatch, but all that matters is that he will terrorize no more. Please come in and have a word with me." He scanned the crowd once, from his left to his right, and centered his look directly at a tall man nearest Hatch. "You, sir, will see to it that no one touches the body save for the undertaker."

"Yessir, I'll see to that."

"The court thanks you."

Plume waited until Hatch reached the porch, and then they walked into the building.

After they had sat down in Plume's office, Plume said, "In times such as this, I am tempted to reconsider my policy of abstinence from a stiff drink."

Hatch took off his hat, sat it on the edge of Plume's desk. "Only trouble with that, Judge, is it's hard to know how much would be required to settle us."

"Precisely…still…" He waved a hand in dismissal of the thought. "Our young deputy is a grievous loss. Post Oak's deadly work I assume?"

Hatch shook his head. "No, it was the other one who wore a face mask. Indian too. I didn't see it. It all happened in a few seconds in the safe car. Ora Lee was posin' as the mail clerk. They had him openin' the safe when I engaged."

"You exchanged gunfire with him?"

"Yes, sir. I come out of hidin' behind a body plate and drew down on Oak, but he shot in that instant, slug clanked off the metal, and then…he just disappeared." Hatch looked at the wall behind Plume, as if he could again see the scene inside the safe car. "All I can figure is that he just let his legs go from under him…like a sack of feed fallin' off a wagon. And then he was gone…just gone—so fast I don't even recollect if he stayed down or got up to run. Just gone. I tended Ora Lee best I could, and he told me to get after Post Oak. He'd already clubbed the other one out cold with his pistol."

Plume listened with his head down, his elbows propped on the desk, fingers formed into a steeple near his nose. "I can't imagine being involved in such an encounter. I have no idea how men such as you deal with it, but I am eternally grateful for you."

Hatch's eyes glistened over and he blinked against the moisture. "Well, Judge, this man ain't sure he dealt with it worth a tinker's damn. That boy was in his light twenties at most…never asked him direct, 'cause he was touchy about it."

"He was twenty-three. I remember when I interviewed him for the job. He seemed beyond his years with his bearing. I was impressed."

"Oh, I was too, Judge. So impressed that I picked him to be in the safe car with me. I'll tell you true, if there'd been any way to switch out where we were in that car, he'd a been the one come out from hidin'. I will regret that until the day I die."

"Would that I could dissuade you of that regret, though I know that I cannot."

"Reckon not."

"So you took Post Oak in the wilderness?"

"Never took him anywhere. I got off two quick shots as he rode away and then he just died there in the woods, bled out after he'd spent his last climin' a tree, way I figure it." Hatch turned his head toward Plume, waited for him to look up at him. "Truth be told, he was better than me.

222

He had me dead to rights. Doubled back on his blood trail and I was blunderin' along it when it came to me what he'd done. I got down, crawled like a snake for a time, then just froze…figured I was had."

"But you weren't."

"Felt a blood drop hit my head, looked up, and there he was right over me, spread out on a forked limb, stone cold dead, rifle dropped in the grass. If I'd a been just a tad faster gettin' back to that spot…maybe a minute or two—who can say?—we'd both be dead now."

"But you are not, Dak. It was God's will."

"Surely feels like that now. Didn't at the time. It was just two men tryin' to kill each other in the woods, one claimin' the right, the other claimin' the same thing as he saw it." The silence gathered for several seconds, and then Hatch said, "Had to be God's will that Ora Lee died to, then?"

Plume reformed the finger steeple in front of his face, drew a long breath, pushed it out. He reached out and placed his hand on a Bible lying between two stacks of paper. "The Apostle Paul tells us that here on earth we are only able to see through a glass darkly."

"I'm in agreement with that."

"You need to go home to your family and rest for a time."

"I intend to." He stood, picked up his hat and settled it on his head. "One more thing. After a fashion, Post Oak got hung after all…which is what I wanted to see done here. I looped a rope around his neck and jerked him down out of the tree. Just as easy to toss it around his foot, but I think I did his head on purpose. I ain't proud of that now."

"The glass is dark, Dak. Forget it. Go home."

CHAPTER 32

Long the mockingbird sang

Hattie had lain naked on Rufus's bed for an hour without moving a muscle. Dusk had succumbed to night; her vigil had just begun. She clutched a buckskin shirt bunched tightly under her chin, breathed in his scent as a delicate fragrance. Then she moved only her fingertips, caressing the smooth hide, trying to remember exactly the feel of it with the man inside it, but it was bereft of warm flesh and blood—an empty vessel—and thus only a vague and melancholy recollection. The window was half raised and from her house she heard the first stirrings of the evening—voices of men, easy-going laughter of the girls, Sally's plunking on the piano—the laughter louder there. She rolled to her side, facing the door, but the open window was all that mattered, for it would either give her the sound of horse's hooves passing by the cabin toward the barn, or it would give her emptiness. So it was that Hattie Wax listened intently, but she only heard the gaiety from the house, and after another two hours had passed, the only sound that she could hear was the delicate tone of her grandfather clock as it chimed eleven times.

The moon was full, yesterday's rain clouds long gone to the northeast, so the room was filled with silvery light, and Hattie walked about, studying his tools and hides and wooden boxes and dozens of other objects both on the wall and the floor. She now wore the buckskin shirt, hanging loose and heavy on her shoulders, and her fingers played through the drawstrings the same way that she toyed with the ends of her hair when Dilla trimmed it. She opened the door and walked out, the packed earth cool on the soles of her feet, the breeze a presence, but not insistent. Above her, high in the tallest elm, a mockingbird began to chirp its quick melody, its song much like a canary, proud on its perch, proclaiming its talent as if from a mountaintop, sure of the knowledge that all of the world's creatures could hear it. She walked behind the cabin and pulled the bottom of the shirt under her buttocks and sat down on the work stump, saw the outline of the cooking spit, the rock ring under it. After a time, she sat on the ground against the stump, and looked to the east, dreaded the sunrise. Behind and above her, the mockingbird sang with not a care in its world. Long the woman sat and long the mockingbird sang.

Sally had slept fitfully. Her last customer was gentlemanly and reasonably quick with his business, and afterwards, he was talkative, chattering on about the scene in front of the courthouse that he had witnessed, and the many details he had learned regarding the failed train robbery—the men living and dead and the one wounded Indian outlaw. He rattled on while the nausea flooded Sally, and finally he said that the wounded Indian was called Rufus, and that he was well known in Fort Smith, and it was then that Sally excused herself to the toilet closet and vomited as quietly as she could manage. Then she told the talkative man that she was unwell and that he should leave.

She tossed aside the sheet covering her legs and sat on the edge of the bed, then reached down to the foot of the bed and pulled the gown to her and put it on. She squinted at the nightstand clock, the hour hand between the Roman Numerals V and VI. It was plain and simple: It had fallen to her to be the bearer of the sad news, and she could wait no longer. She padded quietly to Hattie's room, knocked lightly, and when she heard nothing, opened the door and saw the empty made bed. She closed the door and walked down the staircase, looked first in the parlor and then on the front porch. She went back through the parlor and into the kitchen and when she knocked on Dilla's door it opened so quickly it startled her. Dilla wore a nightgown, but the lamp in her room shone brightly. Sally said, "Oh my, Dilla, I didn't know you were already up."

"What's the matter, Miss Sally?"

Sally grabbed both of Dilla's hands. "Dilla, where is Miss Hattie?"

"She's still in Mister Rufus's cabin, I 'spect. Been waitin' for him all night. I saw her head out there just before dark, and she ain't come back."

"I had a customer that told me he was in town late afternoon, and that there was a train robbery gone bad near Clarksville...men dead...John Post Oak carried dead in a sack on Dak Hatch's horse...two U. S. Deputies dead... and...and he said a wounded outlaw was named Rufus, in the jail…and…goddammit, Dilla, he couldn't have been wrong about things like that…" She looked down, tried to get her breath.

"Ohhhhh….ohhhh, my oh my oh my oh my."

"Dilla, we have to tell her. I don't want her to find out from a stranger. Please come with me. I don't think I can do this by myself."

Dilla squeeze her hands, said, "We both need to go. Come on, Miss Sally…looks like we meant to be the ones."

Arms linked and barefoot, they tiptoed through the gray of the dying moonlight, their eyes fixed on the unlit cabin, a window half open, the bottom of the burlap curtain teased by the breeze in the manner of a gown hem moving with the graceful stride of a woman. They passed the open door, slipped around the sidewall, and when they looked behind the cabin, they saw Hattie sitting on the ground with her back to the stump, knees tucked under her chin, head down and facing away. When Sally and Dilla stopped two steps behind her, Hattie raised her head and said, "Who comes to see me on this morning?"

Sally said, "Miss Hattie, it's me and Dilla. Can we sit with you?"

Hattie extended her right hand, patted the grass beside her, and the women gathered their gowns beneath them and sat down. Hattie said, "There's dew, you might get wet bottoms."

Dilla said, "Don't matter any, Miss Hattie, we've been wet before."

Hattie raised her head, said, "Then tell me what does matter."

They looked at each other for an instant, and then Sally

said, "Rufus…there was bad trouble near Clarksville…a train. He won't be coming back."

"Dead or alive?"

"Wounded, but not bad they say. He's patched up in the jail."

"Is anybody dead?"

"Post Oak is. That lawman they call Hatch carried him to the courthouse in a sack on his horse."

"Others?"

"Two deputy marshals and four more train robbers."

"Who killed the deputies?"

"They say one of the dead robbers shot one…and…well, they say Rufus killed the other one."

From the riverbank came the hoot of an owl, and it stirred up the crows, and they cawed their disdain like a chorus of old men in a madhouse until there were only two madmen, then one, then none. The smaller birds took up the chorus with all manner of chirps and twitters and peeps, but they did not cease, and it was their voices that the three women listened to, were thankful for. They listened for a minute, and then another.

Hattie said, "Well, ladies, life is full of surprises, but this ain't one of 'em."

Sally said, "We're so sorry, Miss Hattie…don't rightly know what to say."

"Ain't a thing else to say, Sally. It's all done." Hattie got up, and when she did, Sally and Dilla stood with her, waited. "Dilla, can you manage to get my buggy ready for a trip to town?"

"Oh yes I can, Miss Hattie, I ain't no stranger to a horse and buggy."

Sally said, "Neither am I, I'll help."

Hattie allowed the women to hold her arms, and she rested her head on Dilla's shoulder for a moment, then said. "I'm beholdin' you came to me."

Dilla said, "Wouldn't had it no other way."

"One more thing, Dilla. When you're done with the buggy, come up to my room and bring your scissors and a sack for a lot of hair."

Dilla and Sally wanted to look at each other, but they dared not, and Dilla said, "Yes, ma'am."

When Apsel Graf turned the doorknob of the courthouse door, he heard the approaching horse and buggy and turned to cast a cursory glance, but instead he froze, took his hand from the doorknob and turned to face it. The driver was alone, and wore an old rancher's hat, and her vestment was far too large—it was like looking at a boy in a man's shirt and trousers. The driver reined in the horse at the hitching post, and it was only then that Apsel recognized Hattie. His body stiffened, and for a moment he considered leaving her and ensconcing himself in his office, but the thought passed quickly. Sooner or later, he would have to deal with her.

She climbed down from the seat and wrapped the reins around the crossbar, and then she went back to the floor of the buggy and picked up a cloth sack. She looked up at Apsel, standing on the porch, and said, "I would like to see him. Just tell me your rules." She held out the sack. "I know this is the first one."

Apsel walked down the stairs and took the bag from her, opened it and probed around in it for a few seconds, before handing it back to her. Her face was plain, untouched with color, and there were deep lines etched around her eyes that

Apsel had no memory of ever seeing before. Her eyes were intent, yet exuding a bone-deep weariness, and from under her hat uneven clumps of straight red hair protruded. He said, "You'll need to come inside and let a lady clerk finish."

Apsel led the way up the stairs, opened the door for her, then quickly took the lead again, walking toward a corner of the lobby, where a woman sat behind a small table on which there were two small stacks of papers. She looked up as they approached, and Apsel said, "Lucy, would you please do the formalities for this visitor. She wishes to see a prisoner."

The woman got up and said, "Certainly." She pointed toward a side door, and Hattie followed her into a small, windowless room. Within a minute, Hattie preceded her through the doorway. Apsel thanked the clerk and said to Hattie. "This way please."

Apsel led her down the front stairs of the porch, and then down another stairway, lined with stone walls. At this door, Apsel lifted from his belt a key ring looped with a small chain and unlocked the door, and after they had entered, he locked it behind him. He nodded at the jailer sitting in a chair against the wall, against which leaned a double-barreled ten-gage shotgun. As Apsel and Hattie walked down the narrow, dungeon-like corridor, a few of the prisoners mumbled words that were lost to Hattie, and she kept her eyes on Apsel's back. At the end of the corridor, he stopped and turned to face a single cell, and pointed toward an opening four inches high and a foot wide at the bottom corner. "You can slide what you want through there."

"Alright. How long can I have?"

"There's no set time limit. Just so everything stays

peaceable." He reached near the base of the wall and pulled a low wood bench forward. "You can use this if you want."

Hattie looked at Apsel and said, "You can rest assured, hangman. Ain't likely neither of us are gonna get unpeaceable, is it?"

She waited until Apsel had walked away before she looked inside the cell. Rufus lay on his side atop the metal bed chained to the wall. On the floor near the bed was a metal waste bucket. He faced the wall, his legs drawn up, and from his top shoulder Hattie saw the edge of a white bandage poking from his shirt, near his neck. It was tinged with dark bloodstains. She said, "You awake?"

Carefully, he rolled over and put his sock-covered feet on the floor, and then sat up. "Wide. Ain't a sleepin' sort of place."

"I brought you a clean shirt and britches, and some jerky and horehound candy." She knelt down and reached into the sack."

"Don't bother. Won't be needin' any a that." He raised his left hand and pointed at her shirt. "I like that. I shoulda made you one to fit. Never knew you wanted one."

Hattie pulled her hand from the sack and sat down on the bench. "Never felt the need to put one on until last night."

He smiled grimly. "You burn it down?"

"I did not. That was just loose, bold talk."

"Figured that. Still...after you found out I wouldn't ever be comin' back, thought you might reconsider."

"Rufus, I intend to hire the best lawyer in St. Louis, or further back East...wherever...because I swear I will do everything I can to see that you don't hang. I read the papers, and I know that Plume has had some of his death sentences shoved back up his ass by the big court, and…"

"Hush that shit and listen to me."

Hattie reached forward and wrapped her fingers around the bars. "Goddammit, Rufus."

"There's no need for a big fuss. I ain't gonna hang."

Her face contorted into a mask of bewilderment, but it quickly turned into one of horror, and she shook head wildly. "No…no, Rufus. Not that, don't do that please."

"It won't take but maybe two weeks, hot as it is."

Hattie rested her head against the bars, and Rufus got up and stepped to her, knelt and wrapped his left hand around one of hers, touched his forehead to hers. "You ain't thinkin' straight, woman. Even if some lawyer got the sentence changed, it would be life." He squeezed her hand. "In a cage for the rest of my life…that's what you want for me?"

Hattie began to weep softly, careful to stifle the sound against the back of her hand. "I just don't' want you to die… any way."

"That's like wishin' the sun wouldn't come up. I'm a dead man walkin', but I'll get dead as I see fit…not stared at up on the gallows, the goddamn hangman loopin' my neck. Fuck him and fuck Plume, they ain't gonna have it their way." He gently tapped his forehead to hers. "So we got us a few good days left and you can come see me, and all we'll talk about is the good times…just the good times, you understand me, woman?"

She sniffed, wiped her nose on her shirtsleeve, moved her forehead up and down against his. "I'll try, Rufus, but you're askin' for a lot."

"I know, but I ain't askin' for long." He waited for her to speak again, but after several seconds of silence, he said, "Listen to me rattle on. Longest damn speech I ever made to you."

"Yes…yes it was. Cryin' shame it took this to bring it out of you."

He cupped his hand around her cheek. "Oh, I ain't sure about that. If I'd made long speeches before, you might've chased me off."

They let the silence grow, moved off their knees to their hips, their heads and hands still touching. Low voices, indistinct and casual, leaked down the corridor, and occasionally metallic clanks carried along the stone wall—messages from the belly of the beast. Finally, Rufus said, "You need to go home and rest now, you look like hell."

She attempted a smile, but it was shapeless. "So do you."

With his unwounded arm, he helped her up, and they steadied each other. He said, "Why did you chop your hair?"

"Thought it might help in not attractin' attention."

"The hell with 'em. Put on your fancy clothes and hat next time."

A faint smile touched her lips. "I will. The hell with 'em all."

From the little kitchen of the house, Iva listened to the sound of Apsel's horse as it clomped toward the shed. She lifted the lid from the frying pan, and with a fork, stirred the beef slices. She looked down at the two place settings and needlessly rearranged the cloth napkins, fingered the edges of the plates. She turned to meet Apsel, who gave her a quick hug, and they went to the table and sat down. She said, "Did she come today?"

"Yes, first thing this morning."

"Did she come…in full…like Hattie?"

"No, I didn't even recognize her at first. She wore some of the Indian's clothes, and her hair was cut short under an old work hat."

"Was anything of substance spoken of?"

"You mean of the boy?"

"That, and anything else…of substance."

"No, not a word about him or anything other than visiting protocol."

How long did she stay?"

"Only for a short while, but she looked like she'd been up all night."

"You'll see a lot of her in the coming weeks…or months. How long is the process?"

"Not long, given these circumstances…still, you are about correct generally."

"Is there any chance that your commitment to Judge Plume will be fulfilled…before…he…before you…" her voice trailed off, and she looked down at the empty plate.

"No, it will be finished before then."

Iva looked away for a moment, then said. "You go ahead and eat if you want, Apsel. I have no appetite just now."

He got up and moved the pan to the edge of the stove. "I don't either. Let's go outside and walk for a time. The air is cooling off and there is some good shade in the trees."

They strolled side by side, Apsel's hands in his pockets, Iva's held together at her waist. They looked around them, did their best to study the fullness of the trees, listen to the breeze move the wide leaves about in slow swirls, but they could not. Iva stopped and turned to Apsel. "Would you be angry if I went on to San Francisco ahead of you…once we get final arrangements made out there? It would only be for a short time, it would seem. I would wait as long as I could before it ends…perhaps a week or two before that."

"Of course I would not be angry. To the contrary, I would understand, and would want for you to go on. And hopefully, with the boy by then. He will come back long before then, I am certain."

"Oh, I do so hope he will, Apsel. I do so hope."

She took his hand and they began to walk again, deeper into the shade of the trees, and the breeze was tender on their faces.

CHAPTER 33

❖❖❖❖

Much happened

After the passing of another day, the news out of Clarksville and Fort Smith was the talk of the town, but it was not until Dabo and Son stopped work for their noon sack dinner that they learned of it. The bearer of news was customer that had arrived that morning on a train from Fort Smith. He had announced his intention to purchase a brace of mules, should Dabo have one for sale, but had quickly dashed off on an errand of less consequence. He was a dapper man, who wore a sleek bowler hat with a silk band and well-tailored clothing, and his black boots glistened in the noon sunlight as he approached with purposeful strides. His round face was red from exertion, and with a white handkerchief, he dabbed at his forehead as he stopped just inside the livery door. Dabo had just bitten off half of a hard-boiled egg, and with the surviving half in his fingers, he lifted it in greeting, finished chewing, swallowed hard, and then said, "Got your errand run I see."

The man forced a smile, dabbed under his eyes, and then folded the handkerchief and shoved it in his coat pocket. "In fact, I did, and I'm ready to inspect your mules, if you would be so kind."

"Yes, sir, that's what we're here for, but if I don't eat my other egg and the apple that's left in my sack, I fear that I might perish from lack of food before suppertime. Why not step on in here out of that harsh sun for a few minutes and then me or my hand here will give you a good look-see around the stalls, where we keep the finest mule flesh in these parts. You'd be a wastin' your time to look elsewhere. Whad you say your name was?"

"I didn't, but it's Lashman." He walked into the shade, took off his hat and fanned his face before sitting it back on his bald head.

Dabo pointed upward, toward the front of the building. "You already know mine, 'cept I go by Dabo, not D.L., who would be my pap, who founded this establishment by knowin' mules and horses like the Lord God knows about his people."

The man stared with his mouth half-agape, his eyes in a half-squint, like a man struggling to add up a long string of numbers. He said, "You are an interesting man—as I've heard you would be—and it would be nice to chat with you for a time were I not in a bit of a rush."

"Ain't no need to rush, Mr. Lashman, for I 'spect you want to load your new mules in the stock car of the 2:41 headed back up to Fort Smith, which leaves us an oodle of time to get it all done." Dabo took a huge bite from a yellow apple, which produced a loud crack. He pointed toward a wooden bench near the door opening. "Rest yourself just a couple minutes longer. Ain't no hurry a'tal, you see. I've accomplished such exact deals as this for years. Why, I'd bet

I could talk to the train men and cause them to hold it for you and your new mules, but 'course that won't be necessary."

Lashman looked at Son, who sat on a small stool, chewing on his own yellow apple, appearing to the man as a boy watching something interesting inside of a tent show, but it did not irritate him. He addressed Dabo, but looked at Son. "Your young hand here doesn't have much chance to talk, does he?"

"Aw, you'd be surprised how he chatters when a customer ain't around. Can't hardly keep his mouth shut." He winked at Son, who smiled and chewed thoughtfully.

Lashman finally relaxed, leaned back against the wall and took off his hat and placed it upside down on the bench beside him, tilted his head back. He released a long sigh—a man resigned to his fate. He said, "Well, I shouldn't be so eager to get on a train, with what happened up in Clarksville day before last." He chuckled at his remark. "However, it's highly unlikely that such a calamity would take place again anytime soon."

Though neither Lashman nor Dabo noticed, Son's jaws stopped moving for a couple of seconds, and then he swallowed. Dabo said, "Hadn't heard of such. We don't have time to read the papers nor listen to idle chatter from the street. What happened?"

Lashman's eyes widened for an instant, pushing upward his unruly brows. "Much happened. Dead U. S. Deputy marshals…two to be exact, some wanted Indian outlaw named John Post, I think it was…killed by that famous black deputy—Hatch it is, I remember that—four more outlaws shot dead, and one more Indian outlaw wounded and now in the Fort Smith jail, which sits directly under the courthouse of the famous hanging judge…Plume, you must've heard of him, for heaven's sake…he was quoted in the news piece about it all, and especially Hatch, who he praised way too much, seems to me. You'd have thought he was the greatest lawman God ever plunked down on earth." He huffed a laugh of dismissal at the silly notion. "Oh yes… much, I'd say."

Dabo's eyes had been locked on Lashman, whose stare had wandered upward toward the roof beams as he recounted what he had heard and read. Lashman looked down and then at the empty stool. "Seems as though your hand became bored with the news."

Dabo looked at the empty stool. "Appears so. I do keep the boy right busy. He's got good manners…didn't mean no offense."

"None taken."

Dabo popped the apple core in his mouth. "Let's go find your mules, Mr. Lashman. I got some sturdy as bridge beams and easy-goin' as cut lap dogs. And you gotta see my Big Luther draft horse, but I'll warn you, you'll try to buy him, but he ain't for sale."

They got up, and side by side, began to walk down the row of stalls. Dabo looked around as they walked, but he did not see the boy.

As the busy day progressed, Dabo gave no thought to Son's sudden disappearance. The boy went about his tasks with his usual energy, and few words were spoken, and the few that were involved only Dabo's brief instructions. The proprietor stayed occupied mainly with customers who sought new stock, or others who wanted to work out a trade. On the ride home, Dabo recounted the deals made, filling in every detail, but Son was mostly silent, staring at Big Luther's broad back—the muscles rippling under glistening hide like waves of brown water.

Dabo reined in the big horse at the barn door, hopped down and said, "Get him freed up and tended for me 'fore you wash up for supper."

Son hopped down and said quietly, "I will."

Dabo looked at him for a few seconds, then said, "I know you ain't no jaybird, but why so quiet? You sickly?"

"No…no, I ain't sick…but…"

"But what?"

"I need to talk to you about goin' back to Fort Smith."

Dabo's features clouded. "For how long?"

"I can't rightly say for sure."

Like a man trying to remember recent pictures he had recently viewed, Dabo thought back over the day at the livery, and then the pictures stopped when he saw Lashman sitting on the bench holding forth on the train robbery news. "Hummm…this is a curiosity for me. Now that I think back on it, you ain't been the same since the mule buyer told us about the Clarksville train shoot-out."

Son looked down at his boots, and he reached out and put his hand on Big Luther's flank, stroked it slowly. Words ricocheted inside of his skull, but he could not sort them out, could not think of a way to explain it to Dabo in an acceptable manner. He did not consider lying to the man who had taken him in to his own home and family, and had given him food and shelter and opportunity. It was bewildering, and all that Son could do was shake his head in little jerks, stare at the ground, and stroke Big Luther.

The seconds oozed by, the silence unbroken, growing

louder in their ears. Dabo could make no sense of it whatsoever—a condition that was always a great aggravation when seldom it occurred. A good mule was a good mule, and if it wasn't, there was a precise reason, or several—all identifiable, all making perfect sense. He could read prospective buyers and traders as easily as if they handed him a note on which they had written down their bargaining shortcomings—a tug on one ear, or the twitch of a nose that they were not even aware of, but which to Dabo made perfect sense. It was simply the way the world was supposed to work for a man who had built his life and business on the sensible.

Dabo took two steps and placed both hands on Big Luther's shoulder and clapped several times. The massive head lifted as the horse gave a little snort, as if to acknowledge his master's touch. "Well then, Floyd…" He stopped, clapped the horse one more time. "Well, I'll be switched with a bundle a briars, but I don't believe I've ever asked you your last name. Good gawd…days gone by, you sleepin' in the house, us workin' our asses off side by side, and I don't even know your full name."

"McCarty."

Dabo waited for only a few more seconds, knew that the boy would say no more. "Well then, Floyd McCarty, I reckon me and you and Big Luther will just have to keep likin' each other w'thout knowing everything there is to know in our own little worlds."

Son finally looked up at Dabo. "I really appreciate that, Dabo. I don't mean to act all secret-like with you…done so much for me and all…and…"

"It's alright, boy, I know you don't mean no disrespect. I don't take it like that. I'll admit it is a helluva curiosity, like

I said, but, by God, Dabo Toomer ain't a man that's gotta know everything about a fellow plodder on this mysterious earth." He turned to Son, and with one hand clapped his shoulder much in the same manner as he had clapped Big Luther. "Time I paid you a wage." He reached into his trouser pocket and pulled out a twenty-dollar gold piece and dropped it into Son's shirt pocket. "No rough-ass tinder car ride this trip. The wife'll pack you some eats in a sack that you might have to fight people off over. We'll just tell her and Pap you need to go back and see some of your people for a time—tend to some business."

"Thanks, I don't know what else to say."

"Nothin' else to say, and you're welcome." He turned and began to make his way to the house, and over his shoulder, he said, "Take care of my big boy now. He's patient, but he's got his limits."

Nothing was said at the supper table that night about Son's planned trip to Fort Smith. Dabo and his wife chatted about how their days had progressed, with Son adding an occasional word to the conversations. Pap felt poorly, and had stayed in his room, half asleep in his bed. Nadine began to clear the table, and then Dabo and Son got up from the table. When she returned for more dishes, Dabo said to her, "Nadine, Floyd needs to make him a trip back up to Fort Smith for a couple of days or so, and I told him you'd pack him some grub for the train ride."

She looked at Son, slight surprise registering on her face, but she only smiled and said, "I think I can manage that easy enough."

Son said, "Thanks."

Nadine caught Dabo's eyes before she turned away, and

with the look, he told her not to ask any questions. She said, "I got your clothes washed up too, and I put in some good pass-down tweed britches of Dabo's that I took up to fit you. They'll be in your knapsack when you get up. Leaving early?"

"Yes, ma'am, first light…aim to catch the first train out."

"Well then, you go on and get some rest."

"Yes, ma'am, think I will."

Son walked into his room and softly closed the door behind him.

Nadine stacked the dishes on the counter beside the pump handle, and waited for Dabo to stand with her. She said, "What's all this about, Dabo?"

"It is a deep curiosity to me, and you know I hate such things." He flapped his hands up then back down. "He ain't exactly an open book, but then again, none of us are."

"You're close."

"Just my nature, I guess."

She smiled. "There's no guessing about it, but I like it, else I wouldn't be standing here doing your dishes." She placed a stack of plates under the spout and pumped the handle. "Hope you don't have to find another hand at the livery. He seems like a keeper."

"Damn sure is, but I don't have an easy feelin' 'bout him comin' back to us."

"Why wouldn't he? He comes to town in the tinder car of a train, hungry as a starved hound, no roof, no job…and you latch onto him. I tell you that would make no sense."

"No it wouldn't." He walked to the table and picked up his coffee cup, took it to the stove and filled it. "I'm goin' to the barn for a while and talk to Big Luther. He might be able to make some sense."

CHAPTER 34

Only decent people shoot mad dogs

The train arrived in Fort Smith just before noon the next day. Son folded the oil cloth around the remains of the bacon and biscuits in his lap, and then picked up his knapsack and stuffed in the wad. From a paper bag at the bottom of the knapsack, he took two pieces of horehound candy and popped them into his mouth, and then folded down the opening of the sack. He wiped his mouth on his shirt sleeve as he watched the departing passengers leave their seats and shuffle to the front of the car. He waited until he was the only one remaining, and then got up and walked out into the stifling heat, pulled down his hat brim, and looked around for a minute before approaching a well-dressed man standing in the shade of the awning, a black satchel sitting beside his boots. The man ignored him until Son stood a step in front of him, and said, "Sir, could you tell me where the jail is?"

The man looked at him as if he had just heard a strange sound, and he cocked his head to the side. "The jail, you say?"

"Yessir."

"Well it's not difficult to locate, if that's where you're sure you want to go."

"It is."

"Hummm." He looked around him, raised his right hand to his waist and pointed with his forefinger before answering quietly. "Four blocks down that street, then go left for two more. Jail's in the basement of the courthouse— pretty hard to miss."

"Thanks."

When the courthouse came into view a half block distant, Son walked another fifty steps and then stopped in the shade of a store awning, edging near the glass front with bold black lettering that read: PIKE & SONS DRY GOODS. He studied the imposing courthouse building, impervious to the broiling sun, hiding its secrets in the heat of noon. Son counted ten windows to its front, all fully or half open to the full-length porch, fronted with eight columns that looked like stone sentinels, all connected by a white wooden railing. A few people milled about on the porch, careful to stay out of the sunlight. To one side of the porch staircase was another, smaller staircase that descended to the basement, and Son reckoned that this was the one that led down to the jail cells.

He stood for five minutes staring at the basement staircase, his thoughts locked on Rufus, somewhere down there, waiting behind the bars and the stones in the close air. Suddenly, as if carried to him on the hot breeze, the urge to find Hattie washed over him, and he turned around and began to walk with long strides toward the road leading out of town.

Two hours after she had cleared the table and washed up all the dishes from dinner, Dilla poured tea into a wide-mouthed glass jar and walked to the front porch, where she knew the breeze would be its most useful. She sat down on the swing and toed the wood floor, and soon the familiar squeak of the suspended chains rose above her. After she had drunk half of her tea, she stopped the swing with both feet and leaned down to put the jar on the floor. When she sat back upright, she cast a casual glance down the long lane leading to the house, saw a person walking toward the house, and she moved to the edge of the swing, squinted into the heat shimmers. When he was a hundred yards away, she popped up and took two quick steps to the railing, and then she whirled around and ran into the house and up the stairs to Hattie's room. She knocked, but opened the door at the same time, saw Hattie, fully dressed in her finery, standing in front of a full-length mirror.

Dilla, breathless, said, "Miss Hattie, you need to come on downstairs now, there's a surprise walkin' up the lane." Before Hattie could say a word, the nimble woman disappeared, and was waiting inside the open front door when Hattie hurried to her side and looked out. He was close enough to see them now, and he raised his right hand in greeting as he began to trot. Hattie's shoes tapped a quick rhythm on the porch stair treads, and then she stopped when she reached the ground, her eyes clouded with tears. Son stopped a few steps in front of her, unsure of the meaning of her tearful look. She said, "Come give me a hug, little man. I do so need one."

Son took off his knapsack and laid it on the ground, and then went to her quickly, his hat falling to the ground as they embraced. She rocked him from side to side, then held him at arm's length. "You do know, don't you?"

"Yes, I know it all."

"Let's go inside. Better yet, let's swing, just like we did the first time." She looked at Dilla. "Maybe we can talk Dilla into bringing out some of her tea."

Son said, "Hello, Dilla."

"Hey to you, little man. I'll be right back."

Hattie and Son went to the swing and sat down. Son said, "When I got off the train, I found the courthouse and the jail, and I thought about goin' to see him, but I knew I couldn't without you."

"You did the right thing. I'm fixin' to set out for there soon, and now we'll go together. He'd want it like that."

"I know he would."

"There are some hard things we need to talk about on the way in. No use sugar-coatin' anything for you."

"Don't want you to."

"Let's go on inside. You can drink your tea in the kitchen with Dilla. I want to finish gettin' ready and go on to him. She'll fix you a bite if you're hungry."

"I'm not hungry at all. Been eatin' some stuff from my knapsack." He tried to form a smile, but could not. "I saved him most of a bag of horehound candy. He's always liked it."

She stood and wrapped her fingers around his arm, slowly shook her head, swallowed. "He won't take it, you save it for yourself."

The boy looked at her quizzically. "Seems like he might want somethin' like that, where he's at and all."

"No he wouldn't. That's one of the hard things I have to tell you about." She squeezed his arm. "Go drink your tea now, and then you can help Dilla hitch up the buggy."

Judge Plume and Apsel sat side by side in chairs

positioned in front of the judge's open office window. They were both coatless, shirt sleeves rolled up to their elbows, and in Plume's right hand was a large, white handkerchief, sodden with perspiration. He rolled it around in his hand and then mopped his brow again. Apsel sat leaning forward, with his forearms resting on his knees, his brow furrowed in thought.

Plume said, "Not a bite nor a single drink of water… you're certain?"

"Yes, sir. The jailers told me about it the same day we locked him up, and I have since personally verified what they tell me. He just shoves the food and water out of the cell…with some force, I might add."

"Well, it can't last. Surely he will get past this…this… initial situation." He waved his handkerchief like a flag. "This oppressive heat…his wound…it just can't last. And make sure water is within his reach every day, no matter what he does with it."

"I will. I tried to speak to him—civilly."

"And?"

"He told me that if we brought the doctor to tend him further, he would bite him like a mad dog, and that if we liked to clean up messes, that we should continue to put food and water in his cell. He spoke as calmly as I speak to you now."

"And that is all he said?"

"No. He also said that we should treat him like a mad dog, but that he knew we wouldn't, since only decent people shoot mad dogs."

Plume looked at the street below, saw the sluggish plod of a horse and rider, and two men walking, all reduced to slow motion, like pieces of meat in a simmering stew. "We have never encountered a situation like this in all of our years, Apsel. What shall we do?"

"I don't see that there is anything anybody can do, Judge. We can't tie him down and poke food down him, or pour water down his throat." Apsel shook his head, mopped his brow with the back of his hand.

Plume considered what he was about to say, and at first hesitated, given the circumstances involving Apsel and his new wife, but need and expediency quickly won out. "His woman, Hattie Wax. She will no doubt visit regularly… perhaps daily. Is there any chance she could be prevailed upon to talk sense with him? The last thing I need is more sensationalism in the newspapers, and those hounds would be all over this."

"I suppose I could try, but…uh…our history is complicated, mostly combative."

"Yes, yes, that is unfair of me. I will speak to her myself. It is my responsibility, not yours. I shouldn't have even asked you."

"I understand, Judge. No offense taken, rest assured. I'll tell her that you want to speak with her."

Plume mopped his brow again, then his entire face. "Ahhh!…I'm assuming that she would even speak to me. That may well be a silly assumption."

"As we know, she's not hesitant about engaging in conversations of all sorts."

"You have a compelling point there. Not at all comforting, mind you, but certainly compelling."

CHAPTER 35

I don't need to say much

Son expertly reined in the mare as the buggy slowed, and then stopped at the hitching post in front of the courthouse, and from behind the buggy, a thin cloud of powder-like dust swirled past them. He jumped down from the seat, secured the reins, went to Hattie's side of the seat and helped her down. She wore a glistening green dress with a bustle, the front of the dress cut low in a half circle, bordered with white silk, exposing two inches of cleavage. Her feathered hat was a matching green, and sat slightly askance on her head, as she intended. Son stole a peek at her—not the first—and she knew that he studied not the hat, but her hair.

She said, "I chopped it off before I came to see him the first time, so's not to attract unwanted attention. But Rufus told me to dress like me. Can't fix the hair in time, but I can my clothes and hat."

"Didn't mean to stare."

"You didn't, little man, you just peeked, and peekin' is alright."

They both looked at the basement staircase for a long moment, figures of stone baking in the sunlight, and Hattie said, "We have to go up in the courthouse and let them check us over first."

When they came out of the courthouse, Apsel stood at the bottom of the stairs, looking up at Son, whose arm Hattie held as they stepped down. She said, "Well…a little clumsy, situations like this, but it ain't no time to be uncivil. Hangman, you can have him for a talk—if he wants—after he visits Rufus with me." She looked at Son, said, "How's that suit you?"

"That'd be alright with me."

Apsel looked at Son, and said, "Thank you…both." Then he turned to Hattie. "I know it would be somewhat difficult, but…if you would be kind enough, Judge Plume would like to have a word with you before you leave."

Hattie closed her eyes for a full second, and then opened them slowly. "I know what that's about, and it would be a waste of his time, but I tell you what, hangman, it might be an interestin' conversation, so what the hell."

"Thank you."

"I don't plan to hurry with Rufus to accommodate him."

"No hurry. He'll wait in his office as long as you like."

She took Son's arm again, said, "Lead the way down, hangman. Time's a wastin'."

As they walked down the row of cells, the shuffling of boots and muttering voices leaked from the cells—all directed at Hattie—but she ignored the commotion. Apsel stopped four cells from Rufus, and Hattie and Son walked

251

on. Rufus sat on the bunk, his back against the wall, and he did not move until both Hattie and Son faced him. Hattie said, "Look who came back to town."

Son felt it rise up within him, filling first his stomach and then his chest—a moving fire, far more intense than the stifling, putrid air surrounding him—and his eyes teared up. He lifted his right arm and extended it between the bars. "Rufus."

Rufus looked at him for only a couple of seconds, and then he pushed up from the bunk with his good arm and shuffled forward, wrapped his hand around Son's forearm, held it for several seconds and then released it. "I need to sit back down. You two pull up that bench if you care to stay a while."

Son pulled the bench forward and he and Hattie sat down. Rufus returned to the bed and said, "My little white man, did you wander far?"

"Little Rock."

"Jumped a train?"

"Tinder pile."

"Banged you around, didn't it?" The hint of a smile creased Rufus' lips.

"Not bad."

"So that's where you heard?"

Son nodded, looked down at the floor.

Rufus looked at Son's clothes and said, "You don't look like you run the streets down there."

"Got a job at a livery. Showed the man I was good with horses...told him I had a good teacher."

"That so?"

"Yep."

"I like that, don't you, Hattie?"

"I do for a fact, Rufus. I like that a lot."

Rufus drew a long breath, exhaled through his nostrils. His raven hair hung wild and loose on his shoulders and covered the sides of his face. His skin gleamed—appearing to Son like the coating of a sculpture in bronze, and the boy wanted to look at him, stare at him until the vision was burned into his brain forever, but he could not stare for more than a few seconds before looking down.

Rufus said, "She tell you how I'm gonna cheat Plume and the hangman?"

Son did not look up, nearly whispered the word. "Yes."

"It's gonna be ugly and there ain't no use in you seein' it—I don't want that—so we need to say what we need to say right now, understand?"

"I do."

"I don't need to say much." Rufus leaned his head against the wall, tilted it to one side. "You have iron, else I would have run you off. Hattie has iron, and she deserved better than me. My spirit is restless now, and soon will I go to the spirit world to see new things and do new things. I believe those of iron will know only others of iron, so both of you will roam with me. There will be no killing there. Spirits do not bleed. This is what I believe."

Son said, "I don't know what I believe, but I hope I believe like that someday."

Rufus said, "You will in time." He looked at Hattie, saw the tear streaks on her cheeks, but she did not weep. Then he looked at Son and said, "I would like for you to stay with her until she finds a decent hand. My cabin will become yours and all that is in it, except for the bird pipe, which is hers. Maybe you can finish learning to play it for her."

"I planned to stay for a while."

"Figured that. Just needed to hear you say it."

Rufus leaned his back against the wall, and it was clear to Son and Hattie that he would say no more to the boy.

Hattie patted Son's arm and said. "Go on now. There's no more to be said here."

Son got up from the bench, looked at Rufus for a few seconds, and then he walked away.

Hattie waited until the sound of his footfalls faded away in a slow cadence. She waited, looked at Rufus, but his eyes were closed, his breathing slow and shallow. She pulled a handkerchief from her dress pocket and dabbed at the perspiration gathered in the hollow of her neck. She stood, wrapped her fingers around the bars. She said, "So it ends like this with me too, Rufus?"

"Unless you want to watch me dry up like a worm out there on the street."

"I want to be with you as long as you want me to be… no matter what."

He rolled his head from side to side. "I know you do, but I don't want you to. I have some pride left. Let me keep it."

"Then…then, I will do as you want."

"One more prideful thing I ask. Do not dig a hole and chunk me in it. The old trapper, Lucian, will take me into the wilderness to a place where no one would ever find me, and bind me high up in a good tree. He will know what to do. Just leave word at the livery for him—he comes to town every few days and always goes there. All they will have to tell him is that Rufus needs him for a favor. He will know, and when it is over here in the cage, he will carry me to your place for binding in my burial blanket and then he will take me into the wilderness. My burial blanket is in the bottom of my cedar chest, wrapped in oil cloth."

Hattie sat back down on the bench. "I'll see to it."

"Good."

"Now, I ask of you one final thing, Rufus. Think of it as something for me…not you. Let me have Dilla make a potion to give you deep rest." She swallowed, gritted her teeth for a second. "It might even finish you, and I can sneak it in. They would never know."

He rolled his head from side to side, said, "No. That is a part of the pride that I have left."

After he had closed his eyes again and turned his head to face the back wall, Hattie stood and quietly walked away, and the murmurs and mutterings of men arose again, then quickly faded away.

CHAPTER 36

Destiny…all laid out before we were seeds squirted in our mothers' twats

Hattie walked up the front stairs and over the porch, and then opened the tall door. She walked to the small desk with a woman sitting behind it, and said, "I take it the hangman told you the high judge wants to palaver with me."

"Yes. Judge Plume is waiting in his office…upstairs."

"I know where it is. Seen it through the window several times."

"Yes, but…I suppose I should escort you…up…" Her voice trailed off as she watched Hattie turn and walk toward the stairs.

Plume looked up when he heard the knock on his door, and said, "Come in." He pushed back from the desk, but when he saw Hattie, he did not stand.

Hattie closed the door behind her, then turned to face him. She said, "So finally we meet—the high judge and the noisy town whore. Peculiar, ain't it?"

He pointed to a chair in front of his desk, said, "Please sit."

Plume leaned forward and said, "I want to talk so that I might implore you to…"

Hattie stopped him. "No. And even if I would agree to go back down there and get on my knees and beg him all night long, it wouldn't make a damn bit of difference."

"Why then? Why bother to come here?"

"Oh, just seemed like it was time we had a talk."

"To what end, may I ask?"

"You just did ask, and that's a good question, but I don't know just yet to what end. Tolerate me for a little while, and we'll see."

Plume swept a hand over his mouth and then down over his goatee as he leaned back in his chair and said, "Consider yourself tolerated…for a little while."

"Don't worry about that. I don't want to be around you anymore than you want to be around me. Oil and water—somethin' like that. You bein' sure you're the water and me the nasty-ass oil. So let's start there. Still curious why you didn't do some high-court sorta thing to me back in March when you hung the young cowboy and I went off on you." She nodded to the window behind him. "Cold mornin', but that window was up, just like it always is when your hangman is busy, so I know you heard me. And it wasn't the first time either."

"It would have only brought you more attention, and it would have been further distraction from the proceedings, which I prefer to be solemn and formal."

"That sounds about like what I thought you would say."
She looked away for a moment, took a breath. "No matter
that, really, just a curiosity. What does matter—or would
have—is if you'd not sentenced the boy to hang. You no
doubt will be surprised to learn that I read the papers about
these events…follow along the process, and what's more—
and this won't surprise you—a lot of informed gentlemen
pass through my front door." She smiled wickedly. "Now
and then, some special ones pass through my bedroom door.
So that one is on you, high judge—that one when that boy
might have served some time in prison, and then got out
and lived the last half, or more, of his life…might've turned
out to be a citizen somewhere, with a wife and young'uns…
the whole damn deal."

"Let me tell you something that will no doubt surprise
you. The sentences that I hand down are agonizing in
every way, even when they involve murderers who have no
remorse—like your very own murderer down in a jail cell—
much less young Dillingham, whose grave I have visited and
wept and prayed over."

"And yet his flesh and bones lay moldin' in the grave,
high judge, and your late prayers don't matter. You want
me to see you like Jesus in the garden, prayin' great tears of
blood, but all I see is a judge who fucked up a sentence and
who tried to make himself feel better."

"You are a blasphemous, contemptible woman, and I
see no point in continuing this." He pushed away from the
desk and stood.

"Sit back down, Plume. I ain't finished. And if you don't,
I'll flop my tits out and go to that open window and dangle
'em while I scream things out to the street so goddamn

awful the news hounds will be there in a flash along with a crowd of citizens, and your good wife will have some readin' material that will turn her face white." She glared at him, daring him to move. "My lover is dryin' up like a bug in the dungeon below us, and I'm in a black mood like I've never been, so keep your ass in that chair and let's continue our talk on philosophy and such."

Plume looked at her as if he saw a wolf poised at the edge of an open cage door, and then he sat back down, placed his hands in his lap.

Hattie said, "Here's the thing, Plume—and I've read and heard a lot about this too—you see yourself as an instrument of God and Presidents of these United States, who was sent to clean up a savage land, and that one day you actually believe that you will get it done. Crazy damn thing to believe such a notion, Plume. You think that the red people are the only ones who tribe up, but I tell you there are tribes all over the entire damn world—red, yellow, black and white, in nice clothes, some fucken near naked—back East, Washington, New York, out West, here there and yon— and they'll be killin' and fightin' and screwin' a thousand years after we're dead and forgot—one tribe will just replace another one, and it'll go on and on and on. You hold yourself way too high." She paused, tilted her head at the thought that just entered her brain. "You know, Plume, I can stand a son-of-a-bitch…dealt with 'em all my life, even liked some of 'em…but I cannot stand a sanctimonious son-of-a-bitch."

Plume took out his handkerchief and mopped his face. "Are you finished?"

"Close, but not quite. And here's another thing stuck in my craw that's about to get spit out. It's called destiny. I know all about you, thanks to those news hounds. You're from back East, wealthy family, connected, sent you off to law school, you shine with your big words strung out makin' regular folks check a dictionary more than they should... you, a lawyer, win cases, get in the papers...small shit gets to be big shit, and years pass and your shit gets bigger and bigger..." She paused, raised her arms theatrically toward the walls. "And here you are. Congratulations, Plume. You made it. Take me on the other hand, who remembers her childhood like a goddamn nightmare. I'll spare you details and just say that men lusted after me long before I found blood in my underpants, and I should have killed them, but bein' a little girl, it was too much of a task, and then one day I wasn't little anymore, and I figured out that instead of killin' 'em, I could get 'em to give me money, and the rest, as they say, is history. And I don't apologize for it any more than you apologize for what you do. And same for Rufus—reckon he was destined to be a lawyer or a banker or a merchant or a doctor, or any fucken thing like that? Don't you see, Plume...destiny...all laid out before we were seeds squirted in our mothers' twats...we're just actors playin' out our parts on a strange stage. Couldn't a been no other way. So you take your moral high ground and stick it up your ass. And put this up there too. I'd wager all I have—which is a lot—that I've done more for the low and needy in this town than you and your wife ever thought about doin'. So study your big black Bible over there and sort that all out if you can...which you can't."

Rivulets of perspiration ran down her forehead into her eyes, and she swiped at them with her handkerchief like a woman trying to kill wasps. Plume raised his handkerchief and methodically mopped his face, then got up and turned around, stepped to the window. "I suppose you want the body after he completes his task."

"What I want is him, not his body, but his body is all I'll get." She got up, tapped her knuckles on the front of the desk. "I wish that I could believe in Heaven, Plume, but I can't quite get there most days, but I do fear Hell some I'll admit. You think you know you'll get carried away to Heaven on your chariot…or by big ole angels flappin' golden wings and singin' your praises on the ride, and you think you know that I'll burn in the eternal fires, but you don't know for sure about either one, no matter what you tell yourself at night in the dark. You keep that thought in your head…as you judge, and watch from your window." She turned the doorknob, but released it and said, "I do have one useful gift for you, Plume. On my word of honor—which is the equal of yours—I will never discuss our little talk here with anybody. It was just between me and you…a personal thing. And I will never again stand under your gallows with or without my bird on my shoulder. That might be the best gift you take from Fort Smith when you head back East to your own kind."

Plume stood motionless, studied the empty street below him, concentrated on the little puffs of dust and the shimmers of heat in the distance rippling like a smokeless inferno, and he did not turn around until he heard the door slam behind him.

When Hattie walked onto the courthouse porch, Son was sitting on a bench against the wall, and he popped up. She said, "Your talk didn't last very long."

"Yours neither."

"Well, I got a lot said. I figured the hangman would take you off to see Iva."

"They got 'em a place outside of town now, said he knew there wouldn't be time. Wanted me to come visit her soon."

Hattie released a long sigh, and to Son it appeared as if she was trying to empty herself of more than air. She said, "You can go see her anytime you want, little man. Stay as long as you want…or forever. Rufus didn't bind you to me. Nobody can bind you to anybody but you."

"I want to be with you for while. That's what I want."

She could not stop the tears now, and they filled her eyes to overflowing and ran down her cheeks and chin faster than she could mop them, but she made no sound. Her voice quivered. "Need a minute to let this pass."

Son looked away, took off his hat, saw a man fast approaching on the boardwalk.

Hattie said, "Let's go to the house, little man."

They walked down the stairs, and at the bottom, Hattie took the boy's arm and led them to the top of the basement staircase, and she looked down the stone steps. She sniffed and blew her nose quietly into her handkerchief. "You're gonna have to stay long enough to get decent on the bird pipe and play me one tune. That's all I ask."

"I will."

They turned away, and when they reached the buggy, the man rushed up to them. He held his bowler hat in place with one hand, and in the other he held a note pad. His cheeks glowed like little red saucers layered with bacon grease. "Beg pardon, ma'am, but I'm hopeful I might have a word with you. Sheldon Lipskey from the Tribune, and I… uh…recognize you, ma'am."

She looked at him. "Many do."

"Yes, ma'am…well, as I said: a question or two, if I may…and…the first would be regarding the fact that—as was relayed to me—you and Judge Plume just conversed in his office, so naturally my journalistic instincts came into play, and…"

"You may not, news man. But I'll toss you one bone and you can write a story as long as you want about it…a whole goddamn book if you're gushy with words." She stared at him, watched his eyelids battle the sweat. "My friend, Rufus, down there will never hang."

She said to Son, "Time to go now. We need to make a quick stop at the livery, and then we're done."

Son helped her into the buggy seat, and then unwound the reins, pulled them back over the mare, and hopped up onto the seat. He eased the reins back and made a little clucking sound with his tongue, and when the horse was clear of the post, he clucked again, gently flopped the reins, and drove away. Sheldon Lipskey took hold of his hat and hurried away with long, purposeful strides, his boots kicking up little clouds of dust.

CHAPTER 37

I did it for me

Iva heard Apsel's horse trot past the house, and she walked out the back door and waited for him. When he neared, she smiled and held up both hands, waiting for his, and then pecked lips with him. He said, "Let's stay out here in the good shade and talk."

"Let's do then. How was your day?"

They began to walk, arm in arm. "Eventful."

"Ummm…that's a loaded word. Tell me about these…events."

"The boy is back. He rode in with Hattie Wax to visit Rufus."

She stopped, turned toward Apsel, her features betraying no reaction, but Apsel knew that her mind churned. She said, "I don't know what to make of that. How did he know?"

"He was in Little Rock, working at a livery, and a mule buyer from here was down there, and spilled it out in general conversation."

"So you must have talked with him at some length?"

"Yes, while Judge Plume was talking with Hattie."

Iva looked at him wide-eyed. "What on earth? Hattie and the judge? Hard to imagine that."

"He asked me if I would ask her to talk with him. There is a problem with Rufus."

"A problem? Has he gone wild…making scenes in the jail?"

"No, not that. He has decided—so far—to refuse food or water. Claims he intends to die like that."

"Dear God…in this heat…down there. Surely she talked him out of it."

"She did not. Judge Plume says that he tried long and hard, appealing to her in every manner that he could think of, but she told him it would be of no use." Apsel puffed a half-laugh past his lips, shook his head. "They talked a good while, and the judge relates that they had a civil conversation, which I wouldn't have thought possible— Hattie Wax being Hattie Wax."

"What she's dealing with now would subdue anyone— even Hattie." She looked away into the deep shadows of the trees. "How long could he last?"

"Another week, maybe ten days. The judge asked Doc Hays about it. The details are gruesome, suffice to say."

"Yes…suffice to say." She put her arm back around his back and said, "Let's walk farther, I want to keep moving just now." After a few steps, she said, "Did you ask Son… about his intentions?"

"Not directly, I thought it best to leave that be for now."

"As do I."

"I asked him if he would come see us here, and he promised that he would, later on."

"Good, I want to see him. Does he look alright?"

"He looks fine—clean, with washed clothes, good hat, boots. Sturdy…he looks sturdy. He looks much older than thirteen…or whatever he is."

"Oh, that is good to hear, Apsel. So good."

"I was pleased."

"Did he steal his way back on a train?"

"No, he said that he had money in his pocket, and that he rode in a coach car." Apsel smiled. "First time ever, he said, 'Just like a regular person'."

"Will she try and keep him now?"

"I don't know. Who can say, things have changed…sea changes."

"Whatever he decides, your concerns about Rufus are gone. At least we have that."

"True."

"And also gone is my wish to go on west ahead of you."

"That I am grateful for."

Iva sighed. "Despite what he did, I don't want to see Rufus suffer so."

"Nor do I, but there is nothing that can be done about that."

They walked slowly, drifting ever deeper into the shade.

Two days passed before Sheldon Lipsky's piece appeared in the Tribune, the details of which were soon bandied about inside of every social circle in Fort Smith, from the highest to the lowest. Estelle Plume sat in her parlor with a copy of the newspaper in her lap. It was folded precisely, so that Lipsky's article was framed, with the headline at the top.

PROMINENT BROTHEL OWNER CLAIMS MURDEROUS INDIAN OUTLAW WILL NEVER HANG

Supper stew was on the stove, but pushed to the side so that it would stay warm. She read the article again, her eyes flashing, and then she laid the paper beside her on the couch, and continued her waiting. At half past six, the kitchen door opened, and she listened to the routine shuffling, heard the cast iron lid of the stew pot being removed, quickly followed by the clank of its closing. He walked into the parlor and looked at her as she raised the paper. She said, "You didn't mention that you had a conversation with that woman."

Plume sat down heavily in a chair and crossed his legs. "It was so inconsequential that it didn't seem to merit mention."

"The connection between this headline—which I of course understand is misleading for newspaper reasons—and certain parts of the article, would seem to indicate merit regarding mention to me."

"The article is mostly innuendo and fiction. I have already voiced my displeasure to the owner. I had Apsel Graf fetch Wax after a visit to the jail in order that I might appeal to whatever decency she might possess, regarding attempting to talk the Indian out of this…this…pathetic intention of his to mock the court. Not to mention torturing himself for no reason."

"And what decency did she possess?"

"She claimed to have no sway with him whatsoever, and that was that."

"The article says that reports have it that she was up there for anywhere from ten to fifteen minutes. It doesn't seem it would take that long for…that to be that."

Plume shifted his weight, switched legs. "The woman rattled on needlessly. She is distraught and shrilly vocal."

"Yes indeed, as everyone knows. Shrilly vocal. Would that she had the decency to be that only on her own foul property and not in public."

"I have the sense that our conversation will end her displays altogether."

"I hope to God Almighty it will be so." She made a noise in her throat that sounded like she was attempting to hock up a fish bone. "'Distraught' you say. Those truly distraught are the families of your two murdered deputies. Just what the likes of her feels, only Satan could know."

Plume said nothing, his only desire being that the conversation end. He stirred in the chair, but she ignored him. The fingertips of her right hand tapped the paper in measured time, steady, like the sound of distant hooves on hard ground. Finally, she said, "I do hope that you made her acutely aware of her place."

"Of course, Estelle, that goes without saying."

In mid-afternoon of the twelfth day of Rufus's incarceration, Dak Hatch followed Apsel down the stairs to the jail. Hatch carried a canvas-covered canteen of water strapped over his shoulder. At the jailer's desk, Apsel nodded and said, "Dewey, we need the key." The jailer pulled out a drawer, poked his hand in it, and held up a ring with a single key. He said, "Don't reckon you'll be needin' me back there with the double-barrel?"

"No, Dewey, no need for that."

As they walked down the row of cells, the strange sounds grew louder, and a prisoner stepped to the bars as they approached and said, "If you boys would see fit to put that poor bastard out of his misery, we'd all be beholdin'. Like listenin' to an animal for the last two days. Goddamn."

Apsel and Hatch ignored the man, continued to walk steadily past. When they reached Rufus's cell, Hatch stepped to the front and looked in. Apsel said, "You still want to do this?"

"Yes. It came to me down in Texas when we buried Ora Lee. Won't leave me be."

Rufus was curled so tightly that he appeared nearly circular—a grimy ball of flesh and hair and clothing soaked in sweat and filth. Black, greasy tangles of hair covered his face and knees and from the middle of the mass came the sounds, faint now, and to Hatch they sounded like an old man praying in tongues that he had heard forty years before—a forlorn, garbled incantation, hovering, suspended in time.

Apsel unlocked the door and Hatch walked in and stood motionless over Rufus, the seconds passing slowly, absorbed by the stench and heat. Hatch removed his hat and sat it on the bunk, and then he knelt in front of Rufus, and pulled the canteen around to the front, unscrewed the lid, and it dangled as Hatch lifted the hair away from Rufus's face. His eyes were half open, his tongue protruding from an open mouth like an enormous lump of meat that had been partially stuffed past his lips. In tiny, ratchet-like motions, his eyes sought the owner of the hands now touching his face, and then his voice fell silent, the only sound a tiny wheezing. Hatch cupped his right hand and filled it with water and slowly poured it over the tongue. Rufus began to tremble, his head and shoulders twitching as the wheezing grew louder. Hatch filled his hand again and again and again, pouring water over the face, spreading it with his fingers, until the canteen was empty.

Hatch said, "What do the preachers say when they baptize a man, Apsel?"

"I have never witnessed that."

"Been a long time since I have. The only thing that comes to mind is about the Father, the Son, and the Holy Ghost."

"That sounds accurate."

"Well then…in the name of the Father, the Son, and the Holy Ghost, I baptize you, Rufus. That's the best I can do."

He stood, put on his hat, looked down. The wheezing grew faint again, ever slower, irregular, and then it stopped. Hatch said, "He's passed."

Apsel waited until Hatch turned around, and then he said, "Of all men, why did you do that for him, Dak?"

"I didn't do it for him. I did it for me."

Apsel took the key from the latch, but left the cell door open, and they walked back to the jailer's desk. Apsel laid the key on the desk, and said, "It won't be long before he's carried away."

The jailer said, "By who?"

"Lucian. He'll be at the livery now I suspect, and I'm headed there now."

"Not the undertaker? Why old Lucian?"

"A last favor for Rufus, he says. He will take him to Hattie Wax's place."

"Friend of yours, old Lucian, ain't he?"

"He is a friend to Rufus and me both."

With his forefinger, Dewey wiped the sweat from his brow and flicked it away, and then he looked at Apsel for a moment, as if he wanted to ask another question, but he looked down at the desk top and said, "I'll be lookin', for him."

CHAPTER 38

And still they watched until it made no sound

Hattie and Dilla sat in the porch swing, just as they had for most of the past three days, and above them, inside the open windows, women in thin gowns sat—some smoking, others with glass jars holding water or tea in hand—peering down the dusty lane. Their faces were unpainted and their hair was unkempt. A week had passed since Son, hammer in hand, had walked fifty yards down the lane holding a wooden sign board nailed to a stake. The sign, painted in the flowing hand of a woman, read:

Closed for mourning until further notice

The sun hung low in the west, but it was still strong even as its rays filtered through the trees. Dilla heard the rumble of the approaching wagon a few seconds before it appeared in the lane, and she touched Hattie's hand, said. "Here they come."

From behind the cabin, Son heard the wagon too, and he began to walk toward the house. He met Hattie and Dilla in front of the hitching post, and they watched as the rumble grew louder and the dust swirled around the wagon wheels. Lucian held the reins in his left hand, his right arm and hand wrapped around his lanky hound, riding on its haunches. Lucian tugged the reins and slowed the horse, and when it stopped, Son went to Lucian and said, "You want me to hitch him?"

"Thanky, boy, but not just yet."

The old man wore a wide-brimmed straw hat with frayed edges, and he touched the brim with a forefinger and thumb as he said, "Ladies. Sorry for this occasion, I truly am." He stroked his long beard, wild and white, except for two lengthy, perfectly matched tobacco stains that would have appeared no different had they been painted on with a small brush. The dog woofed softly and its long tail whipped back and forth. "Mose just wants to say howdy. He won't be no bother."

Hattie said, "No bother to us, Lucian. I appreciate all this." She looked past him at the wagon bed, but the side boards were two feet tall and she could see nothing. She started to move toward the bed, but stopped, looked down and placed a hand on a wagon wheel, ran her fingers over the metal rim. Dilla's eyes did not leave Hattie, and after a half minute had crept past, Dilla went to her side and took her arm. "Miss Hattie, you need to go sit in the swing with the little man until me and Lucian do some necessaries. You come on now."

With Son holding one arm and Dilla the other, they walked her to the swing, and when they got her situated,

Sally walked out of the house and onto the porch, and sat down beside Hattie.

Dilla went to the wagon bed and looked in. The body was covered with burlap, loosely tucked around the sides, but Dilla saw the unnatural, coiled shape under the burlap, and the dread began to build. Beside the body was a collection of tackle—ropes and pulleys—and a long wooden ladder that protruded several feet past the end of the bed, and beside that was a dog travois. Lucian had turned sideways in the seat and when she looked up at him, he cocked his head in apology, and then said very quietly. "Tried to uncurl him, but didn't have much luck."

Dilla spoke barely above a whisper. "Well, sir, we're gonna do better than this here mess...yes, sir. You drive around to the back and on to the cabin. We'll clean him and fix him there."

Dilla scurried ahead of the horse and stopped in front of the open cabin door. Lucian climbed down from the seat, went to the bed, and leaned in and pulled the body toward him, turned it sideways. He picked it up as if it weighed no more than a small, dead tree limb and carried it through the doorway. He looked at the dog and said, "Stay, Mose." Dilla pointed to the bed, where she had spread three layers of blankets, and Lucian laid the body directly in the middle.

Dilla bent over and pulled the burlap down from head to foot, and when she looked back at the head, she sucked in a sharp breath. "Ohmyohmyohmy, Mr. Lucian."

Lucian took off his hat and laid it on a chair, tugged on his beard. "Thought about takin' him by the undertaker to have a go at that tongue, but I didn't. Reckon I shoulda." Dilla just stared, wrung her hands.

Lucian said, "You want me to take it out for you?"

"Huh uh, no, sir, we ain't cuttin' nothin' out or off, except for these nasty clothes for the burn pile." She turned and pulled a woven basket on the foot of the bed toward her, and from it she took a piece of linen cloth, folded it lengthwise several times, and then took scissors from her apron pocket and cut it. She lifted the head with one hand, and with the other, laid the cloth over the tongue, and then she wrapped the cloth tightly around the head and tied it at the side.

"You go around back, Mr. Lucian, and fill that bucket beside the pump."

"Alright."

Too soon, she heard footsteps outside the door and she spun around, stood in the doorway. Hattie stood there beside Sally and Son, and she tried to look past Dilla into the cabin, but the little woman took a half step toward her, shook her head.

Sally said, "We tried to stop her, Dilla, but she was coming no matter what."

Dilla said, "Miss Hattie, you're the boss, and you can run me off if you want when this is all over, but you ain't passin' by me through this here door."

Hattie took a step toward her, and Dilla clamped her right hand around Hattie's forearm, and their eyes met, Dilla's hard and set, Hattie's soft and wet. Dilla said, "You go on back to the porch now, we'll be done before you know it." Gently, she pushed against Hattie's forearm and when Hattie took a little step backward, Sally and Son took her arms and turned her away. Dilla stood until they were twenty steps away and still moving before she went back into the cabin.

Dilla took out her scissors again and began to cut away the clothing, and when she finished, she balled it into a wad and tossed it on the floor. Lucian returned with the water bucket, and she pulled a chair close to the bed and said, "Sit it there." From the basket, she took several wash cloths, a bar of Castile soap, and put it all into the water, swished it around with one hand. She began to wash the body, starting with the head, soaking the matted hair with the soapy water. When she finished, she took from her apron pocket a wide-toothed comb and worked until she had the hair untangled and pulled away from the face. Lucian stood motionless and silent as she worked her way over every inch of the body, and when she finished, she stripped the water from her forearms and hands and then dried them on her apron.

"Reckon you can spare me some of that rope in your wagon?

"I brought lots a rope."

"Cut me six pieces—five about a yard long and then one twice that—and then you're gonna have to help me tie him straight."

Lucian returned within a minute, and then they began the process of tugging and bending and pushing until five ropes had been knotted tightly to the long one, which served as the spine for the system. Dilla took a step back, surveyed their handiwork, and then she said, "Now, that's better. We can wrap him in the main robe now."

She walked to the chest, opened the top and took out the robe. It was made of coyote hides, sewn together beneath the fur, so perfect and hidden the stitching, that it appeared to have been made from a single animal, rather than the dozen that Dilla reckoned. Sewn into the center was a deer-hide image of a human, arms and legs outstretched, and on both sides was sewn the image of a bird of prey, its wings spread wide. The colors of the fur were dusky shades of tan and gray, taken from prime animals in mid-winter, and she ran her fingers through the thick fur as she carried it to the body. Lucian leaned down and slid his hands underneath the body and lifted it above the bed as Dilla arranged the robe, and then he lowered the body. The edges of the robe hung to the floor, and Dilla raised one edge and covered the body, tucked it under, and then she raised the other edge and repeated the process.

"Need more ropes, Mr. Lucian."

"One long one would do better for this. We'll double it and wind it tight, top to bottom. He'll be bound proper thataway."

"That'll be good."

When they had finished with the rope, they carried the body to the wagon bed and laid it down against a sideboard, and Lucian scooted the heavy dog travois alongside it. Mose stirred and nosed Lucian's hand as the man sat down and took up the reins, and then he flapped them once. The wagon turned a wide circle and when it straightened out, it followed along behind Dilla.

The wagon stopped in front of the hitching post, and Lucian climbed down and went to the wagon bed. He stood beside Dilla, and they watched as Hattie, Son, and Sally made their way toward him. Hattie wore Rufus's long, buckskin garment, her arms lost inside the sleeves, and on her feet were moccasins of the same material. Three steps from the wagon bed, Son and Sally stopped, allowed her to move forward by herself. She put her hands on the burial robe, over the head, and held them there as she studied the whole of the robe. Above the porch, all of the windows were open, filled with the solemn residents of Hattie's Place—their chins on arms resting on the window sills, their faces bare and sad-eyed—living feminine figurines of flesh and bone and blood and soul—gloomy and silent—as if they were viewing a tragedy on stage from balcony seats.

Hattie said, "I never knew he had this."

Lucian took off his hat, and said, "It's a fine one. He was good with hides. Best I ever saw."

"He never talked about you much, Lucian, but when he did, he seemed happy."

"He wasn't much of a talker and I ain't neither. We understood each other 'thout any blabber."

"He always said that was the way everybody should be…say what needed to be said and stop—like the coyotes howlin'. Just when you think they'll howl and yip for a long time, they stop."

"That sounds like him, sure 'nuff."

"You say you understood each other. Do you think he loved me?"

Lucian twisted his hat brim, shuffled his boots, and with his free hand, he reached in his britches pocket and took out a plug of tobacco, bit off a chew and poked it into his mouth. After he got it situated with his tongue, he said, "That's a right deep question for the likes of me, Miss Hattie, and I can't say he ever said he did, but that don't mean nuthin'. All I can tell you is that he damn sure talked and acted like he did, even if he never said it." He squeezed some juice from

277

the plug and swallowed. "I loved once, and that's all I could ever manage on the subject."

"She dead?"

"Long dead."

Hattie leaned forward, smoothed the fur with her hands as far as she could reach, and then she lifted them, and took a step back. "How far will you take him?"

"It's a long way, partly by wagon, and when we get to the end of that trail, we'll stop for the night, and in the mornin', Mose will pull the travois the rest of the way—he's damn near to a mule, that dog—to the tree I got in mind."

"I hope it ain't an oak."

He looked at her as if she had just read his mind, then said, "No, ma'am, I done considered that...it's an elm... dandiest elm I ever saw."

"It doesn't seem likely that anyone would ever find him."

"Don't worry with that. Even if somebody wandered right under that elm...even in the bare of winter...they'd never in a Methuselah's life see him way up there. I can find anything in the wilderness that I wanna find, and I can hide anything in the wilderness that I wanna hide even easier."

"I'm sure you can, and I take comfort in that." From a pocket of her garment, she took out four twenty-dollar gold pieces and extended her hand toward Lucian. "The least I can do."

He held up a hand, said, "Oh, no ma'am, wouldn't consider pay. Wouldn't be a favor thataway."

She lowered her hand. "I understand."

Lucian put on his hat, settled it over the mass of white hair, rolled the wad of tobacco to the other side of his mouth and swallowed. "Reckon me and Mose oughta get on down the road. Ways to go 'fore dark."

Hattie extended her hand, and Lucian shook it. He climbed onto the seat and picked up the reins, flopped them once on the horse's back. Every eye both inside the house and outside of it followed the wagon until it rumbled out of sight, and still they watched until it made no sound.

Hattie looked at Son and said, "Little man, go down the lane and get that sign and carry it to the burn pile. The world ain't stopped turnin'."

Epilogue

"Not all those who wander are lost."

"A day will come at last when I shall take the hidden paths that run West of the Moon, East of the Sun."

J. R. R. Tolkien

April, 1912, St. Mary's Sanitarium, Boerne, Texas

The old woman's bed was nearest the window, which was raised several inches, allowing the night sounds to come to her on the placid breeze. From the cypress trees that lined Cibolo Creek a quarter mile away, the creatures that had pleased her most were the tree frogs, their chirpy chorus a constant rhythm in her ears. But now, the sounds had begun to fade inside her head. A vibrant urgency had come to her—a mystery, given her rapid decline over the past two weeks. And with the urgency had come a surge of strength that was an even greater mystery until this moment, and she knew the reason for it, accepted it without dread. She waited for the nun named Sister Regina to finish tending a patient a few beds up the aisle, knew that she would come to her bed to look in on her.

When Sister Regina reached the foot of her bed, the woman raised her hand and patted the side of the bed. "Come sit with me."

The nun sat down on the edge of the bed. "Your voice is stronger and your breathing less labored." She smiled, and in the low, yellow light cast by the lamp, the woman saw as if for the first time the exquisiteness of her face—eyes, soft pools of blue, faultless doll-like nose and mouth.

"You know it's a cryin' damn shame your face is half hid behind that garb. I've seen some real beauties in my time, and you rank high."

Sister Regina ignored the curse word, had weeks before come to accept such words as just another incurable part of the dying woman's life form. Despite the coarse language, and against her inner cautions, the woman had become her favorite patient. "A small price to pay to be a part of The Order."

The woman drew in a long, deliberate breath, suppressed the urge to cough. "I feel strange strong just now, Sister, and I know what that means."

"And what is that?"

"It means that I'm havin' the last conversation of my life."

"Oh, I don't think…"

"Shhh…humor me, it won't take long."

Sister Regina took the woman's hand, squeezed gently, bowed her head.

The woman said, "My life has been some good and some bad—some really bad, and, I consider, some really good."

"As with all lives."

"I'd argue that, but there ain't time." Her bosom rose and fell under the white sheet. "I whored most of my life, Sister, made piles of money, but I gave piles away too…to the poor young'uns mostly. All I kept once I got real sick was enough to come and stay here, and what's left I'm leavin' to you all."

The nun shook her head, started to speak, but remained silent.

"I've heard tell that a nun believes she's married to Jesus Christ…after a fashion, I know."

"Yes, married in spirit to Him and the Holy Church—a total fulfillment of all my earthly needs."

"I reckon—and I don't mean to be disrespectful—that I've done as much good in my own way as you all do in yours."

The nun shifted her position, swallowed, said, "On this earth, I would agree that you have done far more than me… or perhaps all of us here collectively."

"'On this earth', you say—like it don't matter—but how can that not matter since we all got plunked down on *this earth?*"

"It does matter, it's just that the things of earth are so temporal. We flicker through life, eternity never ends."

"I know you believe in Heaven, but do you believe in the fires of Hell, Sister?"

"The holy scriptures address it specifically."

"That ain't an answer."

"It is…a difficult concept to grasp…for me."

"It damn sure is for me too. When I was little, my kin believed that you helped a burn heal by holdin' it close to heat again." She paused, took a raspy breath. "I still remember my screamin' inside my head. So I ask you: If I've done at least as much good as you folks—and any like you—for the most needy and helpless among us, how could I burn and scream forever and you all not?"

Sister Regina shook her head, as if to clear it, placed her other hand on the woman's. "This is all so unnecessary—just believe in Christ, accept him—and all that has gone before doesn't matter. None of it, no matter how bad."

"Or how *good*...that's the hard part for me. I was born with a lot of horse sense, and I can't just make it go away. How can God use all my giftin' to so many of his lowly little children and then toss me into the big fire that won't ever put me out of my misery, all because I'm stubborn and cloudy about what gettin' saved means?"

Sister Regina listened to the low rasp from the woman's tortured lungs, waited for her to recover before she answered. "Why is it that you think you must understand everything so precisely instead of just trusting your spirit?"

"Ah...spirit, you say. The only man I ever loved was a wild Indian named Rufus that I tamed for a time, and he believed in the spirit world as much as you do, and I believe he's there now, wherever that is. And that's where I want to go, Sister—I want to chase after him now." With a fingertip, Hattie touched her chin tattoo, and said, "He marked me in the flesh, Sister, and he marked me inside too." She raised a frail hand from the handkerchief and pointed toward the tiny closet where her personal belongings were stored. "There's a bird pipe in there...it'll look to you like a flute made of wood, but it's a bird pipe that Rufus made for me. He could play it like you wouldn't believe, and he played one tune that I loved the best. I called it *Song of the Bird Pipe*. It was a happy tune. I want you to have it...somethin' happy to remember me by."

"Thank you, Miss Hattie. I will treasure it. What became of him?"

"He got caught by a famous U.S. Deputy named Hatch—great big black feller— after he got stole away from me by a wilder Indian than him, called John Post Oak, and they tried to rob a train. But Hatch killed Post Oak in the woods near Clarksville, Arkansas. My man starved and thirsted himself to death up in the Forth Smith prison. He was too proud to be hung in a public spectacle for white people." Hattie coughed and held the bloody handkerchief to her mouth, and it was a full minute before she recovered enough to continue. "A happier love was a boy, brought to me as a thievin' street waif…would only call himself 'Son' for the longest time. His name was Floyd McCarty and I reckon he was about thirteen, and me and him and Rufus…well…I thought of us as a family—strange one, I know—but family means different things to different folks. An old trapper named Lucian took Rufus way yonder out in the wilderness and laid him up high in a tree, wrapped in a coyote hide burial robe—most beautiful thing I ever laid my eyes on. He was good with craftin' things…anything." She smiled, reached up and touched her tattoo. "I've seen you peek at this a time or two. He marked me perfect…it was just between me and him, this mark." She closed her eyes for several seconds. "Last time I saw Rufus in the Fort Smith jail, he made me promise not to chunk him in the ground." She looked up at Sister Regina. "Anyhow…strange family, but a family to me. Bet you consider the other nuns as family, huh?"

"Oh I do indeed, Miss Hattie. A beautiful family."

"Well, there you have it—families don't have to all be just alike to be…beautiful."

"What became of the boy?"

"He ended up settlin' in Little Rock, workin' in a livery, but he came to see me regular—two or three times a year. I know he was a damn fine horse man, taught by Rufus. I was sure he'd head out to San Francisco to find—listen to this, Sister, I'd laugh if it didn't hurt my chest so damn bad—to find a woman who whored for me a short while before she took up with the famous hangman named Apsel Graf. They'd always wanted the boy to go with 'em…and if he'd gone it woulda been with my blessin' too. Iva Lockwood wasn't no ordinary whore, no ma'am, not by a long shot. Now the hangman, I never really trusted him…hope I was wrong…think I prob'ly was now, lookin' back." Hattie coughed again, deeper now, and spat a great gout of blood. "What do you think of that story, Sister? Prob'ly think I've lost my mind, but it's all true. You can't make up shit like that."

"I believe you Miss Hattie, but you need to stop now, and try to sleep."

"Don't matter…fixin' to take a biiiiig sleep…or maybe not, dependin' on who's got all this forever stuff figured rightly."

"Oh, Miss Hattie…I don't know what else to say to you. I can only pray for your immortal soul." She lowered her head and laid it over their joined hands.

Hattie struggled to draw in a breath that sounded like the tearing of a wet cloth. "You go on and pray then, Sister." She paused, then whispered, "What the hell…it can't do no harm."

From the near bank of the Cibolo, a coyote howl arose

for several seconds, irritating Sister Regina, and she could not ignore it. She stopped her prayers, listened intently as another coyote, far across the creek, began to yip in reply. The chorus quickly reached a crescendo, and then suddenly ceased after a half minute, and it was then when Sister Regina heard no sounds of breathing, and she knew that Hattie Wax was dead. She lifted the frail hands, laced the fingers, and centered the hands over the body. Then she lifted the necklace crucifix over her head, draped it over the hands, and wept for the living and the dead. After a time, she stood, pulled the sheet over the body, and then turned and opened the closet door. Folded neatly in the bottom was a garment fashioned from tanned animal hide, and on top lay the bird pipe. She reached in and picked it up, held it close to her eyes as she inspected the intricate craftsmanship.

Carved on one side were the names *HATTIE + RUFUS + SON.* She hesitated for a moment, made the sign of the cross over her chest, and then she touched the mouth hole to her lips, but did not blow, and she knew that she never would.

About the Author

Photo © 2014 Stacee Clawson

Born in California, Missouri, Steven W. Wise lived in North Carolina from 1971 to 1983, where he met his wife Cathy. Together they had two children and five grandchildren. He graduated from the University of Missouri. He was a licensed real estate appraiser, who held an MAI designation, and owned the commercial real estate appraisal firm of Cannon Blaylock & Wise. Steve enjoyed long walks in the woods, for there, with the wind whispering in the high boughs of trees, stories sometimes came to him. He wrote his stories on a wooded farm near Columbia, Missouri, where he lived with his wife Cathy. Published novels include, Midnight, Chambers, Long Train Passing, Chimborazo, later published with the title Sing for Us, The Jordan Tracks, as well as a published short story collection, From the Shadows of My Soul. On Valentine's Day, 2017, Steve's mortal vessel ended its tenure in this earthly realm. His spirit and stories live on.

Printed in the United States
By Bookmasters